D1249256

ALSO BY HARRY CREWS

The Gospel Singer
Naked in Garden Hills
This Thing Don't Lead to Heaven
Karate Is a Thing of the Spirit
Car
The Hawk Is Dying
The Gypsy Curse
A Feast of Snakes
A Childhood: The Biography of Place
Blood and Grits
The Enthusiast
Florida Frenzy
Two
All We Need of Hell
The Knockout Artist
Body
Scar Lover
Classic Crews
Where Does One Go When There's No Place Left to Go
The Mulching of America
Celebration

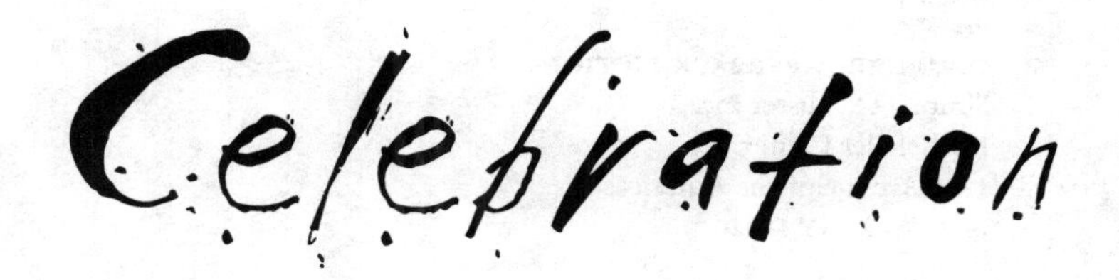

A NOVEL

Harry Crews

Scribner Paperback Fiction
Published by Simon & Schuster

SCRIBNER PAPERBACK FICTION
Simon & Schuster Inc.
Rockefeller Center
1230 Avenue of the Americas
New York, NY 10020

First Scribner Paperback Fiction edition 1999
SCRIBNER PAPERBACK FICTION and design are trademarks of Simon & Schuster Inc.

Designed by Jeanette Olender
Manufactured in the United States of America

10 9 8 7 6 5 4 3 2 1

The Library of Congress has cataloged the Simon & Schuster edition as follows:
Crews, Harry, date.
Celebration : a novel / Harry Crews.
p. cm.
I. Title.
PS3553.R46C45 1998
813'.54—dc21 97-33368
CIP

ISBN 0-684-83758-7
0-684-84810-4 (Pbk)

This book is dedicated to the memory of my mother, who from the beginning told me wondrous stories and, also from the beginning, was the best listener a little boy could have for stories of his own making.

Celebration

To Carol

This thing bites;

be careful

Live long and

well

Harry Crews

Chapter 1

When Johnson Meechum came up the three steps of his purple double-wide trailer and opened the front door, his wife, Mabel, was waiting for him, her thin hands clenched on her hips, her tinted hair standing from her scalp in a tiny blue cloud. He could look right through the hair to her freckled skull.

He made a small adjustment of the .22-caliber target pistol stuck in the small of his back, behind his belt. He didn't even know why he wore it there. It was not as though she wasn't aware he took it with him when he went out in the morning. She knew everything about him. He knew everything about her. Everything. It was very nearly unbearable at times. He often wondered where all the surprises and lovely secrets had gone. He sometimes felt like he'd be willing to open a vein for one tiny surprise, for one inconsequential secret.

It was terrible to know the most excruciatingly intimate details about her person. He even knew the stink she left in the bathroom was inexplicably tinged with the fragrance of almonds. He had no idea why, but it was. And it had taken him the first two years of marriage to discover that she was capable of leaving a foul odor of any kind anywhere. Nothing stank during those first two years of marriage. Now, after sixty years together, everything stank. Even her age, which she wore like a moldy overcoat, stank of mortality. And he supposed he wore the same stinking overcoat, but if he did, he did everything to resist it, by keeping himself washed down in cologne. Mabel wore nothing, not even face powder. She either had no pride left or had just totally given up on everything.

Johnson didn't know, and he was ashamed to ask. But he could smell her fifteen feet away even if he had a bad head cold. That's why he had taken to sleeping on a blanket on the floor. He told her it was for his bad back, but it was really because of the ripe, almond-tainted effluvium that hovered everywhere about her and the sweat that she never seemed quite able to dig out of the creases and folds of her body. Consequently, she seemed to be covered with the coppery odor of impending death.

The thing that frightened Johnson the most was that he knew he must have his own odor of putrefaction, which no amount of cologne would ever cover. For years now, he had feared the stink of death worse than he had feared death itself. It kept him in a state of grinding humiliation and caused him to do inexplicable things like shoot the swamp every morning with his .22-caliber target pistol.

He went around her into the kitchen. She didn't seem to be blinking, or breathing either, for that matter. But she followed him into the kitchen and watched him silently draw a glass of water from the tap. She was close enough now—right behind his left shoulder—that he could hear and smell her ragged Camel breathing (only another odor she carried as though she had been born with it, and since she had been born with it, it was another stink she would be buried with). Johnson had quit smoking five years before, but he still thought he could smell a fine mist of tobacco on his skin.

He knew without turning to look that she still had her marble-size, arthritic knuckles planted firmly on her hips. She was about to tell him she had heard him outside. And he was going to respond by saying . . . well, he knew how he was going to respond.

"I heard you outside," she said.

"It doesn't matter," he said.

"Did anybody see you?"

"Nobody sees much of anything in Forever and Forever."

"That's not what I asked you."

"That's what I told you, though."

There was a silence now while they listened to the fake grandfather clock ticking above the stove. It was made in Taiwan. It sometimes seemed to Johnson that everything these days was made in Taiwan.

Mabel took her deformed fists off her hips and held her open hands in front of her, turning them first this way and then that, inspecting them as though they were something she thought she might buy.

"Do you remember when the sky was blue?" she said.

"Yes, I remember when the sky was blue," he said.

This was code talk they had between them. He couldn't remember how long they had talked of so many things in code. Code made conversation somehow less painful.

When she asked him if he remembered when the sky was blue, she was only asking if he remembered when they still loved each other. And, yes, he did. He did remember.

From far away, a siren started. It was coming this way.

"Another one," he said.

"Maybe not," she said. She was far more optimistic than he in these matters.

"It's another one," he said. "It's been a while. We're due for a turnover." That's what they called it when one of the residents of Forever and Forever passed. Nobody seemed to know how the phrase had started, but it sounded appropriate, at least to everybody but Mabel.

She frowned and said, "I'll not comment on that."

"Good," he said.

"Sometimes you say the meanest things," she said.

"All I said was 'Good,' " he said, but he knew what she meant.

They stood very still as the approaching siren came nearer. At the broad street under the arch reading FOREVER AND FOREVER, the siren shut down, and both Johnson and Mabel knew.

"I guess you were right," she said.

"I guess," he said, drawing another glass of water from the tap.

They saw the ambulance cruise past, the siren dead, the blinking lights off. No lights or sirens were allowed inside Forever and Forever. When the wagon came to pick up one of the residents, it had to come in quietly. It was an arrangement that Stump, the owner of Forever and Forever, had worked out with the company that had the hauling contract. Stump had many arrangements, and no lights or sirens on the ambulance once it was inside the trailer park was one of them. He never explained why.

He never explained much of anything. Why he called his place of business Forever and Forever was a puzzlement. But he never explained that either. He was not a man who seemed to care much about anything, particularly what people thought. Actually, what people thought of him and the way he did things seemed to be right at the head of the list of things he cared least about.

When a problem was brought to him, he would look off toward the far horizon—and all the horizons were far here in south Florida—and say, "Me and my stump don't give much of a good goddam about that."

The stump he was talking about was what was left of his right arm, which stopped below the elbow, near the wrist, in a bright mangle of purple scar. There was much speculation about how he'd come to have the stump in the first place, but nobody had ever found out. And Stump had never been known to say a word about it. The few people who had been dumb enough to ask about it—usually old parties who had recently moved into Forever and Forever—had only got a blank stare that looked right through them. The look was such that they never asked again.

Nor did anybody ask about Stump's wife—or at least everybody chose to think she was his wife, because that felt more seemly to the residents, and for the same reason they never privately or publicly commented on the fact that her name was Too Much. She said she was eighteen and might very well have been—they were willing to give her that—but she would have looked fourteen if she had not had . . . well, too much. Her titties were cantilevered at an impossible angle, and the unbelievable cheeks of her ass chewed constantly and voraciously at her cut-off Levi's, which were much too tight and much, much too short.

And she scratched. That's one of the things she did. Scratched. She never seemed to tire of it. And she not only never seemed to tire of it, she could stay longer and get deeper into the most intimate places than any of the old people could imagine. It shamed, angered, and outraged them. Consequently, they never stopped staring at her when she was outside by the pool or the shuffleboard courts or bending to water the flowers planted about the trailer park. She could bend and scratch at the same time and often did.

Mabel and Johnson, standing at the sink, turned to watch the ambulance slide silently past in the street.

"Who do you think?" asked Mabel.

"I don't know that it matters."

"It's a wonder to me," said Mabel, "that ambulances don't get lost in this place. I've been in towns smaller than Forever and Forever. How they find whoever they're looking for or don't get lost and can't find their way out has always been a mystery to me. Especially way on the back side, where the streets are as crooked as a dog's hind leg."

"Oh, it's happened," said Johnson. "Was a time when it happened a lot, but I understand the company that's got the hauling rights came in here and made their own map, numbering the trailers, so that they could find who they were looking for. I'd bet the shoes I'm standing in that nobody living in this place has ever been on every street in it."

"Oh, I think Stump probably has."

"Stump is the last one that would have walked all the streets of the park he owns. He only wants a quiet, uncomplicated place for himself to live and a quiet, uncomplicated place for the rest of us to die."

"That was an unfortunate thing to say, Johnson, very unfortunate. You've gone off your game. If you'd quit shooting that swamp every morning, things might improve for you and for me. You know people are starting to talk, don't you?"

"I'm just like Stump—I don't give a lot of thought to what people say."

"Stump's got one up on you, old man. At least he owns Forever and Forever, which has got to be bigger than some farms I've seen."

"I've got both arms, though. It all evens out."

"He may not have but one arm, but he's got Too Much."

"Too Much is exactly what he's got, truth be known."

"What would you know about the truth? Shooting a swamp like you do every morning. Shooting swamps is not normal. They lock people away for doing stuff like that."

"No. People get locked away for walking out the front door naked because they forgot to put their clothes on. That's the kind of thing that will get you locked up. As long as you can get to the grocery, cook, wash your clothes, and make sure to wear them when you go out, nobody's going to mess with you. And shooting the swamp? That's nothing, absolutely nothing. And someday I'll give that son of a bitch the coup de grâce. See if I don't."

"See, that right there is crazy."

"Wrong again. That's just eccentric."

Mabel put her hands back on her hips and said, "It's sometimes I get so tired of the way you talk, I could put a hatchet in your head."

"Ditto," said Johnson.

She came to stand closer at his shoulder. The sky was blazingly hot and blindingly brilliant, but they stared at it through the window anyway, their eyes squinted.

"Do you remember when the sky was always blue?"

"Yes," he said, "I do." He drew another glass of water and drank it off. "But things change; even the fucking sky changes. That's the long and the short of it."

"Do you remember when we started cussing so much? Seems like it was a time we hardly cussed at all."

He regarded the empty glass in his hand for a long moment. "No," he said. "I don't remember when we started getting so bad about cussing, but I think it had something to do with moving into Forever and Forever."

"Probably. But you've got to admit Forever and Forever's centrally located."

"I don't have to admit *anything*."

"There wasn't anyplace else for us to go."

"All right. I know that if I don't know anything else. Does that make you happy?"

He didn't wait for an answer but drank another glass of tepid water, which he was convinced was good for his bowels. His favorite joke, which he was sure he had heard somewhere and had not made up himself, though he could not be positive about it (there was so little left in his world he could be positive about), was this: I've reached that stage in life where a good defecation is better than a good fornication. It was a bitter joke, though, because it had come to be the truth.

He filled a glass and offered it to Mabel. "Why don't you drink a glass of this?"

She regarded the glass, and when she spoke, she kept her eyes on it. "My stool is as soft as a baby's. I'll let you see it the next time I go."

"I'll take your word for it," he said, and he poured the water back into the sink.

As he watched the water swirl down the drain, he wondered when they had first started talking about the consistency of each other's stools before breakfast. It so angered and baffled him that he thought about going out and shooting the swamp again. But it was too late in the morning, and Stump had already warned him twice about shooting his swamp, though Johnson didn't think Stump meant it. After all, what harm could it do? It didn't, for that matter, even make any sense, and unfortunately Johnson knew that too.

Chapter 2

Stump watched Too Much getting ready to skin out of her clothes, fixating on her in a kind of killing fury and at the same time loving her as he had loved nobody or nothing else in the world. She was standing in front of the bathroom, where she was filling a tub. She liked her bathwater nearly scalding, and the steam swirled out the door and beaded on the skin of her naked arms and shoulders, while she languidly and without pause scratched herself in a kind of dreamlike state.

Stump had pursued the source of her scratching with a single-minded passion in the two months she had shared his trailer at Forever and Forever.

She didn't have crabs. He knew that for certain because he had checked it out thoroughly himself. After she wandered into Forever and Forever, panhandling for food and a place to sleep, he'd taken her in as a Christian duty and then rode her through that first long night, which would live in his memory forever. She was the most exquisitely formed creature he'd ever seen, and she had skin the clear, bright color of milk. And he'd told her so the first night they were together.

"Clabber," she said.

"What?" He'd been trying to keep her pinned to the mattress, while she had struggled to scratch herself in a way that threatened to throw him to the floor.

"You said I had skin like milk, but it's not. It's the color of clabber. I've been told that my whole life."

"Clabber," he said, trying to keep her hand from scratching the part he was working on himself.

"You hard of hearing or what? I've already told you clabber twice."

Since he wasn't exactly sure what clabber was anyway, he said, "You got crabs?"

"What kind of thing is that to say to a girl when you got her on her back?"

"Could be pretty important, seeing as how I've had dogs with mange that didn't scratch bad as you do."

"Don't think you can take advantage of a Christian girl just because you feeding and fucking her," she said.

"I ain't taking advantage of nothing. I ask a question, the best of my recollection."

"Well, you can rest easy in yourself, because I don't have the crabs," she said, but she kept on scratching.

"You wouldn't mind me getting you checked out by the doctor, would you?"

"Throw your money away if you want to," she said. "But I already been checked several times in the past. You're not the only man in this world with a suspicious mind."

Stump took her to the doctor the next day and the doctor said she was clean.

"Then why in the hell do you scratch like you do?"

"Feels good," she said, and she went on scratching.

He went back to the doctor two days later just to be sure and asked him if she didn't have crabs why she scratched the way she did, and the doctor told him it was probably just a nervous condition and charged him another sixty-five dollars. Paying the extra sixty-five dollars made Stump feel better in his mind, and if the subject ever came up and he felt like talking about it—which he almost never did—he just told whoever he was talking to that it was a nervous condition but it wasn't catching, said that the doctor told him it was no way to catch it off her, which was a lie, but he figured it was all right to tell a lie because he had by God paid a extra sixty-five dollars for the privilege and consequently felt free to tell the lie anytime he wanted to.

Stump was taking his shoes off at the breakfast nook and having himself a Coors beer and at the same time regarding the fetching way Too Much was scratching herself, standing in front of the steamy bathroom door straight down the hallway of his double-wide. Stump watched intensely, his eyes squinted, as her pretty little fingers pressed deeply into her flesh and scratched there until she got satisfaction before she moved on to another spot. Every time she got out of one spot and went into another, she made a sound like a very young calf calling for its mama's teat. Not quite as loud, but the same sound nonetheless. Stump knew this was not without significance. Too Much was nothing if not oral in her various fixations. She made the same sound when he had her in the bathtub and was about to take her around the bend.

She'd hook her bony little heels in Stump's hips and scream, "Look out, Old Son, I'm about to go round the bend!"

Then she'd make the calf sound and start to suck whatever was handy. It was unique in Stump's experience. It was in fact the damnedest thing he'd ever come across in his many years of curious living. *Curious.* That was his mama's word. Before she died, she never tired of saying, "You have lived a curious life, son, and you gone die a curious death. Mind I told you so."

Maybe Too Much was what his mama had in mind. The girl was full of the curious and the strange, and it had occurred to him more than once that she was very likely to be the death of him. For one thing, she had a dangerous stamina, a stamina that when she had a mind to—and she usually had such a mind—could make all the major organs of Stump's body feel as though they were on the edge of stroke. But if that was the way the game was meant to be played out, he was ready to go the distance. He wasn't a man who carried one arm for nothing. He had not come by anything easy, as far as he could tell. In the two months he'd had her, she'd come to grow on him anyway. He had even come to like the desperate way she had of scratching, the way she did it as though her life depended on it.

The only other thing Too Much was as rabidly interested in as scratching seemed to be May Day. Hell, until Too Much showed up at Forever and Forever, Stump had never heard of May Day. But recently she had not only brought it up but insisted they celebrate it.

"May what?" he had asked.

"Day," she said, giving herself a good long dig, which caught and held Stump's attention. "May Day. It's celebrated all over the world, in one way or another. May Day's a mystery, is what it is, going all the way back to the Druids."

"Druids, for Christ's sake?" Stump didn't know what a Druid was and didn't care to find out, but Too Much was still digging in private places, and he wasn't about to let the conversation die. He would have been willing to talk about goats if she would keep on with what she was doing. And he hated goats. "I don't even know what that is."

"You don't know what?"

"What Druids are, goddammit. That's what we were talking about, even if you are making it hard to think straight."

"Can't you keep your mind on anything but where I'm scratching? I read it in my encyclopedia. That is, when I had one."

"One what?"

"An encyclopedia," she said, giving her cantilevered breasts a good long working over, a kind of simultaneous milking, one with the nails of either hand.

"Well," said Stump, in stunned admiration of her double-handed work on her chest. Despite the fact that she had been in Forever and Forever for just over two months, he still was not used to her clever and shameless work with her hands. It was a hard thing to get used to, and he wondered if he ever would. "Well," he said, finally looking off to the far horizon. "You and me are even there, young lady." He still had a hard time bringing himself to call her Too Much, despite the fact that she'd been sleeping in his bed since the first day she showed up at Forever and Forever.

"How are we even?"

"I ain't familiar with'm either," he said.

"Familiar with what?"

"Druids and cyclopedias."

"Damn, you're confusing to talk to, Stump. An encyclopedia is nothing but a book. Quite a lot of books, actually," she said, going behind her now to make a major adjustment to the seat of her Levi's.

"Never much of a reader myself," he said, finding himself wishing that when he died, he could come back as her cut-off Levi's, or else as a bar of soap and be sold to her.

"It doesn't matter you don't read. I know all about the May Day celebration, and we're going to have one right here this year, but we have to hurry because we don't have a whole lot of time to get ready."

"Ready for what?" He wasn't paying attention at all. The young bitch had actually stuck the fingers of her right hand down the front of her Levi's.

"May Day," she said. "But we've got plenty of time if we get right after it."

"Hell, yeah," said Stump. "We got plenty of time."

"Then we're going to do it?"

"Bet on it, little girl."

"I wish you'd go ahead on and call me Too Much like I've told you to. It *is* my name, you know?"

"What kind of mama and daddy'd name their youngun Too Much?"

"They didn't have anything to do with it. Somebody else did the naming."

That was as far as Stump could stand to go with that. He didn't want to know who had named her if it wasn't blood kin.

"You can go on and bet on it, Too Much," he said. He could and would call her by the name Too Much now, because her fingers were in a frenzy behind the waistband of her Levi's and Stump's mind was as near Jell-O as it was ever likely to be and he could have broke a brick with his dick. Maybe two bricks. And consequently, he would have agreed in complete happiness and ignorance to his own execution.

She was starting to skin out of her clothes now, and Stump watched in total happiness and at the same time more than a little apprehension.

She could get out of her ribbed tank top all right. It was tight enough to give her some trouble, but she could do it. Getting out of her bra was no trouble because she didn't wear one. Her skintight Levi's were another matter. He'd have to help her with them. Not an unpleasant chore, and one of the goddamnedest things he'd ever learned in his entire life: how girls got into and out of Levi's that looked like they were painted on.

Down the hall, Stump watched her slip out of her sandals and lie flat out on her back in the carpeted hallway, her breasts standing at full mast, the chocolate-colored nipples rigid. Her nipples stayed rigid. Stump had often thought that if she had been a man, she would have stayed dead-on ready to work.

She raised her head a little to look at him where he sat at the table. "Put that beer down and come on and help me."

He didn't move. "I thought to drink me another of these cold Coors first."

"You know how I like my bathwater."

"Exactly what put me in mind to have another of these beers."

"You want my water to cool off?"

"Wouldn't hurt it none," he said.

"It'd ruin it for me is what it'd do, and you damn well know it. Bring that stump on down here if you mean to." When he didn't answer, she said, "You in or you out?"

She knew the answer to that, so he didn't say anything. He went down the hall where she lay, but he reached in the icebox and brought another Coors with him. She did like her water *hot*.

When he got to her, he bent down and took the brief legs of her cut-offs, and with her squirming to help him, he finally managed to work them off her. The first time she had asked him to do it, he thought maybe he had misunderstood what she wanted.

"Pull me out of these damn things," she had told him.

As it turned out, she put her Levi's on and took them off lying down. He was a little confounded by this, and he didn't like to be confounded. So she explained it to him.

"You don't think those girls you see wearing jeans so tight they look like they're something that grew to their skins put'm on standing up, do you?"

"Hadn't really thought about it," he said.

"Well, they don't. Never get'm on if they tried it standing up. They lie down, suck their stomachs in, and work into those things an inch at a time."

"What if I wasn't here to help you git out?"

"Oh, I'd make it by myself after a while. The girls that don't have any help manage it. Just takes a little more time and trouble. But why should I put myself out, when I've got you here to help me? About all a goddam man's good for anyway is to take a girl's pants off. That's been my experience anyway."

"Damn," he said. He thought on it a minute. "Why the hell do women wear'm so tight anyhow?"

"You've got a dick and you're asking me that? Sometimes I think you might not be too bright."

"You ain't the first one told me that."

"Never thought I was. Now get out of those pants of yours and let me see it. My water's getting cold."

"It's always something to be grateful for."

"Am I going to see your ass or what?"

She never got tired of looking at his ass. Or reading aloud what was written there. There was no use arguing with her. It only wasted time. And sometimes cost him one of her enthusiastic exercises with her mouth to boot. He already had his shoes off, so he dropped his trousers and turned to let her have her look. His cheeks were tattooed, expertly and with some flair, he had been told. He couldn't be sure, because it was hard to tell using a mirror.

Korea was his war, and he had had the work done, pissed off and shot up with heroin, in the bush by a boy from San Francisco who was a tattoo artist and who carried the tools of his trade with him. He loved his work and he loved his tools and he thought carrying them brought him luck, and he'd been hit squarely in the forehead by a .50-caliber round from a machine gun two weeks to the day after he had covered both of Stump's cheeks with a message Stump—who was then called Bubba, not Stump—had thought up himself in a fit of outraged madness and copied on a piece of tablet paper for the tattoo artist to work from. It was done in block letters, and Too Much read it aloud, as she always did. Written across his cheeks was this legend:

> THIS IS THE ONLY ASS YOU'VE GOT TO TAKE HOME. FUCK THE C.O. FUCK THE PRESIDENT. FUCK DEMOCRACY. FUCK THE FLAG, MOTHER AND APPLE PIE. JUST TAKE THIS ASS HOME. IN ONE PIECE.

When the war broke out—or the conflict, as they liked to call it (tell it to the boy with the .50-caliber round in his head, he thought)—Bubba and almost every other southern boy, black or white, went down and joined up, because the service was at least three hots and a cot and there were no jobs at home and, besides that, some gook motherfuckers were trying to do violence to the U.S. of A., and the southern boys were going to go show them whose ass was the blackest.

Bubba joined the Marine Corps, because if he was going to make the trip he was goddam going to make it his business to kill some folks—soldiers, women, or babies, he didn't give a fuck. His MOS was 0300, which in the Marine Corps meant he was a basic rifleman, a grunt, a hard-leg. But shit, he wasn't over there but three months before he saw it was all a big joke. One that wasn't funny at all.

War, his ass. They'd fight like madmen for a week to take a hill because their officers told them it was absolutely mandatory to take the hill and hold it at all costs. They would fight and die and take the hill, and then, two days later, they'd walk off the fucking thing and give it back. The day before Bubba had his ass inscribed, he watched his best friend trip a wire and lose all of himself from the waist down to a fragmentation mine. That's what got him to thinking about taking his own ass back home in one piece and expressing his dead-solid-certain sentiments about the president and democracy and the rest of it. If he hadn't been half out of his mind, though, he would have left his mother out of it, because even if she was a foulmouthed old bitch and a drunk besides, she was *his* foulmouthed old bitch who drank whiskey as though she had never heard of water.

"Are you going to get that arm in here with me or not?" Too Much asked, standing with her feet wide apart on the finest pair of legs he'd ever seen.

That he was. That he was. A whole company of rice-eating gooks could not have kept him out of that scalding water, where she was about to bring him the only heaven any man would ever know on earth. The door to the bathroom was already closed, and he could hardly see her through the steam, where she sat in the huge tub, her breasts floating, hard-nosed and dangerous.

"Well, get on in, dickhead," she said good-naturedly and in a tone of voice a mother might have used with a child.

The tub was the biggest one he could find and have installed the day after she showed up at Forever and Forever and he discovered what her kink was. He didn't like to think of it as kink, because he was a southern boy, born and bred, and had scratched his living from a leached-out forty-acre patch of dirt for most of his life, and southern boys were not into kink, unless you could call fucking an occasional cow kink. That shit—kink, that is—was what New York City boys did with their spare time. But deny it as he tried—and he no longer tried: it had become impossible—he was neck deep in kink with Too Much and loving it as he had loved little else in his life.

And so he was facing a naked eighteen-year-old girl in a tub so big he'd had to have a wall knocked down just to put it in. But whatever it had cost him, it was big enough for the job at hand, a job of joy and fear and great strangeness. Or to say it straight out: *It was not normal.* But shit, Stump had given up on normal the day he watched his best friend blown apart at the navel in a muddle of blood and stinking shit and still live long enough to scream for God to put him back together again. Whatever job of work God—that corrupt little fucker—was doing that day, it was too important for him to hear the scream and smell the blood and the shit and the stinking bile.

"Give me that stump, Stump," Too Much said.

She had her legs spread on either side of his hips. He sometimes thought he'd seen fish ponds smaller than that bathtub, and she was nothing if she was not flexible, limber as a cat. He stuck the stump out toward her through the steam. She took it gently, tenderly, and without even looking, she reached behind her and took the huge, economy-size tube of K-Y jelly off the rim of the tub. She uncapped it and very slowly began to grease the nub of his arm down, her eyes taking on a slight glaze and a very faraway look as she worked.

"Tell me," she said.

"I've told you every day for two months," he said, his whole body going instantly cold in the steaming water. With his good arm, he reached for the Coors he had thoughtfully provided himself with.

"I didn't ask you how many times you'd told me. I said to tell me again."

"You gone tear something one day doing this," he said, his voice not as steady as he would have liked it to be.

"If anything was going to tear, it already would have torn. *Now tell me.*" Despite her glazed eyes, her voice was now one of hard command.

She wanted the story of how he happened to own Forever and Forever, how he, a poor dirt farmer who could barely read, was now rich enough to live in a green subforest of perpetual sunshine and never hit a lick at a snake again as long as he lived if he didn't want to. He had enough money in the bank that he'd quit looking at his statement when it came every month, and she knew it.

She called it *the chance of ultimate possibility.* Despite the way she spoke and very often acted, she was a bright girl and seemed to have read everything. It had taken her the better part of a day to explain to him what she meant by the chance of ultimate possibility, which she always spoke in italics, although Stump did not know what italics were. Whatever they were, though, he recognized in them the voice of a line officer in the Marine Corps when it was time to take the high ground. It did not admit of argument.

So he never really had any choice but to tell her how he'd come by the money to own Forever and Forever, which in his secret heart he did not mind because it made her breathe hard, and slobber, and finally do what he thought of as her circus act.

"Weren't a whole lot to it, actually. Just lost a hand when it got caught in a corn picker," he said, "after I got home from Korea."

"Yes," she said, the only word she ever consented to say while he told her the story, as all the while she greased his nub with the K-Y.

"I was on the tractor, pulling the picker in the back of the field right by myself, when a stalk of corn got caught in a wringer."

"Yes," she said, her voice already getting wet but her hand still gentle on his arm.

"You too young to remember the old-timey washing machines that you run the clothes through two rubber rollers to dry them, but that's the kind of thing the cornstalk was caught in, only a hell of a lot bigger."

"Yes," she said.

"I got off the tractor to git it out. Done it a hundred times in my life, only this time things come up different. When I took hold of the cornstalk, the thing jerked my hand and wrist into the roller. And I was caught. I mean by God caught. Never remember being that scared in Korea. Usually didn't have time to be scared there. But in the back side of that field, I had plenty of time. It weren't nobody coming to help me, that was for dead solid certain, and I was too far from the house to call for help."

"Yes," she said. "Yes."

"Later, doctors said them rubber rollers—the heat of them things—cauterized the veins, or I would have bled to death. I don't remember thinking about it at all. Maybe by that time I was in shock—hell, I don't know. But with my good hand I reached in my pocket and got out my knife, knife I use to cut off hog nuts with, razor sharp."

She could not now speak. She only nodded her head.

"The bone in my wrist was crushed. Hell, I could see it sticking through the skin. Not much blood. The rollers had done stopped that. Using my teeth and my good hand, I opened my knife, and without even thinking, I took a cut at it—my wrist, I mean. Didn't feel much of anything. Took another, harder cut and still no pain, no feeling of any kind. To make a long story short, I cut my goddam hand off, stuck it in my back pocket, and headed for home. Damn near made it too. I was driving into the lane there at the house when I fainted and fell off the tractor. Damn wonder the thing didn't run over me. Ma, drunk as she was, thrown me in the car and taken me to town, where they fixed me up. Hell, I was back home in ten days—doctors didn't want me to be, but I was—setting there on the front porch rocking, not thinking about nothing worth talking about, except that I was gone be a one-armed farmer. No big deal in that, it was a lot of'm where I come from—pulpwood accidents, and first one thing and another. So anyhow, I was rocking there, when I'm a twice-damned son of a bitch if two lawyers didn't show up at the same time and damn near 'bout had a fight there in the front yard over which one was gone represent me in court and sue everybody in sight, including the tractor and corn-picker company, and make me a rich man, and them too, as it happened."

He paused a moment and she did not say anything, but she had him pulled forward, with his greased stump easing between her spread thighs, her bony little heels hooked into his hips and his maypole—it was the only way he could think of his dick when he was in the water with her that way—his maypole rising straight out of the water, its blood-engorged head beating like a heart, or at least it felt like that to Stump.

She eased his nub into her, bent forward with that catlike flexibility, swallowed his maypole entirely to the root, hooked his hips tighter with her heels, and with her throat stuffed all the way past her tonsils with his cock, screamed in a voice as clear and distinct as a man might scream *Fire!* in a crowded theater, "Look out, Old Son, I'm about to get my nuts off!"

In the tub, Stump could never imagine how she managed what she did, because while he was in the water, what little mind was left him was on other things. And out of the tub, he would think about it as hard as he could and it simply did not seem possible. He had even asked her about it.

She only stroked his stump softly, gave him her young-girl smile, and said, "That is precisely it: *the chance of ultimate possibility.*"

Stump drifted on the last edges of deep, sweet sleep and drifted, too, toward a profoundly peaceful awakening to another day that he knew could only be satisfying and good. It had been this way since Too Much appeared at Forever and Forever. His sleep-befogged brain wondered if he would ever get used to it. For another long and delicious night he had not dreamed of the cries of dying men or the stink of the offal that spilled from their ruptured stomachs or heard their ragged breathing as they drowned in their own blood.

He stretched long, still half asleep on his king-size bed, before letting his head slowly roll on his pillow toward the side where she slept. She was not there, and he had not expected her to be. But he could smell—or thought he could—her heavy, almost feral fragrance and feel—or thought he could—the sweet heat of her long, lean body still clinging to the bedclothes. He eased his eyes half open and let the first early light of day sift through his lashes as he gazed toward the blinds, open just enough to let in long sword-thin lines of the sun just beginning to break over the far horizon, and to let in, too, the supple lines of Too Much, wearing gray sweatpants and sweatshirt, a towel wrapped around her neck, as she held her favorite yoga position, still as stone, there on the wide deck beyond the blinds, her deep, steady breathing the only movement that showed that she was even alive.

Both of her feet were behind her head, the tight fabric of the sweatpants giving the beautifully detailed lines of her hamstrings and the round, perfectly symmetrical cheeks of her heart-shaped ass. Both hands were down by her hips, arms straight, elbows locked out, holding her entire body four inches off the deck, her legs impossibly relaxed and holding behind her head, which was dropped back onto her shoulders. Her calm, fine-boned face glowed with the first bright lip of the sun, which was rising now above the distant line of Australian pine trees.

He smiled and felt the wonderfully used nub of his right forearm and the tender, longing soreness of the head of his cock, which seemed itself to be awakening from a long dream of joy, totally satisfied but still ticking with the memory of gripping thighs and hips that thrust and undulated like strong waves coming off a high sea. Waves. Yes, that was it: waves, primal and endless in their strength, rolling forever, and forever rolling, for no other reason than that it was their nature.

She had kept him in the tub—as was her habit—adding steaming water from time to time, until when he finally emerged his skin was as quilted as that of a newly born baby. But when Too Much came out of the water, her firm flesh glowed with the high flush of blood and her skin was smooth and tight and eminently lickable. His tongue had something of an addiction—or that's what it felt like to him—for certain of her secret places when she first came from the water, and she stood good-naturedly on her straddling legs, giving him easy access to her, he there on his knees on the carpeted bathroom floor and she, idly but with easy gentleness, stroking his hair with both of her hands.

He turned his head again and opened his eyes and watched her come out of the yoga position and, once on her feet, strip out of the sweats, standing now in the light of a sun that was full and hot over the far horizon. She wore a bikini that was nearly invisible, clinging in perfect form to the swellings and recesses of her impossibly young body, her skin slightly damp with the thinnest patina of sweat. Stump felt a surge at his heart and a strength in the bone and muscle of his body that he never felt unless he was looking at her nearly naked.

As improbable (impossible?) as it was, Stump knew that what he was feeling was youth, youth he no longer had and would never have again. She did that to him, Too Much did. She made him feel as though he were young and would stay young and would live forever. With his head there on the pillow, he smiled and shook his head at the silliness of it. But silly or not, it was real, as real as the pot of coffee he could smell from the kitchen, which she had put on to brew for him.

She herself did not drink coffee. She would have had a small glass of orange juice before stretching on the deck and then heading for the pool to swim laps in her bikini, her long flaxen hair caught on the nape of her beautifully curving neck by a leather thong. Not a rubber band. Not a bow of some sort. But a thin piece of soft leather. Who else but Too Much would have thought of leather to hold her hair? But then who else would have (could have?) made him proud of his foreshortened arm? Only Too Much. For that reason and others, she could have had anything Stump owned. Surely she knew that. But she apparently wanted nothing. Gifts only embarrassed her, and she refused money. She did not seem to want anything but to belong to him, to please him, and to always be there for him.

It made no sense. And it sent a thrill of fear through Stump to think that undoubtedly, somewhere at the center of his feeling for her, there was something that was a lie, that was rotten and smelled of death.

She suddenly turned on the deck and looked back through the blinds toward his bed, waved, and smiled. The long nails of her left hand ran lightly along the edge of the bikini at the bottom of her flat stomach. In the morning her scratching was light and sporadic, hardly noticeable at all. It was only later in the day that the serious digging started. But Stump told himself that scratching didn't mean an ounce of anything to him anymore. Maybe it had once, but not anymore. Leprosy could not have turned his feeling from her and he knew it. He watched as she stepped off the deck and headed toward the pool, the thinly covered globes of her ass ticking like a clock.

And Too Much knew his eyes were on her ass, could feel them there as if they had been hands touching her. She loved the weight of his gaze on her flesh, loved it because his need for her was so acutely desperate that it made her feel almost God-like. The way he looked at her, the way he touched her, the way he watched her touch herself, gave her a sense of euphoric power that made her heart sing and made the very blood in her veins leap in a way that was hot and quick.

She felt herself magical. She did not understand the feeling or its source, or even its ultimate significance. But she had somehow learned as a very young girl that in the world there was only the quick and the dead. Only that and nothing more: the quick and the dead. And she had the power to make the dead quick. The power to bring life where there had only been death, to bring joy and celebration where there had only been resignation and despair. She rejoiced in exercising that power; it gave purpose and direction to her life. And for her, it was its own reward. Nothing else she knew of in the world could compare with it.

It certainly had nothing to do with physical possessions or money or being well known. She found those kinds of things boring. Rather, she liked to think of herself as a secret shaman, a medicine woman with eagles' claws in her hair. For such a one, chance and possibility were everywhere. She knew that probably only prophets and madmen ever felt as she did, ever felt the very nearly mindless ecstasy of doing what she did with her life. She knew and saw what other people were too helplessly ignorant to see, or perhaps were only too busy to see.

The image of Stump's mangled nub flashed before her. Five minutes after she met him, she knew he was convinced the purple-scarred nub was ugly and worthless, a mutilation that frustrated, angered, and confounded him. Too Much knew that Stump in all likelihood did not even know he felt that way about his arm. But Too Much knew, and she had changed all that. She had made it her business to press his arm between her young breasts and stroke it and to kiss the twisted, gnarled flesh at the end of it. And then there had come the moment, the chance and the possibility—her thighs stretched—of mounting it.

Too Much was almost to the pool now, beside which two extremely old couples were listlessly playing shuffleboard, their rheumy eyes dead and glazed-over with boredom. The couples were not so much playing shuffleboard as they were leaning on their sticks in total silence.

Too Much smiled. They reminded her of the first time she had ever rode Stump's nub to climax. His leaden eyes suddenly lit up like burning coals. The beatific look that flashed over his face was indescribable as the knife-scarred end of the nub pressed against her cervix. Too Much closed her eyes and thought this was what being mounted by a stallion must feel like. It hurt but it was a beautiful hurt, and that feeling, combined with the look on his face, was what caused her to come the second time he stroked her with his arm. Had it been possible, she would have taken him inside her all the way to the shoulder. But while she couldn't do that, she could—and did—change his attitude toward his mangled arm forever.

He carried his crippled arm now the way a king might carry his scepter. When she had arrived at Forever and Forever, Stump always wore a long-sleeved shirt with the empty place at the bottom of the right forearm pinned up. Now he wore T-shirts or tank tops, waving his foreshortened arm, gesturing with it, and generally regarding it as the miracle that Too Much had convinced him it was. There was no payment in the world that could have satisfied Too Much for what she had accomplished.

She stood on the lip of the pool and regarded the old couples as they regarded her, all of them leaning on their shuffleboard sticks. Other old people were coming out of their trailers now, hobbling on arthritic knees or leaning on canes or using three-sided aluminum walkers. Four couples were in motorized wheelchairs. All of them were headed toward the pool, where they watched her swim every morning. They were the Old Ones—known throughout Forever and Forever by that name—and they were her favorite of all the residents in the entire park.

Too Much thought they looked as though they had just stumbled out of a concentration camp. And it was not the first time the thought had occurred to her. She did not like the thought, and she did not like herself for having it. But most of all, she did not like the world for abandoning the old people in such a place as Forever and Forever and making such a thought possible.

Too Much looked across the pool to where they had gathered in a tight little group. The sun, full in the sky now, gleamed off their walkers and wheelchairs in little bursts of light. She waved to them. They waved back, every last one of them in the same instant, as though they had spent a long time practicing the move.

"You poor goddam people are the living dead," Too Much called. She smiled and waved again. The old people waved back, and what could have been smiles twitched on several of their faces.

Too Much waved and called, "Every one of you poor devils are dead and don't know it."

They all waved back, and the same faces twitched again.

"But all you need is joy and celebration to bring you back to life."

She waved and they waved back.

"You think about graves and death too much!" she called.

They waved and she waved back.

"It'll take a little more than this waving to get the job done. I'm going to get the blood and piss pumping in you again or kill every precious soul of you trying."

She took a racing dive into the water and did a rapid, freestyle stroke that she would hold for ten laps, a thin trail of bubbles following her fluttering feet. She breathed on every second stroke, and when her face rolled up for air she saw the old people waving rhythmically, as though keeping time to music.

When she finally finished the tenth lap, she got out of the pool and shook herself like some sleek animal coming out of the water. She stood looking across the pool at the old people still mindlessly waving to her. She smiled gently at them. They were so good and kind and sweet that something really did have to be done for them, or with them, or to them, even if it was nothing but death.

But for now, now they had waved enough. They needed another

movement, another mild exercise to keep their old hearts pumping and their old blood flowing, now that Too Much had got it started here in the first heat of morning.

Gazing at them steadily, she gradually and slowly started to clap her hands. It was only a very few minutes before half of them had stopped waving and started clapping, and even a shorter time still before all of them, every last one, were clapping their hands in slow and steady unison.

Too Much stopped, but they continued. As she walked away, she called over her shoulder in a kind, good-natured voice, "You old petrified bastards, don't worry about being dead. I carry the touch of life, and I'm gone lay it on you every one. Don't worry about a thing."

She walked slowly through the trailer camp, the heavy humidity already moving about her like rising water. At an open square at the center of the camp—a square as big as two basketball courts joined together—she stopped and stood, slowly nodding her head and smiling, as she regarded her maypole. It was a young but tall and very straight Australian pine. God knows how it came to be there, but it was growing in the exact center of the open court, a court that in an earlier time—before somebody had decided to turn the trailer park into a place exclusively for the very old and nearly dead—had maybe been used for boys and girls to play basketball or volleyball or some other sport. Whether that was true or not did not matter. What mattered was that she had found her perfect maypole, growing in a perfect place. It seemed a sign.

True, the tree would have to be considerably altered—topped, and all the limbs cut away from its trunk—but she knew how to get that done. The man for the job, Ted Johanson, a retired lumberjack, eighty years old and recently widowed, was sitting in his trailer not thirty yards away, bordering right on the courtyard she was standing in. That he was universally feared in the trailer park, feared for his size, strength, temper, and profane mouth, did not bother Too Much at all.

If he was the rank, randy old goat everybody said he was, Too Much knew she carried more defense than she could possibly need, carried it between her legs. She gave the tight, high mound under the thin cloth of her bikini a particularly vicious stroking and marveled as she had unaccountable times that something so soft and fragile and damply vulnerable could totally destroy the offensive line of the Oakland Raiders football team—all of them—in less time than it would take to mow a lawn. In that short a time, her gentle pussy could have those huge, powerful, and vicious men collapsed onto their backs and gasping for breath. She knew most women did not think so, but she, Too Much, thought that owning what she carried between her legs was a responsibility of such incredible proportions as to be frightening. It had to be used carefully and with great discretion, because it could be as lethal as a loaded and cocked .357 magnum pistol.

There was an elaborately designed garden surrounding Ted Johanson's trailer. Every plant and flower in it was dead. It had belonged to Ted's wife. And he had never watered it once or done anything else to it that anybody knew of since his wife passed. It was now nothing but twisted and twisting desiccated brown stalks decorated with dead leaves.

Too Much knocked on the door.

Immediately, a voice, loud and rough as a file rasping over heavy metal, boomed, "No! Goddammit, no!"

Too Much smiled, viciously scratched herself, and knocked again.

"Go away!"

"This is Too Much, Mr. Johanson, and I need to see you." She raised her voice, calling even louder. "And one way or another I'm coming through this door."

"I want no split-tail in my house!"

Ted Johanson's voice managed to growl and boom at the same time, and it was shaped by a slight Swedish accent that somehow made it seem all the more threatening to Too Much.

"Even if you are a woman, I break your head for you. Be wise, and leave while you can still walk." Then, as a kind of afterthought: "And take your stinking *thing* with you!"

Too Much put her hand on the doorknob and was not at all surprised to find that it was unlocked. People with a voice and reputation like Johanson's rarely needed to lock anything. She opened the door and stepped inside. The air was so cold, it was like walking into a dimly lit meat locker.

Huge, and wearing a thick, dirty terry-cloth robe, Ted Johanson sat in an overstuffed recliner, relentlessly puffing on a pipe whose stem curved downward over his beard, which was gray and matted and so long as to almost cover his chest. The hair on his head was the same soiled gray as his beard and fell over his shoulders. His eyebrows were long and twisted, and the ridge of his brow was so prominent that in the dim light from the small lamp sitting on a table beside his chair, Too Much could not see his eyes in their deep, black sockets. His hands, bigger than any Too Much had ever seen and laced with veins that were knotted and thick, lay half curled in his lap.

Too Much stood on her straddling legs, about which she had always been vain and in which she had ultimate confidence, briefly touched herself with the forefinger of her right hand, and then pointed the same finger directly at him. "Now, let's get one goddam thing straight, Ted. My fucking thing does not stink." And then, in a gentler, sweeter voice: "If you doubt that, it's easy enough to prove, right here, right now. I don't guess there's but the two of us in here. Do you need proof, Ted?"

"Mr. Johanson to you, you young puppy."

"I'll call you anything you want me to, Mr. Johanson. But while we're on names, I'm not a puppy. I'm the most woman you ever imagined in your youngest and wettest dream, and I go by the name of Too Much, because that's what I am: Too fucking Much. You got that? We straight on all this nonsense, so we can get down to business?"

"I did not order fish," he said. "We have no business. I can tell from here your fish are very bad. Take them somewhere else."

Too Much went across the room until she was so close that she could have reached out and touched him.

"Jesus," she said. "Do we have to play it this way? Aren't we too old for this kind of childish play?"

"What would you know about old?" he growled. He raised one of his thick hands, and for a moment she thought he would touch her. But he was only pointing, and his hand was as steady as that of a young man. There was no tremor of age in it at all. "You speak of old and you walk around in diapers."

She sighed and scratched herself and for the first time saw his eyes flash in their dark sockets. "I don't have time for this, so I'm cutting straight to the chase."

"The what?" he said, his eyes still following her moving hand.

She shrugged. "Manner of speaking. What I've got is a job I want you to do, a job that only you can do."

He laced his thick fingers in his lap and looked down at them. "I don't do no job. Except be old. My job is being old."

"Bullshit."

"You have a very dirty mouth to be still wearing diapers." His lips drew back in what could have been a smile or a leer or both. Too Much saw his teeth move in his mouth. False.

"The word is that you're a lumberjack. A great one. Of course, that could be a lie."

He cut his eyes to the far wall, where the dim light from the lamp barely reached. Hanging on wooden pegs on the wall were the tools of his trade, tools Too Much had not noticed until now: a thick-handled, double-bitted ax, climbing spikes, a wide leather safety belt, and a notching hatchet.

"Ah, then it was no lie. That's the real thing hanging up there."

"What would you know about the real thing?"

"Had an uncle that was a lumberjack. He worked the greatest woods in the world, and he had just the kind of stuff that's hanging on the wall there." The lie came so easily and quickly to her lips, it felt and sounded like the truth to her. In the time it took to say it, she really did have an uncle who was a lumberjack. Too Much was very inventive with her life. Always had been.

Ted Johanson sat a little straighter and leaned forward in his chair. "Your uncle worked the Great North Woods?"

"Oregon," she said, the lie leaping from her mouth with no thought from her. The uncle she had never had was forming stronger and stronger in her mind. If she had been asked—and been inclined to do so—she could have talked at great length about him. An endless number of details were piling up about him. Too Much could see him quite clearly. His name was Johnny, and he had red hair.

Ted Johanson had slumped back into his chair. "If he worked Oregon, he did not work the greatest woods in the world. I've worked all the woods, and I know."

"I'll give you that," she said. "Score one for your side." She gestured briefly at the wall where the ax and the climbing gear hung. "Could you still put that on and do a job?"

His old eyes flared again. "I already told you. I've got a goddam job. Being old. Shittiest work I ever had, but it's full time."

Too Much thought about that and said, "How long has it been since you saw a pair of young titties? Really great and really young titties?"

A forked vein leapt above Ted Johanson's nose and climbed his broad forehead and disappeared into his matted hair. His huge hands clenched in his lap. But he did not answer.

"How long?" said Too Much.

Finally Ted Johanson said in a choked voice, "I would have to think about it for a while."

"Take your time," she said softly. "I've got nothing if I don't have time."

No sooner was the final line out of her mouth than he said, "Sixty years last month. I was faithful to my wife."

"But she's dead."

"Yes, she's dead."

"But I'm not."

"No," he said.

"Would you like to see my titties, maybe feel them with your mouth?"

He did not answer, and the vein in his forehead grew bigger and his clenched fists were now white-knuckled. He opened his mouth but did not speak. His teeth moved, and he closed his lips over them.

Too Much reached behind her back with both hands, and when the brief bikini top opened, her breasts burst free, full and high, standing at right angles to her rib cage. Her nipples were bigger than pencil erasers.

"Jesus, Jesus," Ted Johanson whispered, "help me now and at the hour of my death."

Too Much smiled softly and moved toward him. "Take your teeth out, Teddy."

And he did.

Chapter 4

Too Much stood outside the door of Ted Johanson's trailer. The Old Ones who had watched her swim laps were gathered about her. At Forever and Forever, the Old Ones were not the oldest of the old but were universally called the Old Ones. Nobody knew when or how the Old Ones came to be called by that name. They pressed closely together all day long wherever they were in the trailer park, like a small herd of cattle in a heavy rain.

And they were great leaners. Wherever they were, they leaned on anything that was handy: a tree, a trailer, a shuffleboard stick, and sometimes each other. There were men and women in Forever and Forever who were older than any of the Old Ones. But they had not broken down enough to join them. Many of the Old Ones were deaf as stones, and only a few of them could talk—or at least talk well enough so that what they said could be easily understood.

They had grown attached to Too Much since her arrival at Forever and Forever, probably because she took time to talk to them. They seemed to understand little of her talk—she could never be sure—but it didn't matter to her anyway. They also loved her because she took the time to lead them in mild exercises. And perhaps most of all because she smiled at them a lot and touched them and guided them through the maze of narrow streets of Forever and Forever and allowed them to be part of whatever she was doing.

Too Much loved flowers and plants of every sort. And she let them help her pull weeds and water the soil and loosen the roots with a three-pronged fork. Most of the time, all the Old Ones really did was get in her way, but it never bothered her.

To the two hundred or so other people living in Forever and Forever—the number changed almost daily—the Old Ones were more or less invisible. It was not so much that the other residents treated the Old Ones badly as that they simply ignored them. They wanted nothing to do with them, perhaps because they had the stink of death about them, a stink even stronger than the one the others themselves carried. When an ambulance glided silently into the trailer park, it was almost always to haul off one of the Old Ones. That alone was enough to keep the other residents away from them.

Over three-quarters of the residents of Forever and Forever ambled now about the open space in front of Ted Johanson's trailer, studiously avoiding the Old Ones. Too Much, lean and young and hard-muscled in her bikini, had started her serious scratching and digging, and it so outraged and angered the residents that they desperately did not want to look at her at all. Consequently, they could not keep their eyes off her.

"What's going on out here?"

Too Much turned, to see Stump standing at her shoulder, the purple-scarred end of his nub glowing in the brilliant sunlight as though it were on fire. He wore a long-visored Dolphins cap, khaki pants, and a tank top.

Too Much shrugged. "You wouldn't understand."

"Try me."

So seldom did anything unusual or even mildly interesting happen in Forever and Forever that when it did, the news spread as if by magic, and every resident who could make it out of his trailer was there to watch whatever was going on. Too Much had absolutely no idea how word of what Ted Johanson was about to do got out, but it had somehow, and everybody who could be was here in the open courtyard now to see how it would all end up.

Too Much turned to look at Stump. "I found my maypole is what I did."

"And where did you find this maypole?"

"Right there," she said, pointing at the Australian pine.

"That's the only goddam Australian growing in the park. You ain't got in mind to mess up my tree, have you?"

"Depends on what you mean by mess it up."

"I think you can figure it out."

"Stump, you're not going to ruin this May Day celebration, are you? It's just what your people need."

"What my people need is shade to sit in and time to die."

She said, a little tight-lipped, "I never liked that way of thinking or that way of talking, and you know it."

"Just don't get any notions about my tree."

"Quid pro quo, Stump. Something for something."

"You'll have to talk plainer than that."

"These people need joy and celebration, laughter and happiness. It'll take ten years off their lives."

"If you take ten years off their lives, I'll be out of business, because they'll all be dead."

"You know what I mean."

"I never know what you mean, Too Much."

"Then just stand back and watch."

"Watch what?"

"Ted Johanson's going to top that tree and strip it down to the perfect maypole."

"I could get pissed off about that, but I'm not, because Ted Johanson ain't about to do nothing of the sort. The fucker's eighty years old."

"Not anymore he's not." She gave him the wicked smile he had only seen when they were sunk in scalding water and she had designs on his nub.

"If he ain't eighty, then what is he?"

"The meanest lumberjack that ever pulled on a pair of climbing spikes."

Stump looked up at the Australian pine. "Just as long as he don't mess with my tree."

"Oh, he's going to mess with your tree. Count on it."

"Instead of raising hell and getting all bent about it, I'll just make you a deal. If Ted Johanson can top and trim that tree by hisself, you and him and everybody else is welcome to it."

"Deal," she said.

"Ain't a eighty-year-old man alive can do that."

"Ted Johanson's got some younger since the last time you saw him."

"And how did he manage that?"

"Mother's milk," she said. And again the sly, wicked smile.

"Whose milk?"

"Mine."

"It's a lot of things he could've got off you, but mother's milk ain't one of them. He wouldn't come across that on you."

"To a eighty-year-old man, mother's milk is where he finds it. Another example of *the chance of ultimate possibility.*"

"Bullshit."

She turned to face him now, looking him dead in the eye. "Did you lose all hope, faith, and the power of imagining the impossible in Korea?"

"I didn't lose it there or anywhere else. Never had any of what you're talking about. Nobody where I come from ever did. Among other things, it was starved out of us."

"Let me give you something from Shakespeare. You have heard of Shakespeare, right?"

"As it happens, I have. But I never knew the man."

"Shakespeare said nothing is true or false but thinking makes it so."

Stump held up his nub. "I believe we got a problem right here with this, then."

She regarded him a long moment. "Do you ever feel the hand that used to be there?"

"Every day of my life."

"Then how do you know it's not still there?"

"Because I know what's real and what's not."

"I try not to know anything about that, because it bores the shit out of me," she said, turning to look at the door of Ted Johanson's trailer. "It's time. He's ready."

As if on cue, the door swung open and there stood Ted Johanson, jackbooted, with steel climbing spikes attached to the heels, his safety belt cinched about his waist, a notching hatchet and a small gas-operated chain saw hanging from it. In his huge right hand he held the long-handled double-bitted ax. He still had his curving pipe in his mouth, and he still puffed at it relentlessly.

He had a black knitted skullcap pulled down to his ears. The soiled gray mane of his hair hung from under the cap all the way down to his shoulders.

"Jesus," said Stump.

"Is he something or is he something?" Too Much said.

"What is he wearing that wool cap for in this weather?" said Stump.

"Nature of the beast, I guess. He told me he worked the Great North Woods, and that cap is obviously part of what he always wore. When I talked to him, he didn't strike me as a man who went at anything left-handed or by half measures. With him, it's whole hog or none at all."

"When did you talk to him?"

"This morning. Just a little while ago, in fact."

"When he got the mother's milk." It was a statement, not a question.

"Now you've got everything right," she said.

"And you've done everthing wrong," said Stump, "making that old man climb a tree as tall as that Australian."

"Make him?" said Too Much. "Make him? Do you see a gun at his head?"

"You ought to shut up," said Stump, "and not talk to me. I think I'm pissed off."

"Better to be pissed off than pissed on."

Stump looked at her. "You're a better fuck than you are a comic."

"Does that mean you don't want me in your bathtub again?"

"You know better than that."

"True," she said. "I did know better than that."

Stump had already decided that he was not going to try to interfere. But he was worried. He had never liked Ted Johanson, who seemed to hate everything in the world, but that did not mean Stump wanted him dead. And that old man had no business screwing around in the top of a thirty-foot tree. As big a man as he was, even at eighty, and tricked out in his lumberjacking gear, he still had something fragile, even feeble, about him. Despite his standing in his doorway with booted feet spread far apart, staring at the people gathered to watch him work, staring at them with flashing eyes, his deeply lined face twisted into an expression of utter contempt as he rhythmically, effortlessly, switched the heavy ax from hand to hand—despite all that, Stump thought he looked like a man who very well might pitch straight forward over the three steps leading up to the doorway and land facedown in the dusty yard in front of him. Maybe he could still walk the walk and talk the talk of a lumberjack, but Stump knew that didn't really mean anything. He was only a weak and very old man who was flirting with disaster.

Too Much turned to the Old Ones and started clapping as slow and steady as a clock ticking. In little more than a minute, all the Old Ones were clapping too. Not another of the residents made a sound, and all other movement had stopped. Ted Johanson gave no indication that he heard the Old Ones clapping. For all the notice he took of them, they might just as well have been on the dark side of the moon.

Ted Johanson came down the steps slowly, as if he had sore feet, Stump thought, and made his way in a halting gait across the wide courtyard to the base of the tree. Too Much had stopped clapping, but the Old Ones gathered about her never missed a beat.

"For Christ's sake," said Stump, "look at the way he's walking. And this is a man you want to top and trim a tree for you?"

"He won't have to walk as soon as he gets in the tree," said Too Much.

"I wasn't thinking about walking; I was thinking about falling."

"Lumberjacks don't fall," she said.

"For the last time, he's not a lumberjack. He's an old man. A very old man."

"It was something he wanted," she said.

"This, no doubt, after the mother's milk."

"As a matter of fact, it was," she said. "He said he wanted to do the job. Can you understand that, goddammit—he *wanted* to do it."

"This was with you in his trailer, I reckon."

"Mother's milk is powerful stuff."

Stump looked around him at the Old Ones. They were glassy-eyed and still clapping. Stump wished they'd stop. They were getting on his nerves. This whole thing was getting on his nerves.

Ted Johanson had walked around the tree several times, his head thrown back, looking up into the branches. Suddenly, he stopped, turned to look at Too Much, extended one of his heavy arms, crooked a thick finger, and motioned her to come to him.

After she had walked away, Stump turned on the Old Ones and said: "That clapping is going to drive me crazy! Stop it, goddammit! And do it *now!*"

Several of the Old Ones made unintelligible sounds in their throats, several faces twitched, but they kept on clapping, their eyes fixed on Too Much where she had stopped beside Ted Johanson, who was looking up into the branches of the tree.

The old man kept his head back, his eyes fixed somewhere in the high reaches of the tree, while he spoke to Too Much. "I have to go up and top it first, and then take the limbs off as I come down. If I try to do the limbs from the bottom, working up as I go, I'll have limbs dropping in my face during the whole job." He brought his gaze down to look at Too Much.

Too Much could only stare back at him. "Is that a question? Because if it is, I don't understand."

"It means where do you want me to top it? How high you want this pole to be?"

"Oh," she said, "now I get it. Twenty feet would be nice. Yes, twenty feet would do us nicely indeed."

"You want twenty feet?" he said, his unstable teeth clamping on the stem of his pipe. "You got twenty feet. Now get out of the way and let me work."

Too Much had hardly taken a step before Ted Johanson said in a low, choked voice, "I thank you for your breasts." He paused briefly. "And for the rest."

Too Much smiled and said, "My pleasure." They stood a moment looking at each other, and Too Much thought: You might can't get it up anymore, Teddy, but you sure as hell can still do a job with what you've got.

Ted Johanson said, "I can go to my grave a happy man now. When I lie down to die, you settling yourself on my face while I was leaned back in my recliner is the last thing I'll see. You are a very kind woman, Too Much."

"I'm not kind," she said. "Kindness had nothing to do with it. And from what happened back in your trailer, your grave will have to wait a long time before it claims you."

"Get to it, Johanson," someone yelled. "Show everybody what you got left."

If Ted Johanson heard what was yelled at him, he gave no indication of it. He waited until Too Much had rejoined Stump and the Old Ones, who were still clapping tirelessly, before he whipped the safety belt around the trunk of the pine and cinched it. He hit the trunk of the tree the first time with absolute authority, driving the steel of the climbing spike attached to the heel of his boot deep into the wood. And he was off and moving with singular strength and rhythm. There was no hobbling or gimping here. As he drove himself upward with the steel spikes, he kept flipping the safety belt to a higher position with both hands. A moan of pleasure and surprise rose out of the throats of the residents over the rhythmic clapping of the Old Ones.

"Jesus," said Stump. "What did you do to him, Too Much?"

"Changed him a little," she said softly.

Stump said, "If I wasn't watching it, I wouldn't believe it. He's climbing like a young man!"

Still softly, hardly more than a whisper, she said, "In his secret heart right about now, he *is* a young man."

When Ted Johanson reached the first limb, he uncinched the safety belt and climbed higher, stepping from a lower limb to the one above it, and he did it as easily and naturally as a man might climb a flight of stairs, despite the heavy ax hanging from his belt, where he had secured it before he started up. Even the chain saw and the hatchet seemed no encumbrance at all.

There were shouts of approval and encouragement from nearly everybody below him now, and the Old Ones had picked up the tempo of their clapping.

"He's using his rope up in a hurry," said Stump. "It's got to be close to ninety degrees out here, for God's sake. Why is he working in such a hurry?"

"Because it's in him to do it," said Too Much. She could feel goose bumps rising all over her body. And her spine felt as if it had turned to solid ice. She, Too Much, had done this to Ted Johanson. Magic. It was pure magic. Her magic, and hers alone. The fire that was raging in Ted Johanson had come directly from her. Watching the old man high in the tree, she knew with a rock-solid certainty that the impossible was possible for her if only she willed it. And in that moment, she believed her will was invincible.

"He's not going to make it," said Stump.

"A twenty-year-old couldn't do it any better than he's doing it," she said.

"Problem is, he ain't twenty. He's eighty. Look at his face, red as fire, and the sweat's running off him like somebody had a garden hose turned on him."

Ted Johanson looked down to gauge the distance to the ground. Satisfied, he whipped the notching hatchet off his belt and in two rapid licks cut a perfect V into the trunk of the tree. He slipped the hatchet back into his safety belt, unclipped the small chain saw, and fired it up by pulling once on the starter rope. For so small a saw, it made an incredible noise.

He placed the spinning teeth of the saw in the notch and almost immediately screamed, "Timmmberrr!" But his voice sounded for all the world like that of a drowning man crying for help.

Stump cupped his hands around his mouth and called, "You all right up there, Ted?"

Ted Johanson didn't even look down when he answered. "Just stay out of the way and let me work." But he barely made himself heard over the noise of the chain saw, and there was something childlike and plaintive in the sound of his voice.

"I ought to make him get down from there," Stump said.

"What you ought to do is leave the man alone and let him do what's in him to do," said Too Much.

"He's hurt," Stump said. "Didn't you hear it in his voice?"

The chain saw ripped into the first, highest limb, which came crashing through the limbs below it and landed in the dusty court under the tree.

Too Much pointed to the limb, and even as she was pointing, another limb was crashing to the ground beside it. "Does that look like he's hurt?"

"I hate to keep saying it, but you can't seem to understand. The man's too old for what he's doing."

"That's what you say and that's what the calendar says. But to hell with you and the calendar. His heart tells him he's a man doing a man's job."

"His heart says that, does it?" said Stump. "I say his heart is just about to blow up like a cheap balloon."

She turned her hard eyes on him, anger making her lips go gray. "I don't know how you're even alive, with the rotten attitude you're holding."

Another limb crashed to the ground, and the whole tree was shaking so hard that salt-colored pine needles floated through the air like sifting snow.

The Old Ones were still tirelessly clapping, in a kind of mindless trance. All the other residents were shouting encouragement, some of them screaming like spectators at a horse race or a lynching.

Suddenly, there was a high, piercing wail that cut through all the other voices and the rhythmic clapping of the Old Ones and the ripping noise of the chain saw.

"Goddam, do it, Ted! Do it! Do it for me! Do it for all of us! Jesus, it's beautiful. And do it . . ."

The voice went on like a madness, hysterical, out of control. The Old Ones never missed a beat, but an immediate hush fell over the shouting residents. Too Much, along with everybody else—except the Old Ones—turned to see who it was. A man, not thirty feet from the base of the tree, was hopping from foot to foot as though standing on live coals and waving his long, thin arms as though he meant to fly.

Too Much recognized him at first glance. It was Johnson Meechum. His thin, arthritic wife stood beside him, her face flushed with blood and her eyes wild. She watched Johnson as though he were something in a zoo. The silence that had fallen on the residents held, and they no longer made a sound. None of them moved. Too Much knew that it was Johnson's cursing that had struck them dumb.

Public cursing was taboo and unforgivable in Forever and Forever, especially the kind of cursing Johnson was doing. Johnson cursed the frailty of them all that kept them out of trees, and in the string of words pouring from his mouth he cursed old age and God and death and the loss of love. Too Much admired Johnson's cursing, the sheer inventiveness of it and also the fact that he apparently did not mean to stop anytime soon. Too Much watched his wife, Mabel, put her crooked-fingered hand on Johnson's shoulder and watched Johnson spin and dance away from her without missing a single profane and blasphemous phrase. Too Much wondered where a bank president had learned such language. Perhaps in prison, because prison was where he spent five years after the bank's auditors discovered that he had embezzled a young fortune.

Too Much knew all this because she had gone to considerable trouble to know it. She did, in fact, know more about most of the residents' lives than they knew themselves. Too Much loved the hairy underbelly of other people's lives. She loved all the dirt, the grim, gritty details—all that closest to the bone. And getting the details was an easy thing to accomplish, because given half a chance, the residents would talk endlessly about themselves. Too Much always gave them that chance. And she filed away everything she learned in the deep recesses of her mind, aware that the more she knew about a person, the more power she had over him and the more control, control to help him whether he wanted it or not, control to make him the person he could have been if he had sufficient courage and will and intelligence. Too Much liked to say, "My bag is other people's bags." It was, she felt in her heart, what her magic was made of.

Johnson had come to Forever and Forever straight from prison. He shot the swamp adjoining the trailer park, shot it once a day with a .22-caliber target pistol, because he was convinced that the swamp had a vulnerable place in it somewhere, and if he ever found that spot and shot it, the swamp would dry up and die and not spread to consume and ultimately destroy Forever and Forever. He had a pathological fear of having to leave the trailer park when the encroaching swamp devoured and destroyed it.

Johnson had told Too Much all this when she came upon him one morning on the edge of the swamp. Johnson also said he did not love his wife. He didn't even like her. And because he couldn't like her, he hated himself. And as she was the source of his hatred for himself, he had come to hate her too. "Oh," he told Too Much, "my life will not bear examination. It's twisted and turned on its head and mixed up six ways from Sunday, just like the books those damn auditors found in my bank."

That was also the morning he confessed to Too Much that he often confused the swamp with himself. Not for long, mind you, only for a brief, almost unconscious moment, he was the swamp and the swamp was he, both slimy and muddy and of uncertain depth and filled with living, malformed creatures that loved the dark and hated the light. When he put a bullet into the swamp on some mornings, he expected his brain to explode into a bloody mess with the impact of the bullet. Agitated and wet-eyed, he had said to Too Much, "That's crazy, isn't it? Is that what all this is about: I've gone crazy?"

She regarded him for a moment and said, "No, not crazy at all. Every bit of that is as common as field peas. It doesn't make you crazy and it doesn't make you bad; it only makes you human. You're alive and well. Here, let me show you how alive and well you are." She put her arms around him so that her fingers pressed his spine, and then she leaned in and did not so much kiss him as trace his lips with her tongue. Her fingers felt his spine go rigid, as though touched with a heavy jolt of electricity. When she pulled back, he cried, "Good fucking Lord!"

"You see?" Too Much said, and she walked away smiling, feeling very good about what she had been able to do to and for the old man.

And now, across the way, Mabel had both arms locked around poor Johnson's throat and looked as though she was trying to climb his back. But at least she had shut him up.

The residents had grown tired of or bored or embarrassed by Johnson's leaping and shouting and were again calling encouragement to Ted Johanson. Too Much turned to look up and saw that only two limbs were left, the very lowest ones. Ted Johanson uncinched his safety belt, stood on one limb, and placed the bitted chain of his saw in the V where the other limb joined the trunk, and then he did not move again.

The chain saw roared and the crowd below roared, but Ted Johanson did not move. Not even a twitch. The Old Ones clapped on, but gradually a silence fell on the residents, one by one, and they only stared until Johanson turned and came straight down headfirst and landed in the dirt, the chain saw beside him, still running.

Stump was the first one to him, and when he pressed his fingers to Johanson's carotid artery, he already knew what he would find: nothing. Stump had seen too many dead men not to know one when he was looking at him. And Ted Johanson was as dead as he would ever be.

Stump turned to look at Too Much, who had come to stand beside him.

"You happy now?" he said.

In an almost conversational voice, she said: "You don't understand anything, do you? Every man is looking for his death. Finding the right one is the most important thing in a whole life. Would you rather he died with his climbing spikes dug into a tree, or covered up with his bathrobe and hunkered down in his recliner, with all the shades pulled?"

"Neither. I'd rather he'd not died at all," Stump said.

"It was all as it should have been," said Too Much. "He's going to his grave happy. I know exactly what he was thinking about and what he was seeing behind the lids of his eyes when he closed them to die." She was smiling.

Stump, red-faced, could only stare at her. "If you can know shit like that, you ought to tie a rag around your head and start telling fortunes."

Too Much merely smiled. "I don't need a rag around my head to know what I know."

In a voice that was full of anger, Stump shouted, "Somebody call the wagon."

The chance of ultimate possibility, thought Johnson, as Mabel clamped her crooked-fingered hand about his thin arm so tightly it hurt. Normally the pain in her arthritic fingers was so intense that she could not pick up a frying pan. But Johanson's death and Johnson's own profanity and blasphemy had so galvanized her with fear and anger that she was not only leading but very nearly dragging him through the dusty, narrow street toward their trailer. Johnson did not resist, because his mind was on other matters. She was in an angry rage such as he had seen only a few times in their long life together, and those few times were a very long time ago, when they had still been young.

Her face flushed, sweat pouring down her neck into her blouse, she said in a strange, loud voice he could not remember hearing from her before, "How can I ever hold my head up again?" She looked straight ahead, dragging him along behind her. "You went crazy and acted the fool, and you must have been . . . must have been . . ."

Apparently she could not figure out what he must have been, because she had got stuck on the phrase and kept repeating it as she staggered through the heat, her hand gripping still tighter about Johnson's arm. He wasn't listening, though, and only hoped she didn't have a stroke or a heart attack before he could find out if what he *thought* was happening was *really* happening.

The chance of ultimate possibility kept repeating itself in his head, a mad little chant that would not stop, nor did he want it to. Too Much had explained it to him early one morning as he was walking along the edge of the swamp, his .22 pistol in his hand, searching for the place where he would fire his single shot of the day. Everything is chance, and chance is everything, she had told him. Most people refused to believe that, because chance frightened them. But that was only ignorance. Chance contained every possibility. Of course, some of it might be bad—that was what the ignorant dwelled on and it was what frightened them—but a heartbeat away from what might be bad, unthinkably bad, was what might be unthinkably great, a bliss that even the gods would envy.

Just because a man, naked and alone and dying of thirst in the desert, had never spread his arms like wings and flown away to a green oasis of cool water, just because no man had ever done that, did not mean that no man ever would. Admittedly, it would be an *ultimate* possibility. But that was her point, her only point. And it ought not to bring fear, but hope and happiness.

That was the morning Johnson had not shot the swamp. Listening to her, he had forgotten all about his pistol.

What people called miracles, she had told him, were only the converging lines of chance.

Johnson was not an ignorant man, and there were moments when her words sounded like the rankest kind of madness, but there were other times, when what she was saying sounded like revealed knowledge, something she had from God after going to the top of the mountain.

He chose to believe that it was revealed knowledge. At the very least, it was hope, it was—as she kept saying—a chance. And he desperately needed a chance. He was at the tag end of his life, a physical wreck of a man, a convicted felon who could not even vote, a man who could find no solace anywhere in this place where he had finally ended: a warehouse for the nearly dead.

"For God's sake, darling," he said, "slow down."

Mabel maintained the same headlong stagger through the heat, and the grip on his arm—already hurting—tightened even more. But she did turn her wild eyes on him and ask, "What'd you say?"

"I said, For God's sake, slow down."

"Not that. The other part."

"Darling. I said darling."

She stuck her head forward on her neck as though to go faster, but she was already going as fast as she could. "I thought that's what you said. Now I know you've gone lunatic on me. I've got to get you in the trailer before they throw a net over you. I don't know what ails you, and I don't want to know."

Johnson thought: But you might just have to know. You might *have* to.

He should not have called her darling. That was a mistake that might put her on guard. And he did not want her on guard. He could not remember the last time he had called her anything but her name. And it occurred to him also that there had been weeks on end when she was not even a Mabel, only a pronoun: you or she. It first dumbfounded and then—to his amazement—shamed him to realize that he had for a very long time now thought of her as a pronoun, a bloodless and faceless pronoun. No wonder "darling" had startled her. But these were startling times.

He felt as though he were smuggling contraband, so alien was the fire that raged in his loins. Johnson had felt the first, almost unremembered but not entirely forgotten, stab of heat when Ted plunged his climbing spike into the tree. And the heat only grew after that, grew every time the spike plunged, the hatchet chopped, or the saw ripped cleanly through a limb. And the fire, sexual and savage, was entirely out of control by the time his legs, seemingly of their own volition, started hopping and pumping, and the string of profanity and blasphemy started issuing from his mouth.

Johnson knew Ted Johanson was eighty years old (everybody in Forever and Forever knew how old everybody else was, age being a constant subject of conversation), and there was no way in the world for an eighty-year-old man to do what Johanson was doing—it was impossible, out of the question. But there he was in the stifling heat, climbing and chopping and sawing. And Johnson himself was eighty-two. Two years older! Two *long* years, he had thought to himself, because at the tag end of life, two years seemed an eternity, at least to him. It was at that moment that he realized his wrinkled old cock, hardly bigger than an unshelled peanut, had lifted its head from an unreasonably long sleep. And when it was fully awake, it continued to swell until it hurt with excruciating need. The dreadful climax—terrible and incomprehensible word!—with Ted Johanson dead in the dusty courtyard, only made the sudden and unfamiliar need scream louder for satisfaction. As Johnson was dragged toward the steps of his purple double-wide by his wild-eyed wife, nothing had abated, and Johnson was filled with wonder at what he could only think of as a miracle.

When Mabel got to the steps she turned Johnson loose. The moment she took her hand away, he stopped and stood rubbing the place on his arm where her hand had been. She looked back briefly as he stood without moving, and then went up the steps and opened the door. Without looking back, she said, "Stay out there until you get heatstroke, for all I care, Johnson Meechum. I don't need another thing from you today." Then she slammed the door.

He stayed where he was, the contraband, the miracle he'd smuggled all the way from the courtyard, standing straight up, the top of it securely cinched under his belt. How best to proceed? That was the real and only question. Then the code occurred to him: Baby Rose Bud.

He and Mabel had not gone at each other sexually in five years. At least he thought it was five years. He couldn't be sure. But he remembered the mild couplings that ended in even milder nocturnal spasms. Almost against their wills, it seemed to him, they had continued these awkward—often unsuccessful—fumblings long after all feeling for each other had died. And so Baby Rose Bud had been added to their other various code words and phrases. Without the code, it had been simply too painful, mentally and emotionally, to endure. Baby Rose Bud was bath oil that also lathered up into a heavy suds, and it became part code for their irregular and infrequent couplings, because Johnson always—or almost always—managed to coax or bully Mabel into the bathtub with about a quart of Baby Rose Bud so that it would mask the smells he'd come to find intolerable.

He stood very still, the sun on his shoulders like a weight, and felt how impossible it was to get what he wanted, to get what he *needed.* He was holding not just the unexpected but the clearly impossible: a raging hard-on. But since his hard-on had no nose, it was screaming to him to stop stalling and get on inside the trailer and plug Mabel.

Sure. Right. All he had to do was walk inside, give Mabel a little wink, maybe pinch her on her crippled ass, and say, "I could go for a little Baby Rose Bud. How about you?"

She would go into violent hysterics is what she would do, maybe even pick up the first thing she could put her hand on and beat him to death.

"Take the bitch by main force," his cock said.

"You know I can't do that," said Johnson.

"Take her," his cock said, "the way Ted took that tree."

Johnson said, "A tree is only a tree. Mabel is a whole goddam forest."

"Miracles can take you only so far," said his cock. "The rest is up to you. I'm here now, but I may never come again. Treat me right, maybe I'll be back. It's all up to you. Very dicey situation. Try to play it right."

The rage of Johnson's unfamiliar hard-on was infecting him. He put his hand on his arm where Mabel had gripped it. The more he thought about it, the more Mabel seemed responsible for the entire predicament of his life: the shame of being found out as an embezzler, the horribly long years in prison, being stuck now in Forever and Forever, his declining interest in sex (who could get it up for a bag of bones that smelled like a bag of garbage?), and, finally, the impotence that he had thought permanent.

He kicked the ground with one of his long, thin feet and made a pawing motion with the other, causing a minor dust cloud to rise about him. He didn't have to work at the rage building in him, swirling in his overheated brain. There was no way of stopping it now, no way to alter where he knew it was going to take him. The rage that was coursing through his blood was like embezzling: once it had started, there seemed to be no way to stop it. And in both instances—becoming an embezzler and becoming a raging madman there in front of his trailer—he had no desire to stop, no desire because he knew stopping was impossible. The course had to be run, no matter the consequences. His actions seemed fated; he was only an instrument to carry out what felt entirely foreordained.

He went up the steps and through the door, and closed it behind him. He reached behind himself and turned the little latch that locked the door.

He had thought to find her sitting in the living room, the blinds pulled, slumped in her favorite chair, maybe crying. But the living room was empty. He stretched to stand taller and turned his head so that his good ear could scope around for whatever sounds there might be. And the skin over his heart went cold when he heard the water running in the tub in the bathroom.

Jesus, he thought, talk about fated and foreordained! The whole universe wanted this to happen. No, it was even better than that: the fucking universe *demanded* that it happen; because Johnson now remembered where there was nearly a full quart of Baby Rose Bud bath oil. His cock screamed at him to *move his ass* while there was still time.

Johnson rushed down the narrow hallway to the small closet where they stored cleaning supplies. And he would go to his grave never knowing why he grabbed the long-handled mop with his left hand at the same time he grabbed the Baby Rose Bud with his right. But this was no time for questions. The day belonged to him who seized it. As he rushed down the hall, it dimly occurred to him that he had been dwelling on that very thought—*the day belonged to him who seized it*—when he embezzled the first stash of cash from the bank. But the dim thought was just that, a dim thought, while his cock was a raging beast, tearing at his heart with teeth and claws that drove him into a gimping little run down the hall.

He opened the door quietly, just enough to stick his head in.

Mabel lay on her back in a shallow tub of cool water, with a folded washcloth on her eyes and forehead. He didn't have to wonder about the temperature of the water. Since they moved to Forever and Forever, here on the edge of a swamp in south Florida, she had taken nothing but cool baths, sometimes lying still as death for hours, with the single blind closed over the window above her and a damp cloth folded as it was now on her eyes and forehead.

When he opened his mouth to speak, he did not know—and his cock did not care—whether he would scream or croak or whisper. As it turned out, his voice came out in a feathery little song: "It's Baby Rose Bud tiiimmme."

She did not move, not even her head, and her own voice came back cold, calm, matter-of-fact: "Lunatic."

He said, his tone still light and lilting, "No, my lovely beast, every woman's time comes to her, and yours has just come to you."

She sat bolt upright, the cloth still over her eyes, and in her old familiar harsh and guttural voice said, "Whaaattt?"

And her hand rose to the cloth and tore it away from her face, but Johnson already had the cap off the bottle of Baby Rose Bud and was pouring it over the crown of her head.

"If you think for a min—" She had been struggling to her feet as she talked, but when Johnson threw the mop over the side of the tub and started swabbing her down, she collapsed onto her back. Her lips clamped shut and turned a color that Johnson could only imagine on a corpse. But her eyes were brighter than any he had ever seen and were filled with maniacal outrage. The bath oil lathered up well and quickly, and he had her pretty nearly covered with suds when he said, "Spread your legs and let me work on the old home place."

She spread her legs, and he worked with the mop on the old home place with a vengeance.

"This is illegal," she said, her voice calm again and detached, as though she might be talking of something that was happening to someone else.

Somewhere in his raging brain the illegality of what he was doing had already occurred to him, but his raging cock did not care, and even though he knew he was totally out of control, he felt totally in control, for the first time since he had suffered the humiliation of being handcuffed in his own bank.

"Get up and turn around," he said, "and let me work on the old dirt track."

With some difficulty, she managed to get to her feet, and he went after her from the nape of her neck to the points of her heels, stopping midway between the two for extra and violent consideration of the old dirt track.

"There," he said, reaching up to turn on the showerhead over the tub. "Let's just rinse you off and see what we've got here."

With her back still turned, she said: "I'll tell you what you've got—you've got a world of trouble."

He leaned the mop handle against the wall. "Turn around and see the surprise I've got for you."

"It won't be half the surprise I've got for you," she said. But she turned around anyway.

He had unbuckled his belt and let his trousers and drawers fall to his skinny knees.

"Well?" he said, looking directly into her raging, flaring eyes. "What do you think of that?"

She checked him out briefly and then snapped her eyes back to his. "Think of it, you bastard? What I've always thought: a goddam sickly and sorry specimen."

He looked down and had just enough time to see that his miracle had deserted him and left in its place a wrinkled little peanut almost entirely hidden in his sparse and gray pubic hair.

He was about to look up and try to explain what he already knew in his heart did not admit of explanation, but he never got the chance to even try before Mabel caught him right across the side of the head with the handle of the mop and the lights went out.

Chapter 6

Stump and Too Much were walking back from the courtyard after watching the ambulance slide quietly out of Forever and Forever with the body of Ted Johanson, still dressed in his lumberjack rig. They were in a nasty little argument—an argument that had cooled considerably from what it had been earlier, but an argument still—about the two limbs still left on Too Much's maypole, one of them the limb Johnson had been standing on when he tightened up and then quit moving completely before finally diving from it headfirst, apparently dead when he hit the ground.

Stump was having to fake his end of the argument by now. He was no longer even mildly angry, and in fact his mind kept slipping away to a tall can of Coors, a scalding bath, and Too Much's circus act. After all, he'd only had a tenant die—common enough and the price of doing business in Forever and Forever—and also lost the one Australian pine in the trailer park, but he had never even seen one of the damn things until he came to south Florida. He thought he might as well go ahead and plant some of the long-leaf pine seedlings that seemed to grow up overnight, which he had been threatening to do for a decade now. But he felt compelled to give his best imitation of anger, because he had never had any real notion of Too Much's intentions—and still hadn't. Though he wanted her to know that she couldn't just do any old thing she wanted to in Forever and Forever without telling him straight out about it first and telling him in plain language. That might make her leave. And he didn't have to think very hard to know that he would *give* her Forever and Forever to keep her from leaving. He could get another trailer park, but he wouldn't even know where to look for another circus act of the sort she had, a circus act he had come to depend upon.

Being fifty-six years old and having the ugliest stump of an arm he had ever seen, as well as having both cheeks of his ass tattooed with a message that had only embarrassed him ever since he had come out of the heroin-induced coma in Korea and discovered what he had done, Stump had pretty much given up on sex. He didn't even seem to miss it, and he rarely thought of it. But then Too Much had walked into his life, and now even the thought of hot water caused his cock to leap in a way that startled him.

Too Much stared straight ahead and said in a tight little voice, "I wouldn't even have needed to take his boots off. All I needed was his climbing spikes and that little chain saw, and I could've got them last two limbs off myself. Or to hell with the spikes, I could've shinnied up there with his saw and got'm off. If I'd a done that, I'd have us a maypole now. As it is, I got a mutilated pine tree with two big limbs sticking off it. A freak pole is what it is."

"One freak more or less won't matter here. You'll be the only one to even notice it."

"I think that's the whole point. This is my idea, dammit, and I mean to see it through." She caught his stump, stopped him, and turned to look at him. "What've you got against joy, celebration, and happiness anyway?"

Stump held her eyes and was silent for a moment. "You want the truth, or will a lie do?"

"The truth, if you can stand to tell it."

"In my whole life, I've never got much mileage out of joy and the rest of what you mentioned."

"I don't bring you that?"

"Try not to be put out by this, Too Much, but what you bring me would have to fall under the heading of something I need. Yeah, need. Kind of like eating. I git hungry too, but I fill up fast."

"Well," she said, walking away, "you're an old man."

"You could have gone all day without saying that," he said, falling into step beside her.

"But we wanted the truth here."

"*You* wanted the truth," Stump said. "I only want the truth when I can't have something else. *Anything* else."

"Don't tell me shit like that, Stump."

"Then don't ask."

"I didn't."

"You just want to fight, and it's beginning to bore the marrow right out of my bones."

"Just so I get those limbs off. And soon."

"Justice'll be here today sometime, and I'll get him to do it."

"Even if he shows up, drunks don't climb trees."

"You just ain't known Justice as long as I have. And he's not a drunk."

Too Much only shook her head and spat between her teeth.

Justice was an old black man, who appeared fleshless under his flapping clothes but was strong as a horse. He walked so slowly that Stump said you had to set a peg to see if he was moving at all. He always had a brown paper sack with him, and the sack always contained a bottle of Mad Dog twenty-twenty, from which he sipped continuously. But Stump had never seen him stagger, and slowly as he moved, he still kept up with the grass mowing and the hedge trimming and the raking and minor repairs around the park. He had a tight cap of solid white hair and six teeth, three on the top and three on the bottom, on opposite sides of his mouth. The number of his teeth and their relative position was something he often pointed out to people, many of whom he had already told several times before.

"How do you eat with teeth like that?" Stump once asked him.

"Wine don't hardly need no chewing."

Stump liked Justice, especially liked the answer he had given about wine needing little chewing, and the old man had Stump's complete confidence. One of the few people Stump could name who did.

"Jesus," said Stump, "is that Mabel Meechum sitting on my steps?"

"Looks like it," said Too Much. "Dressed up to go where, do you suppose?"

"Just so she's not here to tell me Johnson's put a bullet in his brain."

"She wouldn't have dressed up for that."

"I've known it to happen," Stump said. "Besides, Johnson's a strange duck. Likes to shoot his pistol out over the swamp once every morning. Once, never twice, and—as far as I've been able to tell—aiming at nothing."

"He doesn't shoot it out over the swamp," Too Much said. "He shoots the swamp itself."

"Want to run that by me again?"

"No."

"Just as well," said Stump. "This day's giving me a headache."

"Somehow," said Too Much, "that looks like some headache sitting yonder on the top step of your trailer, so you better save up a little room for some more to go with what you've already got."

Stump had already thought the same thing, and he slowed down a little, checking Mabel out, as they got closer.

Mabel Meechum was wearing her best pants suit, and her blue hair was in a little wild cloud about her head; her face was powdered chalk white, and bright-red lips had been painted at a slight angle across her lipless mouth. She was crying as Stump and Too Much walked up to her. The crying came in gaspy little choking coughs, and her painted and powdered face twisted with anger and embarrassment.

It was the powder on her face and the paint on her lips that made Too Much know that whatever was wrong meant trouble. Maybe bad trouble. During their walks out on the edge of the swamp, when Johnson told Too Much many things about his wife, Mabel, all about the absence of makeup and the smell of almonds in the bathroom and much, much more, she had listened to it all, listened carefully and with great sympathy.

Stump and Too Much walked up to the steps where Mabel sat. She looked at them, pressed the spoon-shaped ends of her fingers against her puffy eyelids, hiccuped once, and looked off toward the courtyard.

"I guess Ted Johanson was dead," Mabel said.

"I'm afraid he was," said Stump.

"It always seems to be the wrong ones who die," said Mabel.

Stump said: "I don't believe I understand that."

"I never understood it myself," she said.

"Do we have to keep Miz Meechum out here in the sun?" Too Much said, giving Stump a shot in the ribs with her elbow. She took Mabel's arm and helped her to her feet. "You come on inside where it's cool. Stump didn't forget his manners. He never had any."

"Thank you, honey, and you just call me Mabel."

Stump followed them into the trailer, wondering what in the hell she might be there to demand. He was about ready for a hot bath and a Coors, or maybe a shot of Wild Turkey whiskey to wash down two BC headache powders, followed by a nap maybe. What he was not ready for was to find Mabel Meechum sitting on his doorstep dressed in her best clothes, her face clumsily overpainted, and crying. It had immediately connected in Stump's mind with Ted Johanson up in the only Australian pine tree in the entire park—a place where Ted should never, ever have been—cutting the top out of it and then plunging to his death. Something was unraveling, and he had no idea what it was. Forever and Forever didn't feel right, and hadn't for a while now. He couldn't remember when it started or when he first noticed it, but something felt very wrong, even dangerous.

There were times when it seemed he could sense it in the air. It was like those times in Korea when he'd gone out on night patrol knowing that half the men with him would not return. And they didn't.

Mabel had collapsed onto a chair at the dining room table while Too Much busied herself making ice tea. Mabel had protested that she didn't want any, but Too Much went right ahead anyway.

"It'll cool you off, you old honey," Too Much said, getting ice cubes into glasses and cutting a lemon into wedges.

Stump had been standing by the refrigerator, one hand and his nub jammed into the pockets of his khaki pants. What was all this shit about ice tea and cooling off? Why was she here? And what was it going to cost him in time, energy, and worry? Why in God's name wasn't Mabel Meechum telling him why she was collapsed at his dining room table?

Before Too Much had come to Forever and Forever, he would have settled all this right out there where he had found Mabel sitting and been done with it. But Too Much did not like his abruptness with the residents. She couldn't seem to understand that Forever and Forever was a peculiar business. And it had to be run in a peculiar way. The less he knew about what was going on in Forever and Forever, and the less he knew about the residents, the better everything seemed to work out. He only owned a place where they could come to die.

Ah, to hell with this; he had other things waiting. "What brings you over to see me, Mabel?"

"Can't you wait at least long enough for her to have her tea?" said Too Much.

He looked directly at Too Much, whose voice still had the sharp edge from the argument they'd been having about the two limbs that had been left on the Australian pine—or maypole, as she now insisted on calling it.

"No," Stump said, looking directly into Too Much's gold-flecked eyes. "As a matter of fact, I can't wait."

"It's all right," said Mabel, who did not seem much interested in the ice tea in front of her. "The sooner we get through with this, the better."

"Get through with what?"

"First I want to use your phone to call the police."

Stump stood a little straighter. "You mean to call the law here to Forever and Forever?"

Too Much said, "Damn, you can be dense at times, Stump."

Stump did not like the law. Helpful cops was another thing he'd never got much mileage out of.

"Something wrong with the telephone over at your place?" Stump said.

"He's over there."

"Who's over there? You mean Johnson?"

"Is this fucking Twenty Questions?" said Too Much. "Is that the game we're playing here?"

Before Stump could answer, Mabel blushed all the way through her layered face powder and said: "I've been abused."

In a kind of reflex action—without even knowing he was going to do it—Stump snatched open the icebox, took out a Coors, turned it up, and didn't take it from his mouth until he had drained it. One dead from falling out of a tree and one who had been abused. Jesus, it was not only a fucking record for the park, but nothing remotely like it had ever happened since he'd bought the place and changed its name from Sunset Acres to Forever and Forever because what people came there to do was Forever and Forever—at least that was the way Stump had it worked out in his head; but more important, he believed in calling a thing by its right name.

Too Much had pushed a chair close to Mabel's. She had her arm around the old lady's shoulders and stroked the thin blue cloud of her hair with her other hand. "There, there, you darling," crooned Too Much. "Everything will be all right. Too Much will make everything just fine."

"Want to tell me how you were abused?" asked Stump, taking another beer from the refrigerator.

Too Much turned and glared at him. "Subtle, you know that? You're one subtle motherfucker."

"He mopped me," said Mabel.

Stump put the beer down and took out the Wild Turkey and uncapped it. He had the Wild Turkey almost to his mouth, preparing to bubble the bottle three or four hard times, when he said, "Mopped you? Is that what you said? You mean like with a swab?" Then he bubbled the bottle while Mabel answered.

"Yes. He mopped me in the bathtub."

Stump took the bottle from his mouth. This was *National Enquirer* shit. This was a *National Enquirer* day.

"Why would he want to do that?" Stump asked the question without wanting to. He didn't want to get any deeper in this than he already was. But she was here in his trailer, and something had to be done with her. Something had to be done with all of this.

"I don't know," said Mabel.

But Too Much did. Johnson had told her all about the smell of almonds and the foulness that lived in the folds of her hanging skin and other creases and cavities of her body.

"Maybe he just went nuts there for a minute," Stump said. There seemed to be no other explanation.

"I don't care if it was for a minute or forever. I'm calling the police. I've been abused, and by God, I mean for him to pay for it."

"Mabel, darling," said Too Much, "let's just try to think this through for a minute. Do you really want to stand in front of a bunch of men—even if they are cops—and tell them that your husband *mopped* you? How about standing in a public court in front of a judge and saying that, trying to prove that? Believe me, I know something about domestic squabbles of one kind or another, including violence, even, and you just won't get anywhere with that story."

Mabel's face reddened, but this time it wasn't blushing, and her voice was as angry as the look that had come on her face. "It's not a goddam story."

"Do you have any witnesses?"

"I told you we were in the bathroom!"

"Are you marked anywhere? Scratches? Bruises?"

"Did you hear anything I said? I told you it was a goddam mop he got me with."

"All right. Calm down, honey. I'm only trying to help you, just trying to tell you how it's going to be if you call the police. Has he ever done anything like this before and been arrested for it?"

"He never once in his life did it before. If he had, I wouldn't be living with him today."

"Then it's your word against his. That's all you've got."

"The son of a bitch has got to pay. Nobody mops Mabel Meechum in the bathtub and gets away with it."

"I understand that," Too Much said, "and I sympathize with you." Actually, Too Much thought it sounded like fun and was thinking about sending Stump out for a new, fresh mop today. "But there's got to be some way you can make him pay, as you say, without having to be humiliated in front of a bunch of strangers."

Too Much knew very well she had total control over Johnson and could, in fact, hurt him all she wanted to. Like the Old Ones, Johnson liked and trusted Too Much because she took the time to listen to him without treating him as though he was not only nutty but senile besides.

One morning, walking along the edge of the swamp, Johnson had told her of his trust in her and how much he appreciated the feeling that she actually looked *at* him instead of looking *through* him. He also told her how they paid the rent and bought food and whatever else they had to have. It had been on the same morning he told her of the smell of almonds, probably because after he got through telling Too Much about how and why he was so dependent upon Mabel, he had worked himself into such a state that Too Much thought he might have a stroke.

He had ended their conversation that morning by saying, "Justice is a fucking joke."

"I couldn't agree with you more," Too Much said. "That's why some of us try to make our own justice."

"The young can say that," Johnson said. "I'm just a worn-out old man."

"You're out here trying to kill a fucking swamp, aren't you?"

Johnson looked at the pistol in his hand and said, "Well, yes. But everybody who knows about it thinks it's either a joke or I'm crazy."

Too Much said, "I know, but I don't think that. I think you're going to kill the fucking thing. Maybe not tomorrow, maybe not next week, but you're going to kill it, because it's in you to do it."

Johnson put his hand in hers and she squeezed it. They kept walking, his hand in hers, for a minute before he said, "Yes, but you're special."

"I *am* special, Johnson," she said. "And just the fact that you can see it and know it proves you're neither nuts nor senile." Then, in a firmer, harder voice, "Are you going to *believe* me when I tell you to believe me?"

"I believe you," Johnson had said. "Oh, God, I do believe you."

"I could starve the son of a bitch to death," Mabel said with some satisfaction.

"Starve him to death?" said Stump. He had only spoken because Too Much had not. She had leaned back in her chair, her arms crossed over her chest, so that each of her hands ended in an armpit, where her fingers were scratching in a slow and contented way, as though she had solved all their problems. And in fact, he had remained silent and a little stunned at how easily she had managed Mabel, who had clearly been on the edge of hysterics when they found her sitting on Stump's doorstep. Among other things, at least the cops weren't coming. Stump could get six months behind on cops and catch up in about five minutes. "Starve him to death? Is that what you said?"

"I wish you'd quit repeating everything I say," Mabel said. "You don't hear Too Much—and, honey, I never told you, but I think that's just the cutest name—you don't hear *her* repeating everything."

"It's just a bad habit I picked up sommers or other," said Stump. "I certainly don't want to upset you." What he wanted to do was put his good hand on her neck and tear her throat out.

"You're not upsetting me. Johnson took care of that. And, yes, starve him is what I said. How do you think we eat and pay utilities and everything?"

"I try not to pry," said Stump. "I don't know." Truth was, he didn't really care as long as it was done on time.

"You ever hear of Carl Meechum?" said Mabel, her face brightening a bit.

"Can't say as I have," Stump said.

"Carl, he's my son, doesn't own but about half of Chicago. He sends us a check every month. Check's made out to me, letter's addressed to me. He hasn't spoken to his father since Johnson turned out to be a crook. That trailer we live in belongs to Carl."

Stump was trying to make some sense out of this. Their son owned half of Chicago and he bought them a fucking trailer to live in? Something about that didn't work just right in Stump's head. Why weren't they in the city of the living dead, Saint Petersburg, Florida, in a condo overlooking the water?

"Maybe you could call up old Carl and he could help you straighten these problems out?"

"Carl wouldn't take a call from me. He's not spoken to me once because I stayed with his father, the crook."

"But it looks like you left him now. You could tell him that and . . . and that might help." At least it might get you out of where I live and out of my life, he thought. It might do that.

"Too late," said Mabel. "Carl told me when they turned his father loose from prison that if I ever spoke to the bastard again, he was no longer my son. He does send the check every month, but it's not much."

Jesus, Stump thought, great kid you raised there, old Carl is.

"How about writing him a letter instead of calling him?"

"Tried it," she said. "Tried it more than once. Letters come back unopened."

Stump was tired and bored and pissed, and he had nothing else to say. He looked at Too Much, whose fingers were now working under her bikini top, but it didn't seem to bother Mabel, whose mind was no doubt on the revenge she was going to heap on old Johnson's head.

Too Much saw Stump looking at her and knew what he wanted. A way out.

"It's easy," said Too Much. "Piece of cake. Do you own Ted's trailer?" She knew Stump owned some of the trailers in the park and some were owned by the people who lived in them. She also knew they were all full at the moment, except Ted Johanson's.

"Well, yes and no," Stump said.

"That's not an answer."

"Ted owned it but it was deeded to me, so I could sell it and use the money to bury him. He wanted to be buried beside his wife, a marble headstone and slab just like hers, and their favorite gospel to be sung by a church choir. He had it planned down to the last detail, and it's pretty elaborate. I'll probably go in the hole getting the job done."

"No, you won't," said Too Much, "because Ted's not going in the hole. We'll sell his climbing rig, including the chain saw. Two or three hundred will cremate him, and we'll scatter him in the swamp. He wants a song? I'll be glad to sing him one. Or better yet, we'll have everybody in Forever and Forever sing him one while we scatter him in the swamp. Then Mabel can move into his trailer until she decides to make things up with Johnson." Too Much reached out and touched Mabel on the shoulder. "You're not going to let that old man suffer."

"It's more you haven't heard about," Mabel said.

"That's cold, Too Much," Stump said. "That's colder than this." He held up his purple-scarred nub for her to look at.

"But both were necessary," she said. "You had to get your hand out somehow, so you cut it off. Mabel's got to go somewhere. And Ted? Well, Ted won't care either way."

"I had a deal with the man, Too Much."

"I didn't," she said. "You don't have to do a thing. I'll take care of it. He was a tough old man. He'd understand. Besides, he managed to outlive every blood kin he had and every friend too, not that he ever had many friends, or wanted many, for that matter."

"How do you come to know all this?" said Stump.

"We had a talk."

"Well, I had a deal. I can't go back on my word."

"Then get rid of that monster bathtub you had put in. You won't be needing it."

"What do you mean, I won't be needing it?" But he already knew.

"Too big for one person."

Stump looked down at his scarred nub, and when he spoke, he

spoke directly to it. "Get on the phone. Stop'm down at the funeral home. Tell'm to burn Ted instead of doing what all I told'm to do. I'll give the chain saw to Justice to do the job on the tree. But we won't be selling his climbing rig."

"Why not?"

"We'll burn that with him."

"Those climbing spikes won't burn."

"Neither will his teeth."

"He had false teeth, Stump."

"I know what he had, goddammit. Thought I'd just give you a little something to think about. You *can* think, right? Don't answer that, and don't fuck with me. I'm bent."

Too Much said, "I never thought you kept me around for how well I think."

"You got that right. Now get on the goddam phone before it's too late."

Too Much got out of her chair and went to Stump and held his foreshortened arm between her breasts. "You're a good man," she said.

Speaking again directly into the top of his scarred arm, he said, "No, I'm just a man who broke his word."

Mabel wanted to get out of the trailer she and Johnson lived in and over to Ted's that very afternoon.

"Mabel," said Too Much, "a very old, very dirty man lived in that trailer. Don't get me wrong, Ted had his good points." She was thinking specifically about his tongue. "But if you move in today, you're going to see a movie you'll wish you'd missed."

"How's that?"

"Manner of speaking, honey. What I'm saying is, that trailer's going to be the dirtiest goddam thing you ever stepped in. You could find yourself walking through shit you never dreamed of."

"That's nothing compared to what I just went through that I never dreamed of," Mabel said. She looked off down the hallway, where Stump had disappeared, carrying the uncapped Wild Turkey bottle by the neck, after telling them to do as they pleased but by God he was not in the moving business and he'd never had a single stroke of luck trying to fix things between a husband and wife who only had murder on their minds.

"Don't worry," Too Much had told Stump. "I've got it covered. I did all right with that funeral director jerk-off, didn't I?"

Stump didn't answer but only disappeared into the back of the trailer.

Too Much had in fact done singularly well with the funeral director. She always did well with men, maybe because of her unshakable belief that she could make any man do anything she wanted him to do. It was part of her magic and part of her conviction that she was not like other people. She had something they did not have, and while she was never sure what it was, she knew she had it.

"You know what that bastard did?" Mabel asked.

"Who?" said Too Much.

"Johnson, dammit!"

"Mopped you, you said."

"Well, see," said Mabel, "I was down on my back in the tub and . . ." She paused, and Too Much couldn't help but hear the excitement (was it sexual excitement?) in her voice. ". . . and he told me to spread my legs so he could work on the old home place."

Ah, yes, sexual excitement, no question. "And did you spread for him?"

"What else could I do?"

Too Much knew very well what else she could have done. Refused. But she said, "And did he work—as he put it—on the old home place?"

"God, did he ever."

"Did he hurt you?"

"No. It was the principle of the thing."

Sure, the principle of the thing. Right. Too Much decided right then to send Stump out for a mop, the bigger and heavier the better.

"I always admired a woman with principles," Too Much said, telling the lie she knew Mabel wanted to hear.

Mabel said, "A woman with principles can't expect much in this old world."

Starting with getting laid very often, thought Too Much.

But she looked at Mabel and said, "Well, if we're going to get enough of your stuff for you to live on over to Ted's trailer until we can get a chance to move the rest of it, we'd better get started. I'll get Stump's truck. If we don't have too much trouble with Johnson, it ought not take too long."

"Johnson gives us any trouble, I'll knock him on his ass again."

"You knocked him on his ass?"

"Honey, I knocked him colder than a pound of calves' liver with the handle of that mop."

In that moment, Too Much took an instant dislike to Mabel. Johnson was her friend, and if what was between Mabel's legs was not Johnson's old home place, where the hell was it? Johnson's request for her to spread so he could mop it seemed entirely reasonable to her.

As it turned out, Johnson was no trouble at all. When Mabel burst through the door to their trailer, he was hunkered down on the couch, with an ice pack pressed to the side of his head.

"I'm leaving," Mabel said.

"I'm sorry," said Johnson.

"You'll be a lot sorrier before I get through with you."

Johnson said nothing but only hunkered lower and moved the ice pack to cover his face.

"Let's just get the stuff you need and get out of here," Too Much said.

They piled Mabel's things in the bed of Stump's pickup truck, Mabel continually heaping abuse on Johnson as they did, abuse to which Johnson never answered, except for an occasional groan, which Too Much recognized as not groans of remorse or sadness but of physical pain.

Just as she and Mabel were leaving, Too Much stopped in front of Johnson and put her hand on his shoulder. "You all right?"

His voice came muffled behind the ice pack. "First I lost my job. Then I lost my son. Now I've lost my wife. I think I've lost about as much as I can stand to lose." He took the ice bag away from his face and looked up at Too Much. There was an ugly knot as big as a lemon on the side of his head, and his eyes were red. "I've been thinking maybe that spot I've been looking for in the swamp is in me."

Mabel was going out the door with a box filled with the last of the food that had been in the icebox. She had cleaned it out. As soon as the door closed behind her, Too Much put her hand under Johnson's chin, caught him hard by the jaw, and shook his head. "You're talking like a fool. You're my friend, and I don't have fools for friends. I don't know where Mabel'll end up going, but I'm here, and I'm not leaving. No friend of mine ever saw my back. Now, goddammit, *lighten up*. I'll take care of everything."

Johnson's voice was like that of a child when he said, "Would you do that for me?"

She leaned forward and lightly brushed his forehead with her lips. When she straightened up, she looked into his eyes, shot with a web of veins, and very softly she said, "Would you do that for *me?*"

"Yes."

"That's your answer, then," she said. "Now lie back and heal up. They don't call me Too Much for nothing. I'd go to the wall for you or with you. You're one of mine now."

"What does that mean?"

"Only what it says."

The door opened, and Mabel, her blue cloud of thin hair plastered to her freckled skull now with sweat, said, "Honey, are you going to keep me waiting out here till I die of the sunstroke? Let's go. I've got everything." Then she slammed the door.

Too Much winked at Johnson. "She just *thinks* she's got everything."

Too Much drove over to Ted's trailer and backed up to the door. The first thing Mabel said when they stepped inside was "Now, this place has got the strong stink of a good man." And even with her sweat-plastered hair, her face was radiant with pleasure when she said it.

"It stinks right enough," Too Much said.

"There's stink and there's stink. No offense, you sweet child, but you're still too young to know the good stink from the bad."

What Mabel was saying could not have come as a greater surprise to Too Much if it had been spoken in Latin. She could only stare at Mabel.

"Even at his age," said Mabel with obvious satisfaction, "Ted Johanson was enough man to make a woman who suffers from chronic dry socket get wet halfway to the knees." She was walking around, sniffing like a hunting dog on blood spoor. "I'm going to be just fine here."

This balding old ruin of a woman was still horny, and that might be a good thing to know somewhere down the line, thought Too Much. But she said, "You hit the AC and get some air in here, and I'll start unloading the truck."

"You know," Mabel said, "that crazy bastard mopping me down might have been the best thing that ever happened to me. I'd still like to know why he did it, but I don't want to know bad enough to ask."

It came as no surprise to Too Much that a connoisseur of stink could not smell her own rank and rotted juices. It was only another manifestation of the blindness of the world. Was it any wonder that prophets, madmen, sorcerers, and seers were held in such wondrous awe and murderous suspicion? The inclination throughout recorded history—as far as Too Much had been able to determine—was to do one of two things to the men and women who could see the unseeable and say the unsayable: Build statues in their honor or kill them or, more usually, both. But the killing very nearly always preceded the statues built in their honor. Too Much did not spend too much time thinking about it. It was so common as to be boring, another cliché in a cliché-ridden world. But she did give considerable thought to keeping her own head down and to making sure her true nature remained undiscovered.

They had not brought anything much from the trailer Mabel and Johnson shared, and they had the pickup over half unloaded when Ted's chain saw roared into life and shook the humid air inside the trailer where Too Much stood holding a box of Mabel's soiled underwear. She immediately put the box down and turned her head toward the sound to listen.

Mabel, sweating heavily but looking happier than Too Much had ever seen her look, said, "What is it?"

"That's got to be Ted's chain saw."

Mabel seemed to hear it for the first time. "I believe myself it is," she said.

"And that could only be Justice using it."

"The old nigger?" said Mabel.

"Can you finish here?" asked Too Much. "I've got to go make sure he doesn't mess up my maypole."

"Honey, don't you worry about a thing here," said Mabel. "Now that I've made the move I should have made forty years ago, I'm happy. You go ahead and take care of your tree."

"Maypole."

"Right. It's a maypole now."

"Except for two limbs, it is," Too Much said. "And I'm not trusting Justice to finish the job without me watching him."

"Can't blame you there," said Mabel. "He never seemed certain of but one thing to me, and that's which end of the bottle to drink out of."

"I'll be back to get the truck," said Too Much, "or else Stump will."

"Don't you worry about a thing," said Mabel. "You've helped me enough already."

Too Much went out of the trailer without closing the door behind her. She stopped in the brilliant sun and had to blink twice before she could see properly after the dim light in Ted's trailer. As if they had been searching for her, the Old Ones came out of one of the narrow lanes separating the rows of trailers. They herded close together and seemed to lean inward upon each other, and gave a ragged noise that might have been a cheer when they saw her and quickened their uncertain gait until they had surrounded her before she could move.

She could see across the courtyard, where Justice squatted on his thin haunches. His clothing, loose and flapping about his fleshless body, made him look like nothing so much as a pile of dirty laundry. He had his brown paper sipping sack in one hand, and with the other hand he was examining the base of the tree, every now and again raising his yellow palm to look at it. Ted's chain saw lay idle in the dirt beside him.

Too Much pushed her way through the Old Ones and started toward the place where Justice squatted in the dirt beside her maypole. The Old Ones fell into step behind her. When they walked anywhere with Too Much, they all did their best to stay in step with her. Except for a stagger here and there and a few arthritic knees that could not match Too Much's long strides, the Old Ones looked like a platoon of drunken soldiers following her.

It was actually Stump who had pointed it out first. "What in the hell did you say to'm to make them fall in behind you like afflicted troops passing in review?"

"Afflicted troops, you say? Is that what they look like?" said Too Much. It was news to her; she had rarely even noticed them before. She supposed it had something to do with the clapping or waving that she could start them doing by simply clapping or waving herself. And they would go on with whatever she started them doing until she stopped them. She had wondered, at idle moments, how long they could or would keep clapping if she didn't stop them. One time she had left them in the sun clapping, and when she came back, they were right where she had left them and to her amazement still clapping in unison. She had left them clapping in the sun for forty minutes. A God's wonder some of them had not fell out with a stroke. On the other hand, maybe in their mindless way they were *Guinness Book of Records* material. She would have to check it out sometime. Right now she had Justice to deal with.

"Justice," she said.

"Yas, Missy," Justice said, but he did not look up. His jaw worked continuously, as though he might be chewing something with his mismatched teeth. It occurred to Too Much that Justice was nervous about something, very nervous. He still had not looked up at her but kept his eyes fixed on the base of the tree. He seemed to be taking its measure with his free hand while taking long, careful pulls from the bottle in the sack held by his other hand.

"My name is Too Much, Justice. I'd really rather you didn't call me Missy."

"I know yo name be Too Much. I knowed dat. I spect errybody know dat, Too Much, sho now, Missy, sho now."

She had been right about the nerves. Justice wasn't talking, he was babbling. His old thin shoulders bunched closer to his neck as he talked. And he resolutely kept his eyes on the base of the tree.

"Look at me, Justice," she said.

"Justice be on de job. He don go eyeballin nothin or nobody when Justice on de job. Yas, sho now, Missy. Errythin be awright, yo let dis ole nigger do de job."

"Don't call yourself that."

"Sho now. I aint gone call mysef nothin."

Too Much had about lost her patience. "What the hell ails you?"

"Truf is, yo ail me, Missy."

"All right. Never mind the Missy part. Call me anything that pleases you. But your job's up there, Justice, those two limbs. Where you're looking's got nothing to do with the job you're supposed to do."

"I wake fo Mistuh Stump. Ain studin yo."

"Oh, you're studying me, Justice. If you're not, you better be. I don't think you could've got this old by being a fool."

Justice's thin, winglike shoulders folded even tighter on his neck. "Say whut?" And then, when she didn't answer, he said, "Ol Justice ain done nary a thin to yo, Missy."

"I think you've got in mind to do wrong by my tree."

"Got my mind on whut Mistuh Stump say do."

Then Too Much knew: Stump had remained against celebration and joy. She had miscalculated the change she'd made in him. Maybe he did think his stump of an arm was ugly and insufferable, a mutilation that was beyond redemption. And if he thought that about himself, there was no way to keep him from thinking it about the world. And his world was Forever and Forever. The problem reduced itself to simple terms in her mind: Stump wanted the people of Forever and Forever to sit quietly and die; Too Much wanted them to dance around the maypole.

"Look at me, you old fucker," she said.

Justice immediately cut his eyes, yellow and rimmed with mucus, up at her. "Ol Justice know yo mama ain learned yo to talk lak dat."

"What makes you think I had a mama? What makes you think I give a damn about you, whether you live or die?"

"I ain even thought on dat oncet. Had my mind on de job Mistuh Stump sen me to do."

"Then get up there and get those limbs off."

"Mistuh Stump ain sen me fo no limbs. Sen me to cut dis tree down."

"You heard him wrong," Too Much said, trying to hold her temper.

"I ain hern nobody wrong."

"All right. You didn't hear anybody wrong. Maybe Stump did say it. But it is not going to happen. This is *my* tree, and we do it my way."

Justice put one of his hands on his forehead, ran it up and over the crown of his head, and scratched the nape of his neck. "Way I hern it, errybody an errythin in Forever and Forever belong to Mistuh Stump. Way it be tol to me."

"I'm in Forever and Forever," said Too Much, "and I don't belong to him."

Justice said, "I do." He paused and then went over the top of his head to work on the nape of his neck again. "Yo stay roun Forever and Forever long nough, yo will too, I'm thinkin."

"I've got to go see Stump," she said.

"I gots to cut me dis tree down," Justice said.

She turned and looked at the Old Ones standing quietly behind her. She opened her mouth as wide as she could and then clamped it shut. She repeated the movement rapidly, as though biting huge chunks from a sausage. In little more than a minute, she had all the Old Ones champing and clamping in unison, some of them slobbering and groaning. The groaning—because of their furiously working mouths—sounded like growling, which pleased Too Much enormously.

"Lawd Jesus," Justice said, his yellow eyes rolling high in his head.

"You fucking A Jesus," Too Much said. "And you better hope He's listening. I got to go find Stump and get this straight, because you got everything crooked as a dog's hind leg."

"I got to cut dis tree lak Mistuh Stump he done say do," Justice said, his eyes no longer rolling but staring without even blinking, focused hard on the Old Ones, their strangely chewing mouths, and the even stranger sounds they were making.

Too Much turned to the Old Ones. "He"—she pointed to Justice—"touches that tree"—she pointed to the tree—"with that saw"—she pointed to the chain saw, where it lay in the dirt—"you . . . you *eat* him!"

"Lawd hab mercy!" screamed Justice. "Whut yo say?" His eyes were rolling now as though they would never stop.

Too Much had no idea how much the Old Ones understood of what she said. She made exaggerated chewing motions with her mouth. This was all for Justice's benefit anyway. "Will you *eat* him right down to the *bone?*" More than half of the Old Ones were nodding their heads vigorously.

"I want every mouth here bloody if he cuts my tree. Like *this*!" She spun and caught Justice by the wrist and buried her teeth in the heel of his hand.

He screamed, and when she finally released his hand, felt the hot blood on her lips, and tasted the salt of it on her tongue, Justice was dancing a little jig, chanting, "Jesus, Jesus, Jesus."

Too Much, really into it now, running her tongue over her bloody lips, screamed to the Old Ones, "If he cuts my tree, you eat his ass down to the bone!"

She'd done the best she could with it and sprinted off toward Stump's trailer, screaming his name as she ran. She was no more than fifteen yards from the steps leading up to his front door, when she heard the chain saw fire up and the unmistakable sound of the blade ripping into wood.

Stump appeared in the door, unsteady enough for her to know that he was drunk.

"Justice is cutting down my tree!" she shouted, waving behind her in the direction of the sound of the saw.

"Justice always does what he's told to do," Stump said.

"Come on, goddammit. I want you to see what you've caused," she said.

"Hell, I don't know about that," said Stump. "Maybe I can make it that far. Long as we don't walk too fast."

"Walk slow as you want to," she said bitterly. "What's done is done by now."

Stump ambled toward the courtyard, and she stayed with him as though the pace really did not matter, as she knew in her heart it did not. From where they were, she heard the cracking of the tree as it started to tilt, breaking because it had not been sawed all the way through, and she knew why when she heard Justice begin to scream, the screaming nearly drowned out by what sounded like the growling of dogs.

When Stump and Too Much stepped into the courtyard, the tree was down and Justice was down, his gray-black skin flashing now and again from under the pack of snarling and growling Old Ones.

Stump seemed to sober considerably and very quickly. "What are they doing?"

"It looks like they're mauling'm pretty good to me."

"Why? What's he done to make them act like that? Jesus, it looks like they're biting him!" His choked, cracked voice came out as though he had a fish bone hung in his throat.

Too Much spoke calmly, as if reciting something from rote memory, "I told them to do it if he messed with my tree. Someday, somebody in this godforsaken place is going to learn I don't play."

"Mother of God, Too Much, how could you do that to that old man?"

"You thought you could just take me light, didn't you? Do you know now, goddammit, you can't? Do you understand how it is with me?"

"Yes," he said quietly, "I know now."

Justice somehow gained his feet and rose from the midst of the Old Ones. He was stark naked, his mouth stretched open but making no sound, and his body spotted with flecks of blood.

"Hope he's had his tetanus shot," Too Much said in a voice so calm that under the circumstances it brought a stab of terror to Stump that he had not known since Korea.

"Can't you at least stop'm?"

"I'm going to take a long, hot bath." And then, as she walked away, she said over her shoulder, "But not in your tub, motherfucker."

Chapter 8.

Too Much headed straight for Johnson's trailer. When she got to the narrow street that led to where he lived, she looked back once and saw that Stump had taken off his shirt and wrapped it as best he could around Justice's naked hips and was carrying him in his arms as he would carry a child, his nubbed forearm under Justice's knees and his other arm under Justice's shoulders. It could not have been much of a load, because stripped of his flapping clothes, Justice looked small and fragile and starved. He still had his brown paper sipping sack in one hand, but his face was buried in Stump's shoulder, the tight cap of his white hair brilliant in the sun.

Stump showed no signs that he'd been drunk a few minutes earlier or that he had even had a drink that day. His stride was long and firm, and his face was red and twisted in what could only be anger. No doubt about it, he was truly and deeply warped over what had happened to Justice. Well, good. Let him be as angry as he liked and stay as angry for as long as he wanted to. Cut down her maypole, would he? He just thought he knew what being pissed to the gills was. She'd show him before this was over.

Behind Stump and Justice, the Old Ones had herded up again, their faces tranquil, even though a few of their mouths were bright with blood, and they were calmly leaning in upon one another, a few of them twisting their wrinkled necks, no doubt looking for Too Much. Now that the task she had set them was finished, they were ready for another, ready to get on with the day she might have to take them through.

She turned into the macadam lane that led to Johnson's trailer. The Old Ones would be all right. With a task, without one, with Too Much or without her, they carried a mindless contentment and happiness with them, which was a hell of a lot more than she could say about the other residents. Being one of the Old Ones wasn't the worst thing in the world. As a matter of fact, it was pretty damn good in a great many ways, and Too Much had known it from the first time she laid eyes on them.

Too Much paused on the top step of Johnson's trailer and then knocked. There was no sound on the other side of the door, no voice or even movement of any kind. The door was not locked, and she opened it just enough to see inside. Johnson was precisely where she had left him, sitting in exactly the same way, slumped on the couch and holding the ice bag pressed against the side of his head.

"Johnson?"

His head moved almost imperceptibly. She saw one eyelid rise and a single blood-red eye look at her.

"Thank God, you've come back," he said in a whipped, childlike voice.

"I told you I was your friend. This is what friends do." When he didn't answer, she went over and put her hand gently on the ice bag. It was warm. "Don't you have any more ice, Johnson?"

He moved his head, but she couldn't tell if he meant yes or no. She went to the icebox and checked the freezer.

"You're going to get on the wrong side of me, Johnson. There's plenty of ice here, and you're sitting over there with a bag full of warm water. Just what do you think you're doing?"

"Waiting."

"I told you everything'd be all right and that I'd be back to help you."

There was a silence before he answered, "Not that."

"Not what?"

"Waiting for you."

"Then what is it you're waiting for?"

"To die."

For the first time, she noticed the .22-caliber pistol on the coffee table in front of him. It looked like a toy, but one of those tiny slugs would kill you deader than hell if you put it in the right place. She made no sign that she'd seen the pistol. If he was going to kill himself, he would. Again, that was part of the chance of ultimate possibility, a final option, and if he was really going to carry it out, there was nothing she could do about it.

She reached over and took the bag away from his head. The knot did not seem to have gone down very much, and it was now an ugly mixture of colors: yellow and deep purple. And a crooked black bruise ran down into his cheek.

"You look like you've been hit with a goddam baseball bat instead of a mop handle."

"Mabel's stronger than she looks," he said. And then, as an afterthought: "Especially when she's mad."

"Never mind Mabel. She's only a minor nuisance. I told you you'd be all right, but I guess you don't have much faith in me. I don't guess you've believed *anything* I've said."

"I've believed *everything* you've said."

"I guess that's why you're sitting here with a bag full of warm water on your head and"—she pointed to the pistol on the coffee table—"and that stupid little popgun in front of you. Am I supposed to be impressed?"

"No."

"Is the idea that you're about to kill yourself, is that it?"

"No."

"Well, I'm getting plenty of noes here. What I want are some yeses. You've got plans, right? A way to straighten this mess out?"

"Not really."

"Then you've got to be thinking the world is going to pop in the front door and save your ass. It won't, trust me. The world doesn't give a damn if you kill yourself or not. But if you really want to die, maybe I can help you out."

"I wasn't thinking about death."

"You've been thinking of giving up ever since all of this came down. Giving up is death. You're sitting there a dead man already."

Johnson did not say anything. But he stood up, took the bag of tepid water from Too Much, poured it into the sink, and went to the refrigerator and filled it with ice cubes. Still standing with the freezer compartment open, he pressed the ice-filled bag against his swollen and discolored eye.

"Ah," he said. "Jesus, that feels good."

He looked over at Too Much, hoping for a little sympathy, but her face showed nothing but anger. "If you had kept that bag cold, you wouldn't have that knot on your head now. And that busted-up eye would look some better. Remember, the race is not always to the swift but to the one who gets off his ass."

Johnson smiled. "I've blasphemed enough for both of us today. Maybe you ought to leave it alone."

"That is not blasphemy. It's the simple truth. Straight out of the Bible. I just paraphrased the motherfucker a little bit."

"What's got you so angry?"

"Finding you sitting here like a dead man would have been enough. But the fact is, they cut my maypole down."

"Nawww," said Johnson, removing the ice bag to touch his knot with the ends of his fingers. "Nobody would do that."

"Somebody did it. Bet on it."

"Who would've been mean enough to do that?"

"He might not have been mean enough to do it, but he was drunk enough to get the job done. Stump had Justice cut every bit of it down. Not even a stump as big as his own left in the ground."

"That was the only one in the park, so what now? Just give it up, I guess."

"Giving up is not in me. My mind was running more along the lines of a bath and some food right now, then I'll figure the rest of it out from there. A glass of orange juice is all I've had today, and I've put a lot of miles on that. I'm pretty much tapped out."

Johnson had come back to sit on the couch, with his ice bag pressed against his head. "We've got a tub and plenty of hot water, but even the cockroaches'll be leaving now. Mabel stripped the house of food like a swarm of locusts."

"What did you think to do, sit here on this couch and starve to death?"

"You don't have to growl at me, Too Much. I didn't know what else to do."

"I'm going to give you some advice. When it gets to the place where you don't know what to do, here's what you do."

"What?"

"*Something.* Do goddammit *something,* even if it's wrong. Get up and *move.* Next time I see you forgetting that, I'm going to see how much of my shoe I can lose up your ruined old ass."

"You talk to me worse than Mabel."

"Mabel ain't shit. No balls. I'm the one holding the balls, and you're one of my troops. And we're taking this place like Sherman took Georgia. Stump's done stepped over the line."

"Sherman?" said Johnson. "Georgia?"

"You're just trying to get on the wrong side of me, right? I hope by God you're not telling me you don't know what Sherman did to Georgia?"

"Oh, I know, all right," he said. "I know every bit of it, right down to the last detail. When Mabel slammed me on the side of my head with that mop, I think it slowed my thinking down some." Johnson at least sure as hell hoped so, because he couldn't for the life of him make any connection between Sherman and Georgia.

"I don't think I'm going to go any farther with that, because I think you might be lying."

"Do you think for a minute that I'd lie to you?" he said.

"Of course you would. Everybody lies to everybody else. It's one of the things that make living so fucking much fun, trying to get to the bloody, beating heart of a thing and see what the hell it *really* is, instead of all the lies you've been told about it."

"I never thought about it that way."

"Of course you didn't. Nobody ever does. But let's stop with this. I think I've overloaded your brain already. What do you want to eat?"

"I've already told you, there's nothing in the place to eat."

"Try to pay attention. I didn't ask what was in the house. I asked you what you wanted to eat."

"Anything I can chew," he said, "which isn't much. My teeth don't fit like they should."

"Jesus," said Too Much.

"It's not my fault. Carl won't buy me any new ones."

"Don't even mention Carl. I've heard too much about him already. How about Chinese? Can you do Chinese?"

Johnson brightened immediately. "Chinese'd go down good, most of it anyway, stuff like egg drop soup, egg foo yong, and most anything with rice in it."

"Enough," said Too Much. "I got you covered."

"But I don't have any money," he said.

"I don't either," she said, "but Stump has."

"Well, of course," he said. "But why would he . . . ?"

"Let me handle it."

She picked up the phone and dialed Stump's number.

"What are you doing besides fucking with other people's lives?" she asked when he answered.

"Too Much?"

"No, asshole, it's Santa Claus."

"Someday I'm going to teach you to watch your mouth."

"Someday I'll teach you to keep your hands off of what I'm doing."

"It was only a goddam tree, Too Much, and you could've killed this old nigger. That's what I'm doing now, trying to clean him up and tape some patches on him and convince him he's not going to die. It's a good thing the ones that had him down didn't have real teeth, or he'd be dead now."

"It could have all been avoided if you had just stayed out of what didn't concern you."

"Everything in Forever and Forever concerns me. I own the place, remember?"

"So you say."

"What?"

"The maypole being cut down won't stop me; nothing will, in case you're interested. We're still having a May Day celebration."

"Is that what you called to tell me, for Christ's sake? I got a busted-up and bleeding old nigger here, one that's scared shitless to boot. Where the hell are you calling from anyway?"

"Johnson's. We're ordering out for Chinese."

"Does this conversation strike you as crazy? Because if it ain't crazy, I am."

"Just have some cash when I send the guy over with the bill for the Chinese."

"Say again."

"You heard it right the first time. I'm having some food with Johnson to calm him down, and then I'm having a long, hot bath. Maybe after that I'll come home. You might get lucky. It may be that I can stand two baths in one night. Just pay the guy with the bill."

Too Much hung up, with Stump still talking. She half expected him to call back, but he didn't. She supposed he had his hands full with Justice. She hoped the old man wasn't hurt too badly, but sometimes it took blood to get a person's attention. She bet by God she had Justice's now. And Stump's too, for that matter.

The Chinese restaurant Too Much ordered from was just down the street, but their advertisement said if your order was not delivered in thirty minutes it was free. As it turned out, the delivery got there with time to spare.

Too Much had just gone back and started her scalding bath—she turned on only the hot-water tap—when there was loud knocking at the front door. The mop Johnson had used on Mabel earlier in the day was still lying on the bathroom floor, and Too Much took a good long look at it, a vague, improbable notion forming in her mind.

Johnson was totally broken and—as far as she could see—had no options. Unless you considered the pistol on the coffee table an option, which she refused to do, not in Johnson's case. She liked him, but more than that, he was one of her own now. She had no doubt at all that he'd stick his head into a full bucket of water and drown himself if she told him to.

But she had him on scholarship, because she owed him now, or he thought she did, which amounted to the same thing. Before she could leave him tonight, she had to do something for him, get his blood up and his heart pounding. At the moment, she didn't know for sure what she'd have to do, but she thought she had it pretty much figured out. Too Much hurried down the hallway to the front door, where the knocking had become a continuous banging. Johnson, the ice pack against his head, had not moved. When she opened the door, a long-haired young man with bad skin was standing there holding two large brown paper sacks filled to the top with tiny white cardboard boxes. He was trying to get a bill out of one of the sacks to hand to her.

"Don't bother with that," Too Much told him, "because we're not the ones paying."

The long-haired young man said, "Hot damn, when did they start having stuff like you in this place? I've been here a thousand times, and I ain't never seen nothing like you." He waved his hand to include all of Too Much.

Too Much only smiled. "Like the bikini, do you?"

The young man smiled, showing Too Much a ruined mouthful of teeth. Most of them were varying shades of green and yellow and black, several of them broken. "Actually," he said, "I didn't even notice the bikini. Kinda hard to see it, with you standing in it."

Too Much said, "Nicest thing I've heard today. Unfortunately, all you'll be able to do is eat your fucking heart out." Too Much reached for the packages in his arms and took them. "Take the bill to the first trailer on the right as you enter the park. The man who lives there will pay you."

"I caint leave the order without the money," he said, his lips clamping grimly together.

"Get off this step and do what I told you to do, or I might just whip your ass."

"I'd take it as a honor and a pleasure, ma'm."

"No, you wouldn't. You just think you would. I'd kick your ass so hard, you'd be wearing it around your neck like a collar."

The young man gave a sudden braying laugh and said, "Shit,

now that's a good'n. Ain't heard that'n before. But what I'm thinkin is if I got to break a company rule and leave the order without no money, I ought to git to do a little more'n eat my heart out." He showed her his bad teeth again in a way that made Too Much want to kill him.

Too Much watched him for a moment and said, "Think in one hand and shit in the other. See which one fills up first."

She slammed the door on the boy, who still smiled for all he was worth, his heart doubtless full of hope.

Too Much set the two grocery bags on the coffee table; at the same time, she picked up the pistol and sent it sliding across the rug, where it came to rest in the corner of the room.

"If you're going to kill yourself, I guess you might as well eat first."

Her voice was light, and she had meant it as a joke, but Johnson did not move on the couch, his head inclined toward his chest, the heavy bag of ice against his eye. She put her hands on her hips and regarded him for a moment.

"Don't tell me after I've gone to the trouble of getting us some righteously solid food you're not hungry. Seems like everybody's trying to ruin my disposition today."

He didn't look up when he spoke. "I guess I'm hungry. And I know I ought to eat, but somehow I don't have my heart in it."

"Forget your heart being in it. Put your teeth in it. You get your teeth sunk into some of this good Chink shit, and you'll be a new man."

"I don't know whose teeth'll be sunk in it, but they won't be mine. These loose son of a bitches I've got in my mouth came out of a store. And going to be a new man? We both know I'm not going anywhere but six feet, and that's straight down."

"Normally," she said, "I'd get ragged-out and want to slap the shit out of you for wimp talk like that, but you already look like one of the walking wounded from a losing battle, so I'm cutting you some slack. But first I'm going to fix that bag and free up both of your hands so you can get at this stuff right."

She took the ice bag away from his head and emptied half of it in the sink, and then tied it back on, using a belt from a bathrobe. The eye looked a lot better from having fresh ice on it, and the knot had gone down considerably.

While she was knotting the belt, he said, "I really do appreciate how you've helped me out with all this. I know you'd probably say it was only common decency, but I feel like you've saved my life."

"Wrong on just about every count, sweetheart," she said. "I'm not common and I'm not decent. And what comes around goes around. Who knows? Maybe you'll get a chance to help me out someday."

"Anytime. Anything," he said.

"Again."

"What?"

"Say it again."

"Anytime. Anything."

"I thought that's what you said. Do you mean it?"

"I mean it like I've meant few other things in my life."

"Then maybe I've been helping myself as much as I've been helping you, right?"

"I don't think I understand."

"You will," she said. "Now let's get at this stuff while it's still warm."

The food, in fact, was hot. And after Johnson gingerly put the first steaming spoonful of egg drop soup into his mouth, he went after the rest of what was before him with such a single-minded focus that Too Much very nearly stopped eating just for the pleasure of watching him. She knew there was no question; he was on his way back. But she'd bring him all the way back before she was through.

He gulped the soup, wolfed the rice, and then, without the slightest embarrassment, he took his false teeth out and gummed the hell out of four egg rolls. He finally leaned back and palmed his round little belly with both hands. He had put his teeth back into his mouth while Too Much went to turn off her bathwater. His face was radiant, his smile strong, when he said, "Must have been good; we didn't do a hell of a lot of talking."

Too Much said, "You look like you feel some better."

"I know I must have felt better than this at some time in my life, but I can't remember when." He reached up and tore away the wrap that was holding the ice bag. "Hell, I don't need this." He dropped the bag on the floor beside the couch."

The knot just above his temple was only a bump that was hardly noticeable now, and his discolored eye had entirely lost the swelling in it so that it was open and nearly clear.

"I've got to get that bath," she said. "I've been in this damn bikini all day, and I need a good scrubbing."

"Honey, after all you've done, you deserve anything you want."

"What I want is a bath."

"Go for it."

"I will, and if I ever tell you the same thing—to go for it—I want the same goddam answer. Understood?"

"Understood."

"All right. Now I'm going to give it back to you. You deserve anything you want."

Johnson thought on that for a minute. He glanced briefly at the pistol in the corner of the room where Too Much had thrown it. With the fingers of his hand, blue-veined and age-spotted, he gingerly touched his eye, only slightly puffy now.

"Maybe," he said. "Maybe so. But what I want I can't get."

"Well, let's have it, goddammit," Too Much said, leaning toward him over the little coffee table. "Tell me what you can't get, before you start telling me it's impossible."

"I can't," he said.

"You're in love with that fucking word, aren't you? This is Too Much you're talking to. And I do not—repeat: do not—like that word *can't*. Every time you open your mouth, it's something you can't do. You're with *me*, remember? You're one of mine. Now, before I do something crazy, like take you by your ears and bite your nose off, tell me what it is you want and can't get." She held his eyes with her own. "You can tell me anything."

He breathed deeply, and then, in an explosion of breath, he said, "I want to get fucked."

She relaxed and leaned back in her chair. "Well, hell, I could have told you that. And I'll tell you something else. I fed you, but I'm not going to fuck you. Jesus! What are you, eighty-two? And you're blushing. It's only words, Johnson. We haven't spilled any blood, broken any law."

"I didn't mean for you . . . That is, I wasn't even thinking about you when I . . ."

"The hell you weren't. Why are you lying to me, Johnson? You're a man. And I'm a woman with a body that causes car wrecks, holding a pussy that makes trains run off tracks. Would you kindly quit bullshitting me? I find it boring. Some dipshit philosopher said that sex was a young man's battle. Probably thought the same thing about young women. Truth is, the battle ends when they throw the first shovel of dirt onto your coffin. We come out of the womb swimming in piss and shit, and we never quit longing for it." She shook her head and expelled a great breath. "I sometimes despair of the human race. Cowardly, twisted-tongued motherfuckers!"

Johnson was still blushing. He could feel the heat in his face and hated himself for it. "I just didn't want you to think that . . ."

"Don't let it worry you," she said. "I don't think. I *do.* I told you about getting off your ass and *doing* earlier, but I guess you've already forgot about that." Johnson opened his mouth to speak, but she held up her hand, palm out, and it shut him up. "See, Johnson, whether I fucked you or not wouldn't matter. Zip. Nothing. But it'd be like putting a Band-Aid on an open artery. I don't mind fucking you, understand, that's not the point. Sometimes that's what real friends are for. But we've got to do something permanent. Get you back on track. Right now you're a man sitting here with your head in your hands. I want you to be a man with a life, otherwise you're no good to yourself or anybody else, including me. Especially me. So that's what we're going to get—everything fixed."

Johnson looked at her without blinking, the way a bird might look at a snake. Finally, when he could hold the gaze no longer, he said: "What? What are we going to do?"

Too Much gave him a smile that slowly turned into a leer, a lascivious twisting of her mouth, her tongue wet and working, so sexual it was savage. She could see that it frightened Johnson, and that had not been her intent at all.

She said in her most soothing voice, "Relax. Too Much is here. She fixes what needs fixing. I'm not going to leave you here all night, eating your liver alone, when Mabel is just across the way in Ted's trailer, where the smell of his musk has already made her, as she herself said, wet to the knees."

Johnson stiffened on the couch. "What's this about Mabel? What's that you said?"

"That's what she said. Mabel's over there right now, over there by herself and as horny as any of God's creatures ever get."

"Mabel hasn't been horny in twenty years, maybe even forty, for all I know."

"Whose fault is that?"

"Nobody's that I know of. It just somehow happened when I wasn't looking. Just turned around one day, and there it was."

"Good. That's good, Johnson. Placing blame and fault gets you exactly nowhere. Action, on the other hand, does. Can you remember when you first got married? How it was? How it smelled and tasted when you got up in there where it counts?"

The faintest smile touched Johnson's lips. "Like it was yesterday." He paused and looked at the ceiling. "Every night I climbed into her bed and thought I'd gone to heaven. You wouldn't believe it."

"Wrong. I do believe it. I'm the world's champion believer. I believe in everything." Johnson was still looking at the ceiling, the tendons standing out in his thin neck. "Look at me, Johnson." He lowered his eyes and looked at her. "Look at me and believe. The chance of ultimate possibility will take you where you need to go. Don't you dare talk to me of age and death and time, particularly *time.* Time passed and ruined *this.* Time passed and ruined *that.* Time ain't shit. And death ain't shit until you're dead. You just ate a meal like a fucking stallion. So death me no deaths. You want her a certain way? Make it happen, Johnson. You don't live anywhere but in your head. That's where it all starts and ends. So you've got to get your head right."

"I tried," he said. "It didn't work."

"But you didn't have me. I'm going to live in your head, Johnson. When you need me, all you will have to do is close your eyes and I'll be there. Will I always be in your head, Johnson? If you need me, can you close your eyes and taste me on your tongue, feel me on your fingers, use my juices to grease your rails? Can you do that, Johnson?"

"God, I believe I can."

"The right word. The only word. *Believe.* Do you believe, Johnson?"

"Yes."

"Then go for it, Johnson. Go for it."

"I will. By God, I *will* go for it."

His eyes were dilated, his nostrils flared. His teeth moved and clamped and clamped again. Every attitude of his body suggested he was about to get off the couch and bolt from the room. Too Much reached across the coffee table and put her palms softly on his fists.

"Not quite yet, Johnson. It's time to do something else. Now, it's time."

"Time for what?"

"The marriage counseling I have to do for you. We have to set all this in you as solid as bone. You just fell into what everybody in the whole world dreams of, and everybody could have if they only believed in the chance of ultimate possibility."

In a voice that was full of wonder, he asked, "What did I just fall into?"

"Me."

"You?"

"You're going to help me a little, and I'm going to help you a little, and Mabel's going to have a night she'll never forget. Because after this, there is no way that if you need me, I won't be waiting right there behind your eyelids."

"What is it?" he asked. "What in the world is it?"

"Patience, Johnson," she said. "Some long-dead holy fucker said patience is a virtue. And so it is. So try to be patient."

She stood up and in a seemingly single fluid motion she was out of her bikini. Johnson thought his heart would stop. It took several efforts before his constricted throat allowed him to speak.

"God of us all," he said. "What are you doing?"

Her face completely passive now, she said, "I'm about to take my bath. You wouldn't expect me to take it in a bikini, would you?"

She did not wait for an answer—and it was just as well, because he could not have spoken anyway—but turned and walked more slowly than was necessary to the closed door of the little bathroom, where she knew the steam would be thick as fog and the water so hot as to be nearly unbearable.

Before she turned the doorknob she had her hand on, she looked back over her shoulder and said, "Your time will come. Just sit quietly and believe—believe in the chance of ultimate possibility—*believe,* because you are right in the middle of it. Here is your chance, maybe the last chance you'll ever have to give birth to yourself and be entirely new again in a world of your own making."

She opened the door, and Johnson watched her disappear into the thick and layered steam. The door had hardly closed when Johnson thought he heard Too Much call his name. He turned his good ear toward the bathroom door. No, it was his imagination. Why would she be calling him? Still, he would have sworn he heard the sound again, his name, low and lilting, almost like the long and sorrowful cry of a mourning dove. Certainly not a command, which was the only sound he could associate with Too Much's voice.

But command or not, it was her voice, and it was his name she was calling, or rather almost singing. He got up from the couch and went to the door of the bathroom. He could hear the sound of lapping water. She had the tap on again. And there! His heart leapt. It *was* his name she was calling. He took the doorknob in his hand, hesitated a moment, and opened the door only inches. Steam swirled around his head.

"You need something?" he said.

"You," she said.

He didn't know where this was going, and it frightened him. But he could not very well just walk away. And he sure as hell could not go in, because that was a total impossibility for any number of reasons. For starters, he could not have heard her say what he thought he heard.

"What?" he said.

"Come in and close the door."

He did, and he could make out only the vaguest outlines of her body lying in the tub, her knees drawn up and parted. He looked up and stared steadfastly at the wall.

"The mop is right where it was left," she said. "There on the floor. Mop me, you brutal, savage bastard! Mop me within an inch of my life."

"You don't understand," he said, still not looking at her. "Before, that was for—"

"Before be damned," she said, her voice no longer soft and singing, but raw and gritty with need. "Before was for you. This is for me. I'm so horny, I could bump into a table and come. Get my nuts off, motherfucker! Tease, terrorize, tantalize, and brutalize, but get that mop on me."

In an almost dreamlike state—this could not be real, could it?—he bent for the mop and threw it over the side of the tub, where she caught it with one hand and put it between her legs. His eyes were watering, but he could clearly see her knees drawn now nearly to her chest and spread. With her other hand she was draining the last of the Baby Rose Bud onto the ragged end of the mop, which was working and stroking in a mound of lather as if with a will of its own. And Johnson felt the same stab of heat that had struck his loins when Ted plunged his steel climbing spike into the tree. Jesus God, would it never end?

"Yes, there! Goddammit! Now! Hold on, you mean son of a bitch. I'm about to go around the bend!"

Johnson had gone entirely out of his head. Nothing like this had ever happened in his entire lifetime. Or even been imagined. There was no possibility beyond this one. The ultimate! The final absolute end.

Not until he heard her say, softly, "There, there it is. It's done," not until then did he realize that a moan, almost a scream, was coming from his own throat. He did not realize it until he felt her touch him. He looked down and she was kneeling in the tub, and from his trousers, which had somehow come unzippered, there stood the proud and beautiful cock of his early manhood. She had the base of it in her hand, and with her eyes looking up at him, she whispered, "If you ever need to believe, remember this." She leaned forward and briefly took the head of it in her mouth. Then she was on her feet, water and suds sliding down her body, dripping from her rigidly nippled breasts. It had happened so quickly that he could hardly believe it had happened at all. But there—inarguably—was his cock, feeling as though it beat with a heart of its own.

"Put him up," she said. "But be careful with the zipper. He has work to do tonight."

Her voice was cold and flat, an absolute monotone, and her face, even her eyes, looked dead. And strangely, he felt not only unafraid but totally at peace, full of trust. It was a feeling he remembered from somewhere in his childhood, but he could not place it. He let the mop handle drop to the floor and took a step back.

"Not yet," she said in the same calm, dead voice. He stopped. "Now I think it might be better if you kiss the devil."

"I don't understand."

"I think you will," she said. "But only if you want to. Really want to."

She turned her back to him, bent from the waist, and presented to him her beautifully curving, heart-shaped buttocks. The skin was taut and wetly glistening. He had forgotten such beauty was in the world. Then he watched in amazement and disbelief as she reached back with her hands, put a palm on either cheek, and spread herself for him until he was looking directly into the wrinkled, brown, winking eye of her asshole.

"Kiss the devil," she said.

"Yes, God help me, I will," he said.

"But only if you want to."

"I want to."

"Of your own free will."

"Yes."

"Say it."

"I want to kiss the devil of my own free will."

And he truly did. More than anything else he could think of in the world, he wanted most to do that. And his cock's voice that beat in his blood had gone mad with screaming need and demanded that he do it. He bent and pressed his face deeply between her cheeks and kissed the wrinkled little mouth and, without meaning to, touched it with his tongue.

She abruptly straightened and turned, her face again animated and radiant. In her old compassionate and ultimately helpful voice, the one he had always known, she said, "Now get out of here so we can get on with the work at hand."

He went out and sat on the couch, gingerly, because his cock refused to accommodate itself to any other form than the one it had assumed. It *would* have its way. His entire body had to position itself around it. Shortly, she came out as naked and natural as a little girl and put on her bikini. Her damp hair was caught at the base of her skull with a strap of leather.

"Ready?" she said.

"I'm dead-on ready," he said, "and thank you."

"Be careful about thanking people until you know you've got something to be thankful for."

"I know that," he said. "I know that all too well."

He was thinking of his son, Carl, whom he'd thanked when Carl had said he was buying his mother and father a trailer, a double-wide, and would support them while they lived in Florida. Johnson was grateful for that and thanked his son before he found out the trailer was purple—the color Johnson hated most in the world, which Carl knew—and found out, too, that not only were the checks he sent them so small that they had to pretty much live off Hamburger Helper, but the checks were made out to Mabel. And then to cap it all off, "thank you" were the last words he was ever allowed to say to his son, who owned not one but two penthouses, one in Chicago and one in New York City. Yes, "thank you" could turn out to be the nastiest words in the language.

"But knowing what I know, I still thank you," he said to Too Much.

"It really doesn't matter," she said pleasantly. "The deal was struck when you kissed the devil."

"I've heard that expression before," he said, "but I —"

"We won't have any conversation about that. The arrow of the compass is holding steady on Mabel."

"There's no way for me to get to her," said Johnson. "She won't let me in that trailer with her."

"If you're ready, it'll work," Too Much said. "Get off your ass and let's go do it."

"If I'm not ready now, I'll never be."

"Good."

Johnson followed her out into the late afternoon sun. It was still hot, the humidity heavier than ever. There was not a soul to be seen anywhere. All the residents were dozing in their recliners or laid out on their beds, sleeping away the final heat of the day.

The walk to Ted's trailer didn't take long, and when they got there, Too Much said, "You wait here. It'll only take a minute."

Too Much opened the door without knocking and found Mabel with a vacuum cleaner humming across the living room. She looked up, saw Too Much, and shut it off. Mabel motioned to the vacuum.

"Found this in the back under a pile of stuff that I guess had been there since Ted's wife passed. I can tell you this for sure—he never used it."

Too Much said, "I told you from the start it'd be rank in here."

Mabel smiled. "And I told you, if you remember, there's rank and there's rank. I've never felt younger and more alive in my life."

"That's good," said Too Much, "because I've got Johnson outside, and he has some news that I think'll please you."

"He couldn't have," she said. Then she seemed to study the vacuum cleaner sitting silently in front of her. "News? News, you say? Couldn't be from Carl, could it?"

"I couldn't say," said Too Much. "I just told him I'd come in and talk to you for him. I'm not in this except as a friend. It's between you and him."

"There hasn't been anything between me and him in a long time," Mabel said.

"But you'll see him, right?"

"I don't know why I should."

"It'd seem to me that sixty years of marriage would be a good enough reason for starters. Besides, you could at least see what he's got for you. I'll be right outside if you need me."

"You'll wait right there so I can call you if I need to?"

"You know my name," Too Much said. "That's all it'll take to bring me."

"All right. I don't guess it can hurt."

Too Much went back outside, where Johnson was pacing back and forth. He glanced down at the front of his trousers. "He's holding up like a real soldier."

"She's ready for you to come in."

"How do you think I ought to handle this?" said Johnson.

"Just show it to her. She'll handle it."

"If you say it, I believe it," Johnson said.

"I say it."

Johnson went up the steps and through the door without even looking back. Too Much stood very quietly, smiling. There was not a sound from inside for a long minute, but then the silence was broken with a high, startled squealing. Whether of joy or of pain, it was unmistakably Mabel, and it stopped as quickly as it started. Too Much waited, still holding her soft, confident smile. Then she heard something from the back of the trailer, as though a piece of furniture was being shoved about, and over that the sound of Mabel again, but this time it wasn't squealing: it was the deep moaning sound of celebration.

Too Much walked slowly to Stump's trailer and let herself in. He was sitting at the table, the whiskey bottle in front of him, but she could tell he had not been drinking.

When Stump looked up and saw her, he said, "Be quiet. Justice is asleep in the back."

"Jesus, was he hurt so bad he couldn't make it home?"

"Scratches. He's not hurt. But you scared him so bad, he drank himself to sleep on my whiskey. If he wakes up and sees you, he'll go right out of what little mind he's got left. He thinks you're a witch."

"He's subject to think anything. That wine's fried his brain."

"Where the hell have you been anyway?"

"Doing the Lord's work. What God has joined, let no man put asunder. Mabel and Johnson are back together again and over in Ted's trailer right now, fucking like mad Indians."

Stump snorted through his nose and said, "Now, I know that's got to be a lie."

"That's always been one of your biggest troubles, Stump. You think you know things you don't have the slightest notion about."

"It's always the off chance you could be right on that one," he said.

She lifted his nub and kissed the scarred end of it. "One of your most endearing qualities," she said, "is there's always real humility in your ignorance."

"I don't think much about that," he said. "Mostly, I spend my time thinking about pussy. What about it?"

She smiled. "Talk to me. Make my mind right."

"Too Much, I've thought on it more than some," said Stump, "and I decided a long time ago there's not a man that ever shit behind two shoes could make your mind right." He had been chewing on a kitchen match, and he took it out of his mouth and looked at the frayed end. "And talk? I never talked my way into a woman's drawers yet. Always had to slip in on the sly, if you know what I mean." He put the match back into his mouth and winked at her.

"I got no notion at all what you mean," she said, "but I'm a fool about your bullshit."

He spit the match out onto the top of the table. "Let me tell you something that ain't bullshit. Git serious with you for a minute."

"Do it," she said.

"It'd take God His own self to say which is hornier, my nub or my dick. Now, that's gospel."

"That's also enough. Let me go turn on my tub."

"We got to be quiet, now," said Stump, catching her by the wrist and stopping her as she passed him. "We wake Justice up and he gits one look at you, he's gone wreck my goddam trailer getting the hell out of here. I ain't shitting you when I tell you that he was just about scared to death today, and he's still scared. If you can't keep this quiet, we'll just have to save it for another time."

"Where is he now?"

"Where he passed out in the back room on the floor, after getting on the outside of nearly a whole quart of my best whiskey. That's how bad you scared him."

As she walked away down the narrow hallway toward the bathroom, she said, "Don't worry. I'll even try to muffle my scream when you take me around the bend."

"Trying won't hack it," he said. "You've got to goddam do it."

"Trust me," she said. "Everything'll be fine."

And it was. She did everything she said she would do, including muffling her scream with a washcloth when she was getting her nuts off. Johnson's mop had only primed her for the nub, and while a mop was unique in her experience, a mop was still not Stump's nub, and Too Much wanted to keep Stump happy. Happy men, she'd found, had a way of not paying much attention to what was happening around them.

After they were finished in the tub and were stretched out on Stump's enormous bed, Too Much lay quietly and patiently beside him until he was sunk in a deep sleep, a soft, regular snoring rattling in his throat. When she had first come to Forever and Forever, Stump had been a light and fitful sleeper, with a bad habit of coming fully awake in the middle of the night screaming for medics and morphine, but within two weeks after the huge tub had been installed in the trailer, the screaming stopped and his sleep was profoundly deep and peaceful.

So she made no particular effort to be quiet when she got out of the bed naked and went to the closet where Stump kept his Polaroid camera and stack of film. The camera had been his idea, and he had pictures of her naked in pretty much every position he could imagine. He'd been embarrassed when he brought the camera into the trailer one day and made his proposition.

She only waved off his embarrassment and, in her most supportive voice, said, "Hell, I don't mind. I want a few shots of that brutal nub of yours myself, and then you can take whatever shots you want of me."

"It's only to have something to remind me of when you're gone," he said.

"I'm not going anywhere," she said. "You'll be gone before I am."

"I never thought otherwise," he said. "The worms'll have me before you even reach your prime."

"I wasn't talking about death," she said.

He did not respond to that, or perhaps even hear it. Too Much had found that a man with a camera in front of a naked girl on her back doing clever things with a sausage doesn't hear much or, for that matter, give a good goddam about what he does hear. It wasn't the first time she had been naked in front of a camera, and the only curious thing that struck her about such work was the boring sameness of every man's lust. Crushingly boring. It did utterly nothing for her, and from the first time she had suffered a man to use her in such a way, she had thought it was about as exciting as chewing gum.

She took the camera and went down the hall to the tiny room at the back of the trailer. The door was open, and Justice was sound asleep on his back, the dark hole of his mouth open and his false teeth resting on his chest. She took five quick pictures—the flash disturbing Justice's alcohol-induced coma not at all—and then gently closed the door behind her. She slipped into one of Stump's robes when she passed the little closet beside the bedroom, then went into the kitchen. She placed the pictures across the dining table to finish developing, while she poured half a pint of milk into a pan and heated it briefly on the stove.

She touched the milk with the tip of her finger. Ah, she thought, just the right temperature for a baby's bottle. She took the pan off the stove with one hand and opened a drawer for Stump's favorite butcher knife, a knife he kept especially sharp for carving roasts and turkeys. Then she went out into the early evening dusk and sat on the bottom step and put the pan of milk beside her. It was only minutes before he appeared, an enormous, totally black tomcat, which she playfully called My Little Black Heart.

"Ah, yes, come," she crooned. "Come to your mother, My Little Black Heart."

The cat came to where she was sitting and directly began lapping milk from the pan. This was not the first time she had brought the cat milk in the early dark. But it was the first time she had also brought a knife.

"The theory is," she said to herself in a whispery voice, "that one dies best on a full stomach. Why else would the professional killers of every prison in this sorry country offer up to their victims a final and wonderful meal?" She picked up the knife from where she had placed it beside her and, in the same whispery voice, said, "So drink, My Little Black Heart. Drink your fill."

Chapter 9

It was little more than first light when Too Much awoke. She turned her head to listen carefully, because it felt like some sound had awakened her. But the only sound in the trailer was Stump's soft, rattling snore. As she lay there, she knew it was not a sound that had brought her abruptly out of a deep sleep, but rather a kind of quickening in her blood, a happy anticipation for the day, an anticipation that had a quality of the unknown in it, that sent a jolt of adrenaline coursing through her blood.

Things were starting to happen. Her life was becoming deliciously entangled with the lives around her. And she liked that. She liked that a lot. God knows she had gone to enough trouble to get it all started. Every life that touched hers was like a road leading off in some strange direction, toward some unknown destination. And along every road were uncountable moments of unpredictable surprise, moments of joy and love and celebration, but of course, too, moments of betrayal and violence and death. Yes, death. Always that.

She got off the bed, lighthearted and happy, and finally worked her way into a pair of Levi cut-offs and pulled on a bright-red tank top. She thought this morning she would skip her stretching, her yoga, and her laps of swimming in the pool. If she changed her mind about a swim, she could always come back for her suit.

But she did not see how there would be time for that this morning. She really had no inclination for such activities today. She had arranged things so that she had managed to stave off that which she feared most: boredom. It felt as if the very air around her was crackling. And by God, she meant to keep it crackling, now that she had got it started. She took one more quick look at Stump, bent briefly to savagely scratch a delicious itching high on the inside of her left thigh, and left the room.

On her bare feet, she went quietly down the hall and opened the door to the back room just enough to glimpse the legs of Justice. He was still asleep on his back, his long, thin feet pointed toward the ceiling. A satisfied smile touched her lips as she closed the door and went back down the hall to the closet where Stump kept his camera. She opened the door and took down a shoe box and opened it. A small stack of pictures was inside. She took out the pictures and replaced the box on the shelf, so that she could spread the pictures in her hands as if they were cards she had been dealt in a game of poker.

Ah, you sweet, mean bitch, she said to herself, you might have missed your calling. Perhaps you should have been a photographer. Clear, clean work.

There were fifteen pictures in all, and she had to finally shuffle slowly through them one at a time to get a good look. But it was hardly necessary. There was not a blurred shot among them. Five were of Justice, his mouth open, asleep on his back. There were five of My Little Black Heart, the huge tomcat, lying on his back, his legs splayed and his throat cut. Deeply and broadly cut across the entire width of his throat. Too Much looked long and hard at the cat. She rather liked that his lips were drawn back so that his amazingly white and sharply pointed teeth could be seen. Such a beautiful animal. He really was.

Then she turned to the final five pictures and studied them. They were of the cat and Justice together, the cat lying on his back on top of Justice's chest, so that the cat's grinning head rested just below Justice's chin. Justice's false teeth had been placed in the red open mouth of the bloody cut across the cat's throat. Yes, indeed, from start to finish, absolutely brilliant work. She selected the picture she thought was the best—the clearest and cleanest—of the cat and Justice together, and then returned the rest of the pictures to the shoe box on the top of the shelf in the closet.

Cut her maypole down, would they? Insist upon Forever and Forever being a quiet and boring warehouse for the dead and dying, would they? Resist joy and celebrations would they? And—worse, far worse—doubt her powers, would they?

As she walked down the hall to leave the trailer, her teeth were clamped so tightly together that her jaws hurt. There would be laughter, and there would be celebration, if she had to wreck the entire goddam place to get it. She hated death and dying and every notion of it, but more than that, she hated the fear and trembling, the slobbering and quaking terror, it induced in people. She had not an inkling of an idea what had brought her in off the street into this place, but she felt she was fated to be here. It was not an accident. Her work was here, and she would do it.

She went outside and walked the two hundred yards to the wooden dock where airboats and—when the water table was as high as it was now—shallow-draft motorboats could be launched out onto the sea of water and mudflats, and saw grass that made up the swamp stretching away toward the horizon.

This thumb-shaped part of the swamp that ran right up to the place where Forever and Forever was built had thick stands of trees, mostly Australian pines, growing along the edges on either side of it.

In the distance, along the edge of the swamp where the Australian pines stopped and the saw grass and water started, Too Much saw Johnson, and for the first time since she had arrived at Forever and Forever, Mabel was with him. They were both looking hard into the edge of the swamp, and—wonder of wonders, at least to Too Much—they were holding hands. Johnson was holding her right hand with his left, and in the other hand he carried the pistol.

They would stop from time to time and turn to face each other, obviously talking, then after some study, Johnson—first very slowly and carefully approaching the edge of the swamp and testing it with one of his feet—would shake his head, and they would move on, slightly bent at the waist, staring in fierce concentration as though searching for something rare and dangerous. Their backs were to Too Much, and they seemed completely oblivious to all of Forever and Forever, behind them on the slight rise of ground where the swamp ended.

They moved easily and lightly along the line of the shadow cast by the Australian pines, moved with an agility that Too Much had never seen in either of them but had always known was there. Never for a moment had she doubted it. The energy only had to be released. They only needed a direction that was important to both of them. And now that they had found the energy and direction together, they might have been young lovers out for a good frolicking walk in the first bright light of day as the sun broke above the far horizon.

Too Much felt the entire inside of her chest lift, and she was flooded with a light-headed happiness. Less than twelve hours earlier, Johnson and Mabel were alone and bitter, with nothing to look forward to but long, silent days and even longer nights, filled with tossing in an empty bed with no one to touch and no one to listen if they needed to talk.

Now look at them! And it was her doing and hers alone. Too Much had brought them to this place, where they happily walked and talked and held hands like young lovers, as if age had not slowed them and death did not exist.

Consequently, Too Much thought, a deal was a deal, and a trade was a trade: They both owed her. She knew it, and she knew they, Johnson and Mabel, knew it.

Suddenly, out on the edge of the swamp, Mabel stopped short and pointed, her arm rigid, her crooked forefinger extended. Johnson moved up beside her and looked where she was pointing. Then he slowly raised his pistol and fired. The shot made Mabel jump and grab her ears, but only for a moment. She threw her arms about Johnson's neck and hugged him while he was placing the pistol where he always carried it, under his shirt in the small of his back behind his belt.

It was then that they turned back toward Forever and Forever and saw Too Much. Both of them waved, but it was Mabel who waved the longest. For ten or fifteen paces, she waved vigorously with her right arm while she clung to Johnson with her left. Too Much raised her hand to acknowledge them and then sat down on the end of the wooden dock and had herself a good scratching where her cut-offs fit the tightest.

She glanced toward the trailer. Would the report of the pistol have awakened Justice? She did not think so, and she certainly hoped it had not. What was to be done ought to be done quickly, while the memory of Too Much and the Old Ones was still hot in Justice's memory. She did not have to worry about Stump. He was so accustomed to the pistol going off every morning he did not hear it. Even when he was awake he did not seem to hear it.

The thought of Stump waking up reminded Too Much that she had not put his coffee on. She would have to go back inside and do that. He always awoke to the smell of fresh coffee in the trailer, and Too Much did not want this morning to be different from any other morning. At least for Stump.

"Speak of the devil, and who do we see?" called Mabel as she and Johnson were coming up the little rise of ground that led to the dock. "Your ears must be burning off, child. Johnson and I have been talking about you on and off all morning."

"Part of last night too," said Johnson.

Mabel gave Johnson a playful punch in the ribs. "You hush about last night, you old billy goat."

"It's really good to see the two of you together," said Too Much. "The two of you together make a beautiful morning like this even more beautiful."

"Oh, God!" brayed Mabel. "Have we been together!" She stuck out her hand and crossed two of her twisted, arthritic fingers, one on top of the other, as nearly as she could do it. She lifted her almost crossed fingers up in front of Too Much's face, and in the same voice that was too loud, seeming to border almost on hysteria, said, "That's me on the bottom! Honey, I can hardly walk!"

"Only what God intended," said Too Much, giving them her broadest, brightest smile.

But what she was thinking was this: Nothing on the face of the planet can stay as horny as long as an old woman. Their natural state is a state of continual rut. They may suffer from dry socket, but they can grease up and get down and dirty in a heartbeat. And an old man who can accommodate one is a miracle, a piece of work that is pure magic, a wonder to see.

Johnson looked as if he had dropped twenty years off his age somewhere between the last time she had seen him and now.

"Honey," said Mabel, reaching out to touch Too Much on the arm, "God never intended nothing like Johnson Meechum, I don't believe."

"That'll be enough, Mabel," Johnson said. His voice was stern, but there was a crooked smile over his loose teeth.

"Yes, dear," Mabel said, her whole attitude quieting in the time it took for her to answer him.

There it is, thought Too Much. She's willing to play the dutiful role of the accommodating wife. But Mabel is, and has always been, the stronger of the two. And she will remain the stronger as long as they live. Johnson, though, is all too willing to believe otherwise. It's probably necessary for him—and all those like him—to believe otherwise for the world to work, given the way everything got arranged over the long and sordid history of men and women. Otherwise we would all still be sitting in trees, peacefully munching whatever fruit we could find.

"He wanted me to come out with him this morning," said Mabel, gesturing vaguely back toward the swamp.

"I *insisted* you come along with me," said Johnson.

Don't overdo it, old man, thought Too Much. But she said, "It was really good to see the two of you out there together."

"Nothing like getting the blood up and pumping in an early morning walk," said Johnson. He lifted his thin chest and stood a little straighter. "It's the reason I'm the man I am today, always being up and out of the house before the sun. No, sir, the sun's never caught me in bed."

So many bankbooks to juggle, thought Too Much, and so little time—right, Johnson? "I always thought the morning was the best part of the day myself," said Too Much. "Now, Stump, he could sleep right through the whole morning if he was let do it."

"Stump's a good man," said Mabel, "even if he's not got but one hand."

Too Much reached over and squeezed Mabel's shoulder gently. "Now, Mabel, you know as well as I do that a really *good* man never needs more than one hand."

Mabel squealed and did a little jig of a dance on her arthritic legs. Everything moved but her feet.

"How you *do* go on!" she said.

Too Much stood watching her until she had quieted. "Mabel," said Too Much, "you mind if I talk to Johnson a minute . . . ah, you know, just the two of us? He's helping me with a little surprise for Stump, and we need to get some things worked out. Don't get me wrong, stay if you like, but it's kind of a secret we're going to spring on not just Stump but maybe on everybody in Forever and Forever. And you being such a good friend, I thought you'd understand . . ."

Mabel held up her hand, her crooked fingers spread. "Honey, you go ahead on and have your little powwow with Johnson. I got work to do myself, getting my things together. I'm moving back over with Johnson and get out of that place of Ted's." She winked and clicked her teeth at the same time. "After last night with Johnson, the smell in Ted's place doesn't have the same attraction it once did, if you know what I mean."

"I think I do," said Too Much. "Yes, indeed. Moving back over, you say? Today?"

"She thinks so," said Johnson. "Soon as possible anyway. We've got some plans, Mabel and I do. We think one way or the other we've got to get Carl down here, reestablish family. That's important, family is."

Too Much reached out and patted Mabel on the arm. "Oh, you can get him down here if you really want to. You're his mother. You suffered his passage into this old world, and you've got more power than you think you do."

Mabel gave a satisfied smile and sighed, a little wearily, Too

Much thought. It had been a long night for the old girl, and Too Much was genuinely happy for her.

Mabel said, "I think there is power in me I never knew about and never used." She looked at Johnson affectionately. "Last night convinced me of that."

"You still a lot of woman, girl," Johnson said playfully. "Every bit of woman you ever was, and I'm not going to let you forget it."

"Promise?" said Mabel.

"Promise," Johnson said.

"Then you two go on and get your business done," Mabel said, "and let me go over to Ted's trailer and get started putting my things together." She looked off toward the swamp a moment and then said, "This is a strange old world we live in."

"Stranger than most people will ever imagine in their wildest dreams," Too Much said.

Mabel turned and hurried off on her slightly crooked stride as Too Much and Johnson watched her until she was out of earshot.

Too Much turned to Johnson. "I take it that every time you needed me last night I was there."

"Like magic," he said. "Every time. Without fail."

"I never failed you, and you never failed Mabel, right?"

"Right. It was a fucking miracle."

Too Much smiled. "That's a nice pun, Johnson."

"No pun intended," he said. "I wasn't saying anything but the literal truth."

"Well," said Too Much, "I never put much stock in truth, literal or otherwise. But I'm glad everything worked the way that it was supposed to work, the way that it *had* to work."

"Listen," he said, "you don't know the half of what went on. We—"

"I can do without it. I've got other things on my mind."

"Would you believe Mabel mentioned the mop and the bathtub again. It looks like she wants—"

"Yes, I'd believe it. I told you I was the world's champion believer."

"I mean, we didn't get into it again last night, but it seems—"

"You take it from here, Johnson. I don't mean to keep cutting you off, but I don't need the details. Went all the way to the chance of ultimate possibility. That ends the conversation, at least for me. There are other things we need to talk about."

"Strange," said Johnson quietly, as if talking to himself and not quite believing what he was saying. "The odor thing, you know, me smelling . . . well, her . . . never once got in the way of anything. I don't remember once even thinking about it. It wasn't until this morning that I realized—"

Too Much took him roughly by the shoulder and turned him to face her. "Are you going to pay attention? Or am I going to have to slap the shit out of you first?"

Something seemed to shift in his eyes, which had been focused far away to the place where the sun was now full above the tree line in a sky unmarked by a single cloud. "What?" he said.

"Try to shut up and listen to me," she said. "You had yours. Now I want mine. Something for something. Understood?"

"Understood," he said. But his voice was still not fully recovered from the dreamy memory of last night's miracle.

"You need to get your head out of your ass, so you can think."

"I can think, Too Much. I'm right here with you all the way."

"I hope so. I need you to do a little job. Practically nothing. But you do not want to get it wrong either. Get any job I set for you wrong, and you better leave Forever and Forever, because you won't like it when you have to see me again."

"This isn't necessary," he said. "You don't have to be hostile."

"I'm not hostile," she said. "I'm Too Much. Too fucking Much! And that's worse than hostile. If you don't know that by now, you're senile and you ought to start herding up with the Old Ones every morning."

He threw his shoulders back and struck his bony chest lightly with his fist. "I'm not senile. I know we made a bargain, and I mean to hold up my end of it."

For the first time, she smiled at him gently. "Brightest thing you've said all morning."

Johnson stood straighter still, and it was a moment before Too Much realized that the slight tremor in his rigid body was anger.

When he spoke, though, nobody could have mistaken the anger in his voice. "I may be just a ruined old man to you," he said, "a ruined old man who needed help with a limp dick." Then, more slowly, a little space between each word: "But you would be wise to remember I'm a good deal more than that. You can't take everything from me. I will not give it up." He took a deep breath and let it out slowly. His face had gone gray as blood drained from it. "Now, what's the job you want me to do?"

Too Much threw herself on his skinny neck and pressed her breasts flat against his rib cage. Her breath was hot, her lips brushing his ear when she hissed, "There, that's a *man*! That's the kind of backbone I want to hear in one of my own. I can't use a ruined sucker with a whipped heart."

He lifted his hands and eased them gently onto the rounded mounds of her hips. But otherwise he did not move, and once his hands were lying lightly on her swelling flesh, they did not move either.

"You said you had a job you needed me to do," Johnson said. "Want to tell me what it is?"

Too Much stepped back from him. "Good," she said. "I like that too. I like that even better. Let's, by God, get it on."

He looked over her shoulder at the far horizon, making a sucking noise with the tip of his tongue, moving his teeth in his mouth. "I guess we better. Unless you want to stand around out here and talk it to death."

"At least one of my troops is a tiger," she said, with some satisfaction.

"Your troops?"

"Manner of speaking. You know Justice?"

"The old nigger works for Stump? Doing nothing mostly but sipping wine from a sack? That one? I wouldn't say I *know* him. But I know who he is, what he looks like."

"All that's required. He's been passed out all night from whiskey in the back room of Stump's trailer. In a little while he'll be leaving through the front door, probably heading home. I want you to hand him this."

She held out a Polaroid picture. There was a ten-dollar bill wrapped around it so that Johnson could not tell what the picture was of, but it was easy enough to tell that it was a picture from the ends that stuck out on either side. She handed him the picture wrapped in the bill, and he held it lightly between his forefinger and his thumb after glancing briefly down at it.

"Just hold the bill out to him," Too Much said. "When he sees it's money, he'll take it without asking anything about why you're doing it. When he sees a ten, what he really sees is enough wine to stay half blind for twenty-four hours."

"A state much to be desired," said Johnson, "at least at times."

"Listen to the job at hand. Don't drop lightweight shit like that on me."

"It's not lightweight shit, and you know it better than most," Johnson said, his voice tight again. "But I heard the job. Is that it? All of it?"

"You haven't looked at the picture that the ten's wrapped around."

"I'll look at it when you tell me to look at it. And I'll ask you again: Is my job just to hand the old nigger what you've put in my hand?"

Johnson's stoic, unquestioning acceptance of what she had placed before him made Too Much's spine hot with pride. "With five hundred like you, I could rule the world," she said.

"Now who's talking shit?" asked Johnson.

"I accept that. I am, of course. No, there's one other thing you have to do."

"What's that?"

"As soon as he's got it in his hand, say, 'Too Much buried you with the cat. You better go see her.'"

Johnson's expression did not change at all. He stood very still for a brief time and then said, "'Too Much buried you with the cat. You better go see her.'"

"That's it," said Too Much. "And then get away from him, just turn around and walk."

"When will he be leaving the park?"

"No idea. Part of your job is to put yourself somewhere so you can see the front door of Stump's trailer. When Justice comes out, *put it on him.*"

"Done."

"I'll get Stump's truck and help Mabel."

"Thank you."

"Hell, I took her over there. I'll bring her back." She gestured toward the Polaroid picture wrapped in the ten-dollar bill, which Johnson held now between the thumb and forefinger of each hand directly in front of him, as though it were something very rare and very valuable. "You better look at the picture now."

"I don't think I need to," said Johnson.

"Look at it," she said.

Johnson carefully folded back the bill and looked at the picture a long time. When he lifted his eyes, for all that showed in his face he might as well have been looking at the picture of some proud parent's child.

"You kill the cat?" he asked.

"Yes."

"I knew that cat. Been around here a long time."

"Yes."

"Not that it's any of my business," said Johnson, "but why are you doing this to the old nigger?"

"I may need him, or I may not. But if I need him after he sees this picture, I'll own him."

"That so?" said Johnson matter-of-factly. He folded the bill carefully back around the picture.

"That's so," she said. "I buried him with the cat, a black cat under the full of the moon. Only *I* can dig him up again. Only *I* know where. I'll tell him that when he comes to see me."

"That wouldn't mean a thing to me," Johnson said.

"It will to him."

"When you want something," said Johnson, "you're willing to do some pretty strong stuff, aren't you?"

"When I want *somebody*," she said, "I am willing to do anything. That's the way it works." They stood for a moment facing each other, until she finally asked, "Any questions?"

"One."

"Ask."

"Do I get to kiss the devil again?"

"Do you want to?"

"It comes and goes. Sometimes I want to very, very badly."

"Do you need to?"

"To keep what I've got, I think I have to."

"Not good enough. You've got to want to."

"Hands down, that's what I want to do," he said.

"In that case, I'd count on it if I were you."

Chapter 10

Too Much left Johnson standing on the dock and went back to Stump's trailer to make coffee. She walked heavily up the steps and across the little porch and let the door slam shut behind her as she came out of the bright day, into the dim kitchen. She heard a hitch in Stump's snoring after the door slammed, but then it settled right back into a deep, peaceful rattle.

She took down a fresh can of Luzianne coffee with chicory, which was the only coffee Stump would drink, and made no effort to be quiet as she plugged in the electric can opener and got the paper filter from a cabinet and let the door slam shut. To hell with noise. She wanted everybody up and doing, now that she had set the day in motion. Things were happening now. A sense of powerful movement shook the air around her. She could feel the day was going somewhere, although she did not know quite where. Nor did she care.

The journey was everything, the destination nothing, somebody had said, and whoever he was, Too Much knew he was not only bright but he was also somebody who had been around some very bad, even lethally dangerous, blocks. But whoever had first said it had failed to point out that you have to control the journey without *ever* knowing the destination. That is what scared the hell out of everybody. But it did not scare her. It had not scared her when she was growing up with her grandfather, and it did not scare her now that she had buried him and was alone in the world.

Well, no, that was wrong. She would never be alone, *could* never be alone, because of what he had taught her. What he had taught her did not admit of ever being forgotten. He would always be alive in her, just as she was alive in him, even though by now the worms had doubtless been at his eyes until there were no eyes left, not even a memory of eyes. She did not find this a matter of despair or of depression or even of regret. What she felt about his loss was part of his teaching, part of her debt to him.

She cocked her head for a moment, standing there in the kitchen beside the perking coffee, and thought about fear. The only thing she could think of that truly scared her witless was boredom, her own or having to witness anybody else's. Boredom, it seemed to her, was unforgivable in a world where there demonstrably existed the chance of ultimate possibility. What else could anybody—assuming he could lay claim to sanity—want?

She heard a hacking cough coming from the back of the trailer. Justice was stirring around to the music of his own phlegm-filled lungs: gasps and hacks and wheezes and coughs that sounded like very old paper sacks being torn and ripped apart and then wadded together again. She heard him spit. Jesus, in order to get rid of the wine-soaked phlegm Justice was leaving back there this morning as he woke up, Stump would have to burn the room. There could be no cleaning it. Fire would be the only thing that would cut through what was being splattered about back there.

She wondered if Justice knew where the bathroom was, or if he was just watering off against the walls. It did not really matter. Not ultimately anyway. Ultimately, very little mattered. He was just a skinny, semimoronic old nigger whose single goal in life was finding another bottle of wine. Nothing very unusual in him doing what he was doing. He might be useful to her later on and he might not. If it turned out she needed him, he would be there, ready to serve her. At least, she was fairly sure he would.

There was a moment waiting somewhere down the road that would give the answer. She could wait, because she fully realized that when a general was assembling his troops, he took whatever he could find, the good with the bad, those with blind, impossible courage along with those eaten up with equally impossible cowardice. Only the battle itself could separate the coward from the hero.

She heard Justice now, coming down the hall, his old sliding steps, his shoulders bumping now and again from wall to wall on his unsteady legs, his gaspy, tearing cough stopping him every few steps while he hacked up a piece of phlegm. Too Much went right ahead with what she was doing: toasting a wheat English muffin and pouring a small glass of orange juice for herself. When she knew he was about to emerge into the kitchen, she turned and faced the hallway, waiting.

Justice seemed to have heard somebody in the kitchen, or sensed someone there, because he had stopped. She could almost hear him listening as he leaned in the direction of the kitchen, and see him, his head cocked, one of his old yellow-palmed hands cupped behind his good ear.

"Mistuh Stump?" Justice called softly, and then went into a coughing fit. When that subsided, he called again, a little louder. "Mistuh Stump, that be yo?"

Too Much only smiled and did not answer.

"Mistuh Stump," said Justice softly, "yo aint got jus a wee taste to git ole Justice over dis mornin, is yo? It aint nare drap lef in de bottle back yonder where I'as sleepin at."

Still he did not move. There was a considerable silence, interrupted only by occasional bouts of wheezing and rasping coughs, full of the unmistakable sound of tearing mucus.

Then finally: "Mistuh Stump, if yo aint in yo kitchen, who dat be I be hearin in yo kitchen?"

Then Too Much heard a couple of groans and thumps from Stump's room. The thumps were Stump beating his nub against the mattress. Actually, he thought it was the hand he did not have that he was beating against the mattress. He had done that a lot when Too Much first came to Forever and Forever. But he had gradually stopped beating his phantom hand against the mattress in the morning, at about the same time he had stopped waking up in the middle of the night screaming and calling for artillery fire and air strikes onto his own coordinates, onto his own company—his own people—because he was surrounded and since there was no chance anyway, he thought he might as well take a few gooks with him. But he was not brave in those nighttime battles. He was a lump of quivering, sweat-soaked fear that would sometimes shit itself in the act of calling in the numbers of his coordinates and waiting for death.

"Justice, that you?" Stump had finally come fully awake.

"It be ole Justice, Mistuh Stump, an it be somebody messin in yo kitchen."

"For Christ's sweet sake, go back to sleep or go home. I aint ready to git up, and you're just about to turn me the wrong way."

"You got jus a teeny taste fo ole Justice to make it over with?"

"Above the stove, it's a bottle up there. Take it and get the hell out of here. You say anything else to me, I'm giving you back to them Old Ones that had you under the tree. In case your brain is been sucked dry by that cheap wine you drink, you was just about torn into little pieces by the Old Ones out by the tree. One more word out of you, and I give you back to them."

There followed a long silence. Justice could not talk to Stump, for fear of being eaten by the Old Ones. There was somebody in the kitchen, between him and the bottle over the stove and the front door, and he did not know who it was. But since the whiskey was in there too, he had no alternative but to keep going straight ahead. Too Much knew all this. Listening to his damaged breathing in the hall, she knew that the thought of leaving the whiskey behind was intolerable to him. Her heart went out to the poor old bastard.

And God help him, he still had to see the picture of the throat-cut cat lying on his sleeping chest, his own false teeth jammed into the open wound, and—on top of all of that—hear that the cat had been buried under the full of the moon with the picture clutched between its stiffened paws, with the grinning cat showing its needle teeth. The old man needed the whiskey for that, if for nothing else. Too Much opened the cabinet over the stove and took down a bottle of Jim Beam. She stepped out into the head of the narrow hallway, and there was Justice, not fifteen feet away, seeming to stand in a half crouch, or maybe it was only the way Stump's clothing fit him, loose and flapping as though the clothes were filled not with a body but with old coat hangers.

Justice took a quick step back and said, "Whoa! Whoa, dere!"

Too Much held the whiskey bottle out to Justice. "It's only your whiskey."

"I ain't said no whiskey."

"I've been making Stump's coffee. I couldn't help hearing you ask for whiskey. I got it from over the stove. It's the bottle he was talking about."

Justice's eyes rolled, showing nothing but white. "Yo set dem ole deef-and-dum folks on me lak a pack a hongry dogs."

"I told you, Justice, to leave my tree alone. I don't play. When I tell you something, I mean it."

"I wake fo Mistuh Stump. Mistuh Stump own dis here Forever and Forever. He done tol me dat, an he tol me to take dat tree down."

"And I told you not to."

Justice's gaze held on the whiskey bottle. His hands were trembling violently. His whole body shook with a tremor. Too Much knew drunks. The same thing that made them sick made them well. Justice was desperate for a drink.

Too Much had about run out of patience with him, though. "Take the damn whiskey, Justice. The door is right behind me. Take it outside and bubble it a few times before you have a stroke."

"I be thinkin I mought druther hab me a stroke dan take drinkin whiskey out from yo han. Yo han be some more tainted."

But he still had not looked at the door. The focus of his gaze had never wavered from the bottle.

Too Much set the bottle on the tiny dining room table and backed away from it. "There," she said. "My hand's not on it. Now will you take it and get out of here?"

"No, on account a yo hand *been* on it. Taint go through glass, metal, wood . . . right through de livin body its own sef, right on down to de blood." But he spoke looking at the bottle, not at Too Much.

"Then I guess you're just going to have to leave it here," she said. "And I don't care if you stay or go. Stand right where you are until you die, if that's the way you want it."

"Don be tellin ole Justice he gone stan here till he die."

"That's not what I said, Justice. You're just hung over and still twisted from last night."

For the first time, Justice's eyes swung from the bottle on the table to Too Much. "How come yo set dat passel of ole folks on poor ole Justice, set'm on me lak a pack a dogs?"

"Don't make more out of it than it was," said Too Much. "There wasn't a decent bite taken out of you anywhere. It's only so much damage false teeth and gums can do. You probably hurt yourself more trying to get up than anything they did to you."

Stump appeared in the hallway behind Justice. His hair was matted from the bed, and his chin and throat were dark with a stubble of beard. He wore nothing but the pair of boxer shorts he slept in. His eyes were angry, but he stood for a quiet moment rubbing the hair on his chest with the scarred, purple end of his nub.

"Justice," Stump said.

Justice, who did not know Stump was behind him, turned with surprising quickness and agility. Too Much saw the quickness and agility and knew it was the adrenaline of fear cooking in the old man's veins.

"Mistuh Stump, yo sposed be in yo bed."

"Exactly what I came out here to tell you. Justice, what in the world is all this talk about?"

Justice's eyes shifted to the floor. "Which talk it be yo wantin to know bout, Mistuh Stump?"

Stump, in a voice entirely too soft and even, which meant he was liable to explode at any time, held up his good hand and counted off the things he had in mind. "I haul your ass out from under a bunch of crazies, tote you to my own house, let you drink my goddam Wild Turkey, clean you up like a baby, get all the blood . . ." Stump stopped talking and turned Justice toward the light coming in from the kitchen window over the sink. "Where the hell did this blood on the front of your shirt come from?

There's even some on the bottom of your chin." He reached up and ran his thumb hard across the crusted blood under Justice's chin and on his throat. "Aint even your blood either. Now what the fuck's going on?"

"Aint studin blood. Studin gittin me a taste to git over. Git over, I go on home."

"Well, if you're not studying blood, that's sure as hell fine with me. There's the bottle on the table. Git it and go rest up."

"You mind puttin yo hand on it and passin it to me, Mistuh Stump?"

"I'm not even going to ask why. I'll give you anything in the house to get rid of you." He walked over to the table and took the Jim Beam by the neck. "Here, go on home, and when you're able to work again, get your ass back over here."

Justice snatched the bottle from Stump's hand, hugged it to his chest, bolted for the door, and went out, letting it slam behind him.

"Well," said Stump, exasperated, "not a thank-you, or kiss my ass, or go to hell, or nothing. Ain't like Justice." He looked at Too Much, who was pouring him a mug of coffee, and said, "What have you been saying to him, Too Much?"

She turned and handed him his mug of coffee, smiling as she did. "Why does it always have to be something I've done, Sweet Cheeks?"

"Just seems to work out that way, don't it," Stump said, sipping his coffee.

Too Much sat down at the little dining table with him, absently turning a small glass of orange juice in her fingers. Finally she said, "You're not joking, are you?"

Stump blinked his eyes against the steam rising from his coffee and also from sleep that he had not entirely left in bed. He did not think well in the morning and knew it. And he particularly disliked this kind of commotion when he first woke up. If the morning couldn't be peaceful, when in the name of God was peace supposed to come? It put him in a bad mood and kept him there, sometimes for the whole day if the morning was bad enough. Right at the moment, he felt like this whole day might be bad.

"Joking?" he said. That was about as much as he had heard of what she said.

"I said you weren't joking about things being my fault."

"Too Much, now that we just got Justice out of the house, we don't have to get right back into something to rattle my brain, do we? I don't think my brain'll take any more rattlin this early in the morning." He yawned, got up, and poured himself another cup of coffee. "Maybe I was joking." He sat again at the table. "Yeah, I think I was joking." He sipped his coffee and looked off toward the far wall, squinting. "Come to think of it, though, things have been happening right along, ain't they? Ted falling out of a goddam tree and breaking his neck. My only pine—which I kind of miss now that it's gone, by the way—getting cut to total shit. Johnson, the crazy pistol shooter, mopping his wife, her moving out and into Ted's trailer, which—strictly speaking—I didn't have the right to let her do, me going back on my word and burning Ted instead of burying him. Yeah, there's strange shit coming down all over the place."

"And somehow I'm supposed to take the heat for all of it, right?"

"Hey, I said to lighten up. You don't have to be anything but Too Much. That seems like a full-time job to me."

"Well, at least you got something right. It *is* a full-time job. You'll never say anything truer in your life."

"I just like to sort of keep track of what's going on around me. I don't want to keep too close a track, mind you, but some. Another way to say it is that I like to pay attention. Because I've seen too many times what not paying attention can do to a man, and seems like lately, I haven't been paying real good attention. What am I supposed to make out of my old people ripping the clothes off Justice and then—*then,* by Jesus—biting him? They bit him all over. That's going to take some thinking about."

"That won't take any thinking about," Too Much said. "I told him not to cut down my tree. You told him to do it. I told the Old Ones if he touched it, I wanted them to eat him."

"Did you say *eat* him?"

"My very words."

"You said you told'm to maul'm. That's what you told me you said anyway. You didn't say anything about telling'm to eat him."

"The only way they could make him stop was with their mouths. Their mouths are still the strongest thing on them. Even at their age, they've still got about four-hundred-pounds-per-square-inch bite in their mouths."

"Too Much, you're strange."

"You knew that five minutes after I walked into Forever and Forever off the street."

"True. I got no comeback to that." He looked off toward the wall as if searching it for some message that might be written there. Then: "You think we could let the dust settle on this until it gets later in the day and my blood's pumping a little faster than it is now?"

"That's easy. Consider it done. I got to get out of here anyway and go help Mabel. Think I could use your pickup?"

"You know you got it anytime you want it. But what are you doing with Mabel?"

"Taking her home."

"I'm getting lost all over again. But I don't much think I want anything explained to me."

"I'm just taking her and her things back over to live with Johnson, get her out of Ted's. Nothing to get excited about."

Stump stiffened on his chair and looked for a moment as though he had quit breathing. "The hell it's not! Now that we burned up Ted and put him in a bottle, or wherever they put him after they burned him up, I got his trailer that I was supposed to sell and use the money to bury him the way I promised, in a coffin in the ground, not scatter him around like so much fertilizer. And it was all because Mabel needed the trailer to live in. You leaned on me to let her have it. *Now, one day later, she's moving out!* And Ted's still in a bottle instead of where I promised to put him. And you say it's nothing to get excited about?"

"Like Janis Joplin said, Different day, same shit."

"What's that supposed to mean?"

"Nothing. I think that was her point. It means absolutely nothing." She shrugged. "But forget about that for a moment if you can. I need to ask you about something else."

"More trouble, right?"

"Not really. Depends on you."

"By God, I'm glad *something* depends on me. I was starting to feel left out of things around here. And I don't think I much like that, because the last time I checked, I owned Forever and Forever."

"You think I could have the use of Ted's trailer?"

"The use of it? To do what?"

"Live in."

"You live here. Leastwise, I thought you did. Unless you thinking on leaving me. That what you doing?"

"Never crossed my mind. I'm not leaving you; I know I live here," she said. "I just want a place to call my own once in a while when I need it. A little space. I couldn't leave you, Stump. You know that. You also know me well enough to know I could never let that tub go to waste after you knocked down a wall to put it in here for the two of us to start with. But you wouldn't begrudge me a place to go and think and be alone when I need it, would you? I'm not exactly asking for the moon."

"Then everything would be just like it's been between you and me?"

"Bet on it. Nothing's changed. I just want to fix that place up. Make it feel like it's somewhere I can go and get in a rocking chair and think when I want to. Don't you ever want to turn everything loose and just kick back and rock away most of the world you're carrying around in your head?"

"All the time, Too Much, all the time." He took a sip of his coffee. "As a matter of fact, that's how come me to buy this place to start with. Called Sunset Acres at the time, but I seen that for the bald-faced lie it was and changed it to Forever and Forever, a name that at least has honesty on its side."

"That still doesn't tell me why you bought the place."

"If you'll pour me the rest of that coffee and quit interrupting me, maybe I *could* tell you."

Too Much poured his coffee and set it down in front of him.

"Thank you."

"Don't thank me, Stump. I like doing things for you. It sort of makes me—oh, I don't know—kind of feel like a wife."

Stump slammed his coffee cup hard against the little table. "Don't—repeat: don't—ever feel like a wife around me. Or if you do, keep it to yourself. I don't want to hear a goddam thing about it. OK?"

She shook her head slowly and pursed her lips. "That's easy enough to read. You had a wife and she fucked you over and now you blame every other woman in the world for what she did. Don't make a big thing out of something as common as cowshit. Why don't you tell me about it? If you got a mind to, that is."

"Ain't a hell of a lot to tell. You probably could figure it out if you thought real hard, clever girl like you."

"Never figured you for low-rent sarcasm."

"Sarcasm's got nothing to do with it." He held up his scarred nub. "She left me after I got this—after I got it but before those two lawyers made me rich. The bitch tried to come back. You know, ease her way back into the barrel of money I was holding. I thought about killing her, probably should have. But cutting the bitch's heart out wasn't enough to git locked up over, so I come south with my money and found this place. I knew it was the kind of place I ought to buy right off. Little something to keep my mind occupied but not enough to get in my way. I needed peace is what I needed. And hell, nothing going on here but death. I can't imagine anything more peaceful than the dead and dying."

"Most of what you just said is completely wrong," Too Much replied, with some heat. "I'd help you get your head straight if I had the time. But I don't right now. Maybe later."

"Take your time," he said.

"Mabel's waiting on me over there to help her, so I got to get out of here. But I promise you this: Come May Day, there'll be no thought of death and no thought of the dead and dying. At least on my part anyway."

"You've written a big order for yourself, little girl."

"I may be little, but we both know I'm no girl."

"I misspoke myself," Stump said.

"We all do, sooner or later. No big deal. I'd stay and talk, but the sooner I get Mabel out, the sooner I can make it a place of my own."

"Take the truck and go get her."

"Then you don't think me wanting a place I can go and be by myself once in a while is unreasonable?"

"What would be unreasonable would be if you didn't want it. It don't mean jackshit to me, as long as I see you."

"As much as you want."

"Then I guess we got a deal."

"You want me to make another pot of coffee before I go?"

"I been making coffee all my life, Too Much. I think I can manage."

Chapter 11

In a single week, Ted's trailer and the grounds around it bloomed like an oasis in the middle of a desert. It was a miracle, and many of the residents spoke of it as such.

"It's a miracle," they would say.

"Too Much has the touch," they would say.

"If it can be done, that Too Much can do it," they would say.

What Too Much had been able to do in so brief a time had radically changed their attitude toward her. She was a good sweet girl with good sweet intentions. They had forgiven and forgotten her scratching. It *did* feel good, just as she had been quick to tell any who asked about it, and—as she had been equally quick to tell them—they were all old enough to scratch where it felt good no matter where they were or in whose company they found themselves. It was just one more of the many benefits of living to a fine old age.

Scratch where it felt good, and tell the rest of the world to go to hell if they didn't like it. The closer the residents got to her, the more they admired her, the better they understood that what they had taken for a foul mouth—cursing as she did—was really just good straight talk that nobody could misunderstand.

"Tell it like it is, by God," she told the residents. "And you've lived long enough in this old world to know in your secret hearts that the way it is is pretty god-awful bad. And as far as I'm concerned, to beat around the bush by using cute language is telling a lie. But you do as you like."

What almost every one of them liked, as it turned out, was to start telling it like it was. Overnight, the language in conversations throughout Forever and Forever sounded like a boatload of sailors after six months at sea. And many of the residents had taken up Too Much's scratching habit. Old people clawing at themselves in intimate places while they played shuffleboard or ambled down the macadam lanes between rows of trailers, changed the whole look of Forever and Forever.

None of it had escaped the notice of Stump. Very little of the landscaping work had been done by Too Much. The entire herd of Old Ones swarmed about Ted's trailer like bees around a hive, working tirelessly but slowly, very slowly, at whatever job they were given the opportunity to do.

Too Much discovered that Johnson was a gardener, and an extremely good one at that. Gardening, as it happened, had been a hobby he had cultivated with a vengeance, even while he was still a banker and a habitual embezzler. The reason was simple enough. Working in the walled and private garden on his estate kept him away from his wife, whose odor even that long ago had developed to industrial strength, or at least that's the way Johnson had put it to Too Much. So, he had told Too Much, he had kept to his garden rather constantly before he was finally handcuffed in his own bank and taken away to prison.

But what completely dumbfounded Stump was Justice. The old man no longer carried his sipping sack, and he worked as though his life depended on it. He did not shamble and amble. Not anymore. There was spring in his step and purpose in his stride. He bounced around, drenched in sweat, the ridge of his fleshless spine showing through his shirt, moving in a way Stump would have thought impossible if he had not seen it with his own eyes.

"What in the hell have you done to Justice?" Stump asked.

"Nothing," she said.

"God help us, you haven't been giving *him* mother's milk too, have you?"

She only looked at him calmly for a moment and said, "Would there be something so terrible about it if I had?"

Stump thought on it for a moment. "We're not going to have some kind of liberal–conservative, white–nigger argument here, if that's what you're looking for, or even a discussion about it, for that matter. I just asked a question. If I don't get an answer one way or the other, I'll still sleep pretty good. You got that?"

"I got it. And the answer is no, no mother's milk for Justice."

They were sitting at the dining table in Stump's trailer. He stood up and got himself another beer, sat back down, and popped the top. Today was the day Too Much was moving her things over to Ted's place. To make it feel more like something that belonged to her, she had told him. But Stump still admitted—if only to himself—that this whole business had put him a little off his feed. A little, he kept telling himself, but not much.

"Well," said Stump, "Justice damn sure don't move around the way he used to. Something pretty strange has got to be at the bottom of all this."

"Oh, something very strange *is* at the bottom of it."

"What might that be?"

"Me."

"Answer enough as far as I'm concerned. I don't need no details. But you probably want to know the reason I wondered about the mother's milk."

"Not really."

Stump went on as though he had not heard her.

"Justice is a damn fine man, old and a little thin in the shank, but fine. One of the few men in this world I'd trust with my life. Trust with my life but not with my titty. There's something about my mouth following that goddam mouth of his with the six mismatched teeth that rubs me wrong in the stomach. Did he tell you about his six teeth?"

"Several times. And I expect to hear about them several more times before it's over. No surprise in that. It's just something that makes him different from the other people he knows. It's something unique to him, and he's proud of that. Pride and guilt run this lousy world, in case you haven't noticed."

She left Stump sitting at his tiny dinner table and went into the back of the trailer, but it was no more than a minute before she returned with the same bag she had carried slung over her shoulder when she first walked into Forever and Forever. It looked exactly like a sailor's sea bag, only it was about a third smaller. Everything she owned was in that bag, and she had made it obvious from the first night with Stump that her bag was off limits to everybody, including Stump. It did not bother Stump at all. He didn't need to know anything about it. He tried to keep his nose where it belonged, on his face, not in other people's business.

Too Much put the bag on the floor beside the table and sat down to finish the ice tea she had been drinking. Stump got up for a beer out of the icebox, but he never took his eyes off the duffel bag, as she preferred to call it, even after he sat back down at the table.

He gestured toward the bag. "You travel light. I've always admired a person that traveled light."

"My granddaddy told me to never own more than I could jump on a moving freight train with. That advice seemed sound then, and it seems sound now. I like to keep it simple."

"Your granddaddy sounds like a damn fine man. He give you some pretty good advice there."

"He was more than a fine man, a lot more. I wouldn't be what I am today if he hadn't raised me."

Though Stump would have liked to hear more, to know more—why was she raised by her granddaddy?—he had always tried not to ask pointed questions about people's personal lives. Hell, he did want to know where she was from—had always wanted to know—but he'd always found one thing or another to keep him from asking. Now seemed as good a time as he'd ever have.

"Where do you come from, Too Much? I always meant to ask you but never did."

"No," she said. "You never did."

The two of them balanced each other on a little tension that had sprung up from somewhere. When it became apparent that she was not going to say anything more, Stump said, "For some reason, now that you're moving out of my house, I'd kind of like to know."

She gave him her most open smile and slowly shook her head as though he had just told the biggest lie God ever imagined. "I'm not *moving* anywhere, Stump. I'm moving my *stuff* from here to Ted's trailer, a distance that the most crippled and damaged resident of Forever and Forever could cover in about ten or fifteen minutes. But since you asked, I'll tell you. I'm not from a place; I'm just from a place near a place."

"Pretty cute way of putting it, but it doesn't tell me much."

"It's a lot of things, but it's not cute. As a matter of fact, it's not even mine. I stole it from a great writer, dead now, dead way too early, and a character in one of her books says that. When somebody asks him where he's from, he says, 'I'm not from a place, just from a place near a place.' "

"You read too much, you know that? Anybody that's got to answer a question from a book they read is somebody who reads way too much."

"Watch what you say. Granddaddy gave me her stuff to read. He recognized it for what it was: the cold hard truth. Besides, what I said is the only way I can say it, unless I want to lie. I'm *not* from a place, just a place near a place. I'm talking here about way the hell and gone in the swamp, where most men would need a bloodhound to find their way out of."

"Forget it, then," said Stump. "It's not important."

But it was important to Stump. He secretly wanted to know everything about her, so he could come closer to knowing who and what she was, because it had not been long after she moved into his trailer that he discovered she was a single monstrous mystery to him. And since that time, the mystery had only deepened. "Let's get back to what's going on right now. Have any of the residents asked what it is you're doing with Ted's place?"

"Of course."

"What did you tell them?"

"The truth."

"Which is?"

In a great explosion of breath that was half from anger and half from frustration, Too Much said, "Damn, Stump, we've had this conversation before, remember?" She watched him as he sipped his beer. "All right, you don't remember, or there's something you can't believe. What I wanted is what I told you: someplace that I could call my own, a place to go and think or *not* think if I don't want to, maybe just go there and chill. What's the problem with that?" Stump opened his mouth to speak, but she held up her hand to stop him. "Just let me finish. Do you want to know if I lied? Yeah, I lied, but not to you. The residents wanted to know what was going on with Ted's trailer: fixing it up, putting in all those plants— By the way, that Johnson is a magician with every living thing that grows in the ground; he can transplant anything and not only make it live but blossom too. So anyway, they asked, and I told them I was making it into an office for myself."

Stump had been about to lift his beer to his lips, but he left it on the table instead. "Did you say an *office* for yourself?"

"I had to tell them something. Hell, you and I have been living with a lie since the first day I moved in here. They preferred to think we were married, and we never told them anything different. They're so old, they come from a time when it was absolutely evil for a man and a woman to just move in with each other and live together. But that's what we did, and we never tried to straighten them out when they got it wrong about you and me being married. I didn't want them to think I was leaving you, which, like I told you, I'm not, so the first thing I thought of to tell them that made any sense was that I was making Ted's trailer over to use as an office to keep your accounts, do your correspondence, try to keep the IRS off your ass, and so on. And as it turns out, lover, that's exactly what I'm going to do. When I spend time over there, they'll just know I'm in the office taking care of business. And you know what the residents' reaction was to that? They said it was about time somebody ran Forever and Forever, because you sure as hell didn't. And they're right; you don't. Now, don't get your nose out of joint about this. I'm only trying to help."

Stump finished his beer and looked at the duffel bag, then at the door, and finally back at Too Much. "Forever and Forever runs itself. It's the greatest thing about the place. I told you that you could have the use of Ted's trailer, but I don't need anybody to manage for me, no offense intended but I'm doing just fine, thank you."

"Where are your books, Stump? Where do you keep the accounts of what you've bought for this place that are legitimate tax write-offs? Where do you keep a record of who paid you rent, how much they paid you, and when they paid you? Could you go to a ledger right now and tell me which resident is behind in his rent and by how much?"

With a little edge in his voice, Stump said, "I told you, I was doing just fine."

"Pardon me all to hell and gone, but that's bullshit. You've got that huge settlement from those insurance companies for getting your arm mangled, therefore you don't really need the money, therefore you don't keep records of anything, therefore you're in a trick of shit."

"You don't know what you're talking about. The only record I need is the one I keep in my head."

"Have you ever been audited by those fucking Nazis who operate the IRS?"

"Never. Why would they want to audit me? I don't cheat. I pay what I owe. What reason do they have for wanting to fuck with me?"

"The IRS doesn't need a reason. To do *anything.* If you think the money you've got in the bank will save your ass, you're dead wrong. The IRS will take that too, if the shit comes down just right. They don't even have to let you know it when they go into your bank account and take every nickel you've got. To get it back, they don't have to prove they're right. *You* have to prove they're wrong."

"That can't be right," Stump said. "Shit, I fought for this fucking country in a time of war, and they didn't have to come looking for me either. I went down and signed up."

"You know what that counts for?"

"A hell of a lot, I say."

"It counts for nothing, zip, jackshit, that's what it counts for. The motherfuckers at the IRS want numbers, numbers you can prove with receipts. So if they come, you're dead meat. They'd take everything you've got and probably put you in jail besides. So let's just consider this conversation over. You've got a manager, and I'm it. I'm running Forever and Forever from this minute on. I'll save you money and keep your ass from getting locked up, on top of it." She paused and looked hard into his eyes. "Unless, of course, you're telling me straight out that I can't."

"I didn't say that."

"Then Forever and Forever is mine to run, to put in proper and efficient order?"

"If that's what makes you happy," he said.

"What makes me happy is keeping you out of jail and hassle out of your life."

"I couldn't hardly argue with that."

"Good. Then it's done."

"You haven't said anything about a salary. What's this costing me?"

"Not a nickel," she said.

"Where I come from, we say, 'Labor deserves its hire.' I can't work you for nothing. I'm not exactly broke."

"I know that, but that's not the point. The point is that there's a job that needs doing and I can do it. As far as what you owe me in salary is concerned, if you're really into keeping a record of who owes who how much money, then hell, I'm the one that's in debt. Who's been feeding me? Who's been putting a roof over my head. Who's been fucking my eyes out with the sort of nub that nobody else in the world has? I could go on, but I think you see my point. My guess is that I could manage this place righteously for a year and still be in debt to you. You're a generous, kind man, Stump, and if you don't watch out, somebody is going to come along someday and walk away with everything you've got, including your ass."

Stump watched her a long moment over the beer he was holding. "If I was the sort that blushed, I reckon that's what I'd be doing. You're pretty crooked in your thinking, though, girl. I ain't kind and I ain't generous. You wouldn't let me be generous if I wanted to be. I've tried to give you spending money, and you wouldn't take it. Name one goddam thing you've ever asked me for."

She flashed a quick, full smile. "A bikini. I told you I'd gone to the store and seen the one I wanted and how much it cost and I asked you to buy it for me to swim laps. Now, did you pull the money out of your pocket without even changing words with me, or what?"

Stump looked out the window and felt his face getting hot, and he wondered if he was actually blushing. "All right," he said. "I did do that."

"Say it, Stump," she said. "Say, 'I bought you a bikini, Too Much, a very pretty one that you really wanted.'"

"I bought you a bikini," he said, still not looking at her.

"That won't do. You've got to say it all."

Now his eyes swung back to hers, and he was frowning. "I got to say that whole thing?"

"Every word of it."

"You're fucking with me, Too Much."

"Yes, I am, Stump, you darling man. I'm fucking with you."

"Tell me again what I got to say. It was too long to remember."

She told him.

He repeated it.

"Thank you."

"You're welcome, but don't do that again," he said. "Ever."

"I can't promise anything about the future. We'll find out when we get there. Now, back to business."

"I thought we'd finished with that."

"Not quite. Let's see what kind of job I do, what kind of money I save you and make you, and then we'll talk about a salary."

"Then you're not against taking money for the job?"

"I'm not an idiot, Stump. Where'd you get the notion I was against taking money for a job?"

"You've done about three times as much work with the flowers and grass and shrubbery around this place since you've been here as Justice has ever done—changed the whole look of the park—and you never asked a dime for it."

"I love things that grow in the dirt, and things that grow in the dirt love me. I did what I did out of the love of doing it, darling. That's allowed, you know, for me to do stuff that gives me pleasure."

"Shit, I can't talk to you. I get beat every time."

"Go on and admit it," she said. "You love me to beat you."

"Ain't bad, actually. But so I don't have to get tangled up with talk again, just go on and take the job. Forever and Forever is yours to manage the hell out of it."

"We probably ought to get somebody to make us a contract of some sort."

Stump nearly choked on his beer, but when he'd cleared his throat, he said, "A contract? Between us? You've lost your mind."

"Just to keep it legal. I might steal you blind, you know."

"I'd rather take a beating than sign my name. And I break out in hives if I even *see* a legal paper. That's why I keep stuff in my head to start with."

"Then somewhere down the road we may have to make some kind of arrangement so I can sign for you. A business can't be run without somebody who has the power to sign whatever needs signing."

"Christ, don't I know it. Every time I turn around, as much as I hate it, I've got to sign some damn thing. So do whatever needs doing. Just leave me out of it."

"Then it's a deal?"

"It's a deal," he said, without the vaguest notion of what deal he had made, but he knew he didn't know, and also that he didn't want to know.

"I guess I ought to take my stuff on over and get settled in," she said, looking at her bag on the floor by the table.

"So this really is the day you're moving out?"

"Going to the office, Stump. Going to the office. Why don't you just say that to yourself every now and then? Maybe you'll get the idea after a while and stop making something out of this it's not. You really are being dense about the whole thing."

"I never heard a person as young as you are that wanted a place to *think*. Hell, it ain't even natural for somebody young as you to want to be *alone*."

"I somehow thought you were brighter than that, Stump."

"Than what?"

"Than to think I was natural. As far as I've been able to tell—and I've thought about it a lot—there's not a natural bone in my body."

"I wasn't going to say it myself. But as long as you brought it up, I don't guess I would want to argue with that."

"Good."

"I mean, I wouldn't want to go as far as to say you were unnatural. I mean, you ain't crazy. Or if you are, you've kept it under your bushel basket pretty good."

"No, I wouldn't say I was crazy either," she said. "But then that wouldn't mean a hell of a lot, would it? There's not many crazy people who admit to being crazy. And the crazier they are, the less likely they are to admit it. At least that's been my experience."

"Mine too. I knew this guy in Korea that . . . No, I won't bore you with that, but he was crazy as a bedbug and thought he was the sanest man in the outfit. You're about to walk out the door, so if you're not natural and you're not crazy, how is it with you? I can't figure it."

"Don't try, Stump. Waste of time. And even if you knew, what would that prove? Besides, I'll be back in your tub and your bed tonight."

"My tub and my bed," Stump said in a musing voice. "That's got a nice ring to it."

"I'm sure as hell not sleeping on the floor over at Ted's."

"There wasn't a bed over there?"

"Well, of course there was a bed. Ted didn't sleep on the floor either, but Jesus, what a bed. I know you've been around a lot of blocks in your life, but I'd bet my last nickel you've never seen anything like what Ted slept on. It was the first thing I got out of there. You really ought to come over and see the place, but not just yet. Let me do a few other things. I've stripped that sucker to the wall, painted it, and now I'm making it my very own nest. My place, which was the whole point to start with, right?"

"If you say so. But how did you manage all that? Are you a painter and carpenter as well as the best fuck east of the Rocky Mountains?"

"Don't talk to me about fucking in the morning. You know what it does to me. And right now I don't have time for the nub God blessed you with just so I could find it and take the best ride I ever had."

"Don't talk to me about riding my nub in the morning," he said. "You know what it does to me."

"Don't make fun of me."

"Whatever I might have been doing, I sure wasn't making fun of you."

"Good. Let's just drop that for now and let me answer your question. That is, if you still remember what it was."

"I remember. It was about you being a carpenter and a painter."

"A painter and a carpenter? The answer is I'm anything I want to be. But I didn't do any of the work over at Ted's. Let me set you straight on something. You listening?"

"I'm listening."

"Forever and Forever is a gold mine. Stump, when you walk around the park, all you see are wrecked and ruined people, people who are dying or people who already ought to be dead. As you've heard me say before, it doesn't make you bad; it only makes you human. Did it ever cross your mind that right here in this park you've got architects, poets, bricklayers, and concert pianists? Did it?"

"Never."

"You do. You name the craft or art, and I'll go find the man or woman who is the master of it. And I'll never have to leave Forever and Forever to do it. They're the ones who have made Ted's place into something you wouldn't believe. And they did every bit of it for nothing. They're starving for something to do besides wait for death. And I'm going to give it to them. Before I'm done, I may organize Forever and Forever like the frigging Prussian Army."

"You mean the Russian Army."

"No, the Prussian Army."

"Never heard of it."

"It doesn't matter. I haven't decided yet. Besides, I don't like to decide things with my head. I like to act first and then let the act be the decision. Just the opposite from the way the rest of the world does it. Which, as far as I'm concerned, is reason enough to do it my way instead of theirs."

"What you just said is a hell of a lot too tangled for me to talk about. I think I'll leave it alone. I feel a little bit like a drunk coming on."

"You're old enough. It's allowed. I've got to get out of here anyway." She got up, slung her bag over her shoulder, and opened the door, but then she paused and looked back at Stump. "About me and natural and all that stuff we were talking about? Maybe you'll rest a little easier if I just tell you that early on in my life I was taught that the human race was about as nasty as it could get and it had nobody or nothing to blame but itself and that I would do well not to give much of a good goddam what it told me to do or not to do. I was little when I first got wind of this, and of course I didn't even know what I was being told. But I stayed with the voice that told me that for a long time, and I decided finally—on my own, really—that what I'd been told was right." She started to go, but stopped yet again to look back briefly. "But if you don't listen to those of your own kind or follow what those of your own kind tell you to follow, what voice do you listen to? I'll just give you this for nothing: Your own voice gets unbelievably tiny and very hard to hear when it's all by itself."

She let the door slam, as Stump called out behind her, "I think 'crazy' turns out to be the word we were looking for after all."

Too Much only smiled and went across the little porch and down the three steps into the brilliant morning sun. The humidity was already high, even though the sun had just crested above the dark wall of Australian pines at the far edge of swamp. So Stump thought "crazy" might be the right word to describe her after all, did he? Fair enough. What Stump and the rest of the world thought of her—or thought to call her—caused her no concern.

What did concern her and give her great pleasure was that this place, Forever and Forever, now had the indelible stamp of her hand, in the same way that every place did where she had stopped for any length of time since she had first taken to the road, three days after her fifteenth birthday, the day on which her grandfather died. It had taken her three full days to leave him as he wanted to be left.

Since they had lived alone in the deep swamp, she had been forced to do all the work herself, following as nearly as possible the old man's carefully written instructions, instructions written in green ink in a spidery script nearly filling a child's spiral notebook.

He died with his hand in hers. His last words were "You are the Appleseed of happiness. Nobody will like it, because nobody will understand it. The world knows what to do with grief. It has never known what to do with happiness and celebration."

Then a deep, long shuddering took his heaving chest, and he was gone.

Chapter 12

When she had felt her grandfather stretch rigid and the shudder take him and the last long breath start to explode from his mouth, she bent to cover his mouth with her mouth and take his dying breath into her lungs. It had all been done as he had instructed her to do it, and it had all been as he had said it would be, the breath strong and sour and long, but the act itself so personal and, by its nature, unique that she would never forget even the tiniest detail of it, so indelibly was it impressed upon her memory.

She was walking now directly toward the courtyard, toward the courtyard where Ted had killed himself at the base of a tree that was now only a ragged stump eight inches high where Justice had cut it down before the Old Ones could pull him off it with their mouths.

A black cross was painted on the top of the gummy surface of the stump. Too Much did not know who had painted it there and did not care. The cross could just as well have been a swastika. They were both signs of allegiance and fidelity. Both were misguided, failed, and fucked-up. As much blood had been spilled under one sign as under the other by fools with neither particularly good nor particularly bad hearts, only particularly human hearts.

The lines of the cross, thick and uneven, had been done with an unsteady hand. It was probably the work of one of the Old Ones, although Too Much wondered at times how much the Old Ones understood of what was going on around them. And she wondered, too, about their memories, especially the memories they would go on talking about at great length—the Old Ones who could talk—telling of the world and the way it had been forty or fifty or more years ago, while a week ago or even yesterday or the day before was a totally blank page to them. The best they could give you about what had happened in the last few days was a dead, bewildered stare. Too Much had always been concerned about them, and now that she was manager of Forever and Forever, they were her responsibility, and she intended to make some changes. She couldn't make them live any longer—which she would not have done had she been able—but she could make the time they had left a little easier for them, which, in her own way, she had been trying to do all along.

She turned from the cross on the stump and looked long and hard toward Ted's trailer, which was—even at this early hour—a shimmering of the sun, as were the Old Ones, and Johnson and Justice, who moved among them, starting them at tasks, closely directing them, and then stopping them in time to keep them from ruining something.

At first Johnson had come to her and complained that they only got in his way. "With the time it takes to get them started, stand over them to see that they don't mess something up, and then stop all of them—one at a time, mind you: you can't stop them all together by just telling them to stop, hell no; with them it's a one-on-one kind of situation—with all the time it takes to do that, Justice and I could've finished whatever they were doing to start with, and in half the time too."

Johnson took Ted's heavy curving pipe out of his mouth and looked at it. He had taken to carrying it around caught in his uncertain teeth, not smoking it but simply sucking on the dry stem and taking it out to look at it in a slow and contemplative way now and then. He said it gave him enormous satisfaction and that he might buy some tobacco one of these days and actually take it up as a kind of hobby. He said he needed more hobbies. Mabel said he needed more sense. But she indulged him with the pipe. She indulged him these days with just about everything.

"Just work them," Too Much had told Johnson. "Whatever they can do, make them do it."

"Oh," said Johnson, snatching the pipe from his mouth so hard that he almost brought his teeth out with it. "You don't have to *make* them do anything. Just get'm started. Show'm the way. Hell, they'd eat that trailer of Ted's—"

"Trailer of mine," said Too Much. "My trailer from now till I move or something else changes."

"Right. But what I was saying is they'd eat that trailer right down to the blocks it's resting on if I only took the first bite. That's the way they are. Just show'm and stand back and let'm go."

"Good. It'll keep their old hearts pumping anyway."

"Easy enough for you to say, but it's, by God, hot standing out here in the sun all day."

Too Much fixed him with what she had come to think of as her command stare, because by damn, now *she was in command.* "You're not, are you, arguing with me?"

"Arguing? Me? When have I ever argued with you?"

"That's what it sounded like to me."

"Then you heard it wrong."

"There," Too Much said. "That's arguing right there."

Johnson took his pipe out, looked as though he might speak, but clamped the stem back between his false teeth instead.

"That's better," she said. "If you worked half as hard as Justice, there wouldn't be any work left to be done by now."

"Justice has something to deal with I don't know about or care about. You didn't bury a cat under the full of the moon with his throat cut and hugging my picture and scare the hell out of me. But you've just about scared that poor old nigger to death."

She said, "I did something a whole lot different and a whole lot better for you."

He looked away across the swamp toward the black wall of Australian pines far away. "Yes," he said finally, "you did."

"How are things between you and Mabel?"

"Little problem, actually. I'm losing interest, and she's starting to stink," he said, so softly it was nearly a whisper.

"What you mean is that she's starting to stink *because* you're losing interest. Lust has no sense of smell, or of taste either for that matter. Actually lust has no sense. Period."

"I only answered your question. You asked, and I answered."

"And I just answered yours. You *didn't* ask but I answered anyway."

"Could you fix my little problem, you think?"

"Show me you can work," she said. "Show me you can get things done the way I want them done. Then everything'll take care of itself."

"I'll show you," he said. He took Ted's pipe out and turned it in his freckled hands a moment before looking at her. "And thank you."

"Don't thank me," she said. "You don't know the tiger you've got by the tail, so don't thank me."

"I wish you'd stop threatening me," he said. "It's unnerving."

"Then let me see some goddam results," she said. "And keep on seeing them. You were privileged to kiss the devil. Have you forgotten that?"

"I couldn't if I tried," he said.

"But you've never tried, have you?"

"Just the opposite. I *try* to remember. But it gets harder and harder. The more time passes, the more difficult it all gets to remember. I was hoping we could fix that for me."

"I can," she said. "Just get the work done."

"I will," he said.

And he had been as good as his word. It had been he, not Too Much, who had discovered that Forever and Forever was a gold mine of artisans of every sort, plumbers and carpenters and stonemasons and all manner of professional people, including an uncommon number of teachers. That there were so many teachers had not surprised Too Much at all, and it would have pleased her grandfather beyond saying. He had gone to great lengths to tell her all about teachers.

The bullshit system of values that kept the entire nation working for so long for all the wrong reasons needed an army of teachers to shape its young to believe what was essentially unbelievable. Progress was the name they gave it, and progress had as its sole purpose to serve that other huge nonword: civilization. Progress and civilization were then combined to become an unbroken upward spiral toward something called The Good Life, a.k.a. The American Way of Life, but usually shortened to simply The American Way.

But the people in charge of the entire apparatus—which every group thought it controlled and understood, when in fact no single group or combination of groups understood or controlled it—the people who thought they were running the apparatus had enough sense to understand that it had to keep these drudges called teachers impoverished and powerless. Where else could teachers end their lives but in places like Forever and Forever, many of them keeping their slack flesh intact and their foul breath coming and going in their ruined lungs by subsisting mainly on dog food? Everybody knew it, but nobody talked much about it.

Too Much had all this from her grandfather, who had quit his law practice and retired to a cabin he had built himself and filled with books deep in the Big Hurricane Swamp in south Georgia, and it had been he who had raised Too Much when she had been brought to him after her parents died together at an unmarked railroad crossing. She had gone there when she was two years old and walked out of the swamp when she was fifteen, with a duffel bag on her shoulder and her grandfather's dying breath in her lungs and firmly rooted in her brain and heart the old man's single conviction: The only system that worked was no system at all. And it was all because of the nature of the human beast.

Good could be done but only in the tiniest of increments and for the briefest of moments. Evil, on the other hand, was boundless and could be made to last over millennia, again all because of the taloned and bloody-mouthed human beast. Her grandfather had told her over and over again that he did not know, and there was no way to foretell, whether she, Susanna French—for that was Too Much's name in those days—was destined for good or for evil. But she ought to know the nature of each. There would be those who would tell her to listen to God (and here he would enumerate ten or fifteen gods, and never the same list twice), and He or She (because, of course, many of the gods of the human beast had been female) would show Susanna The Way. Oh, yes, and there would be many who would tell her to listen to God and she would hear and know the truth. The rankest kind of foul deception.

If the gods spoke, they spoke only to one another. Where was the god—or anything that could be called godlike—that would demean and besoil Itself by speaking to the rapacious human beast, which ruined and perverted everything it touched? No, listen to your heart and head, and hope for the best, her grandfather had told her. And what was the best? The tiny, the infinitesimally tiny, increment of good that she might achieve for the briefest of moments. That was all. That was everything. Beyond that was the unknowable abyss.

But the fact that the abyss was unknowable had not kept a tiny number of the vast horde of men and women who had trod the earth since the beginning of time from trying to know it, and many of this tiny number had left a record of their fruitless search in the scribblings and scratchings brought together in books, and each of us was free to make his own search throughout these books—as her grandfather had done over the fifty years since he retired to the cabin, only to find, as he had come to believe, that there was nothing to find.

The cabin was huge and shaped in the form of a Greek cross, and every wall from floor to ceiling was covered with books. He had read every day all day and into the night, mumbling a constant stream of curses and filling the margins of the books with the same curses, although he seemed to be more elaborate and inventive when he was writing the curses down instead of just saying them.

In his book collection he had the known and the unknown, the good and the bad. As far as she could tell, he gave no more credence to one book, or set of books, than he did to another. He never, to her knowledge, took a bath, and except to run his trapline or build a fire to cook or amble off into the bushes to squat and curse the heavens by offering up his excrement as sacrifice, he stayed with his books, which he profoundly doubted and profoundly hated and yet could not leave alone.

Susanna—she would not be called Too Much until she stopped in Tampa, Florida, with a motorcycle gang called the Outlaws—Susanna could read by the time she was four but had quit entirely by the time she turned thirteen, because in her twelfth year she had discovered—or more accurately, it had been brought to her attention—something that her grandfather had never mentioned: her sexuality. As deep in the swamp as they were, she had been sniffed out by an even half-dozen illiterate brothers, who had thought to make her their whore but whom she had turned one against the other until they killed themselves off to the point where only one remained, and he was given two life sentences, to be served consecutively.

The discovery of the power she stood astraddle of had finally proved more valuable to her than her grandfather's books, his cabin, his care, and his teaching, all of which she had left in one huge pile of smoking ashes—following to the letter his instructions—when she walked away from it all at the age of fifteen, carrying nothing with her but what was on her shoulder now in the duffel bag.

In the flowering garden that opened in symmetrical rings around Ted's trailer, the Old Ones were stooped and digging shallow trenches in the dirt with their hands. Johnson stood on the edge of the garden, puffing on the curving stem of Ted's pipe, the bowl of which was still cold and empty, while he stared out over the garden toward the swamp beyond. Too Much wondered if Johnson still went out along the border of saw grass and mud each morning to fire a single shot from his 22.-caliber target pistol, aiming carefully at nothing. Surely he must. It was an old habit, and—as he had told Too Much himself—it gave direction, and sometimes even meaning, to his life.

Too Much felt something at her shoulder and in the same instant smelled Justice. She turned to look, but he wasn't there. The sound of tearing phlegm brought her eyes down, and there was Justice on his knees in the dust at her feet. It startled and frightened her.

"What the hell are you doing down there?" she demanded.

Justice pointed toward the Old Ones with his long chin, the skin of which was lightly salted with a white stubble of beard. "Be doin what dey be doin." As he spoke, he started digging a shallow trench in the powdery dirt with his hands.

She shouldn't have raised her voice to him. There was no fun in beating a cripple, and particularly a cripple who was bewildered, frightened, and half destroyed from too much alcohol and too little food.

"I can see what you and the Old Ones are doing," she said patiently, "but why are you doing it? That's what I meant to ask. Why?"

"I do whut dem ovuh dere do," Justice said, pointing to the Old Ones stooping and scratching between the rows of flowers. "Dat whut I do. Whatevuh Mistuh Johnson say do, dat whut I jump on an do." He paused to rip up a piece of phlegm with a long hacking cough. "I know he wake fo yo, so I mind to do whut he say."

Too Much cocked her head and looked down at him. "And who do *you* work for, Justice?"

"Fo de cat," he said.

"And who's got the cat?"

"Missy, yo know yo got dat cat. Don play wif ole Justice."

"I *do* have the cat, Justice. And I never play. That's why I have you."

"Now I sho ain sayin nothin contrairwise to dat. Yo got Justice like Jesus had Peter."

"You know a lot about Jesus having Peter, do you, Justice?"

"Ony whut I hern, Missy. Ony whut I hern."

"Then let's leave Jesus the fuck out of this."

"Jesus be gone," said Justice. "When yo come in, He go out. Yea, now, Missy."

"You call me Missy one more time, and I feed the cat."

"Great Godamighty!" Justice said, looking wildly around. "Whut dat mean, feed dat cat?"

"You won't find out till I do it. But just keep on calling me Missy."

Looking straight up at her from where he knelt, his eyes rolled back in his head, Justice said, "Yo Too Much now and yo be Too Much foevuh."

"Now you've got everything right, Justice," said Too Much with some satisfaction. "Just make sure you keep your old ass dead on the mark."

Justice nodded his head violently. "Justice gone keep his ole ass daid on de maak." Then his head stopped, and with his whole body very still, he cautiously looked at Too Much. "Whut do daid on de maak mean?"

"Try me and find out."

"Whoa, dere! Ole Justice ain tryin no Too Much."

"Then get on back to whatever the hell it is you're doing."

Justice stuck both hands in the dirt and started digging with a will. "Now yo know ole Justice hern dat."

"Good," Too Much said. "That's good."

She looked across the garden at Johnson. He had not moved, but he was no longer looking at the swamp. He was looking at her. His thin neck was wet with sweat and very red. He was no more than twenty yards away, but he looked as though he did not recognize her. He looked as though he had passed out standing up and did not recognize anything.

She raised her voice and called: "Johnson?"

"Too Much," he said, speaking so softly his voice barely reached her.

"Something wrong, Johnson?" she called.

His lips moved. She heard his voice but understood nothing.

"I didn't understand you. What?"

"I'm dying here."

She walked over and stood without speaking.

"You don't have to look like that," he said.

"How was I looking, Johnson?"

"Like you smelled something that stinks."

Too Much squinted against the sun. "Like something dead and rotting? You mean like that?"

Johnson took out a handkerchief and wiped at his face with it, and he acted now as if he meant to eat Ted's pipe. "Yeah, maybe like that."

"You think I might've smelled you?"

"There's no call for you to talk like that."

"I wouldn't if you'd quit whining." She stepped closer to him, so close that she could smell the taint of Ted's pipe on his breath. "Listen, Johnson, you'll die soon enough without talking like that," said Too Much. "Come on with me into the office and cool down."

"My place is here if you want this job done right."

Too Much turned to look at the Old Ones bent and digging with their hands between the rows of plants and flowers.

"If I want the job done right?" said Too Much. "I don't even know what they're doing." She paused a moment and looked back at Johnson. "But whatever it is, wouldn't it be easier if you gave them hoes?"

"If they had hoes, they'd chop down everything in the garden. You can set'm to chopping and by God they'll chop until you stop'm, but there's no way to make'm understand what to chop and what to leave alone. Hell, they'll chop each other if you don't keep an eye on'm."

"Give them a break and tell them to go find some shade. I need to talk with you, and we might as well do it inside, where it's cool."

"I can't tell'm anything," said Johnson, his loose teeth champing noisily on the stem of the pipe. "You're losing touch with'm since you turned'm over to me. They have to be led, Too Much. They have to be shown."

"I've not forgotten anything," she said. "What are they doing anyway?"

"Digging a shallow trench between the rows for an irrigation hose."

"I don't believe I've ever seen one," she said.

"It's like a regular water hose, only flatter than it is round, and has tiny holes that leak water into the ground around the plants when it's hooked up to a faucet."

"Where did you come by irrigation hose?"

"Midnight requisition," he said.

She knew the phrase from her extended stay with the Outlaw bikers in Tampa. "You stole it?"

"I stole it. Or at least Justice and I did. Justice didn't want any part of it until I threatened him with the cat."

"Don't do that anymore," said Too Much. "If he has to be threatened with the cat, I'll do it."

"Right," Johnson said.

"If you're ever in doubt about anything, check with me first," she said.

"That'll take a hell of a lot of checking."

"Do it anyway."

"It was the only way we could keep those plants. This soil has a limestone base and—"

"I don't need the details," she said.

"—it won't hold water, so we *had* to steal the hose. Only way we could get it."

"And that's why I need you to come in the office and talk to me."

"And do what with the Old Ones?"

Too Much looked around and saw Justice watching her from where he knelt across the garden. "Give them to Justice and tell him to find them a shade."

"Justice is not very kind to the Old Ones," said Johnson.

"It won't take long. They can stand it." She looked again over the backs of the stooping Old Ones amongst the flowers and plants. "I think, of all of us, they stand everything best."

She turned and walked away from Johnson. As she was going up the three steps into the trailer, she could hear him calling to Justice. She made a mental note to remember that from Johnson's tone of voice he did not seem very kind to the old nigger. And there was no reason for it. If anybody needed beating, she—Too Much—was the one to wield the whip.

And the whip was *always* needed. Her grandfather had gone over and over that hard fact with her from the time she was old enough to talk. Doing good, or the state of goodness, had nothing to do with the absence of pain. Many times, perhaps most times, whatever was good could only be brought about through pain and suffering. If a man had cancer in his foot, he had to suffer it to be cut off and thereby be made healthy again. There was a great deal of what her grandfather said that Too Much did not believe, that made no sense to her. But goodness by its very nature demanding pain and suffering did make sense, and Too Much believed it with all her heart. Her entire experience since leaving the smoking ashes of her grandfather's cabin had proved the truth of it to her over and over again.

She stepped through the door and stopped. All the walls had been torn out of the double-wide, so that it was now one enormous room, and the entire inside of the trailer had been painted a light lime color with peach trimming, Too Much's favorite colors. The work had been done by a man who was eighty-six years old and nearly blind, but the job was immaculate, every line of trim plumb-bob straight, not a drop or the tiniest splotch of paint anywhere out of place.

Too Much had been able to buy the paint with the money she made when one of the residents, an obese man of seventy-seven who had lived his entire life in Miami and who had made and lost several fortunes selling junk as antiques to Yankee tourists, managed to sell off Ted's furniture, all of which was made of heavy oak and may even have been built by Ted himself, or at least by the obese resident, whose name was Jim Bob but who was universally called Biggun.

At the far end of the trailer, a tiny Chinese man slowly, very slowly, worked with a wood rasp on the arm of a huge structure that might have been the throne for a king. It was, in fact, a chair he was finishing for Too Much that would sit behind her desk, not yet built but already planned in great detail by the tiny Chinese man, whose name was Tryve Tron Doo. The high-backed, wide-armed chair looked as though it had been carved from a single block of wood. But Too Much knew it was made from bits and pieces of lumber the old man had found or begged or stolen and then fitted together and sanded and stained so perfectly that not a crack or seam showed anywhere.

The Honorable Mr. Doo, the only name to which he would answer, had his own elaborate set of tools that he kept in velvet-lined boxes: chisels and mallets and wedges and tiny steel saws and hammers of various sizes and shapes. All of the tools were cared for so carefully, they gleamed like pure silver. He had been a master woodworker all his life, and it deeply offended Too Much that such a man had to scavenge, beg, or steal the materials with which he worked.

She walked over to the Honorable Mr. Doo, whose back was to her, and stood quietly, watching him work. He was dressed in black baggy trousers that were very loose in the legs but tight at the ankles and a clean but wrinkled white shirt with tiny red and blue flowers embroidered across the shoulders. He had a tight cap made of black leather on his head from under which a gray, finely braided pigtail of thin hair hung down almost to the small of his back. On his feet were slippers made from what Too Much thought was crushed black velvet, trimmed with exquisitely stitched white characters of Chinese.

Everything about Tryve Tron Doo looked as though it had been planned with the most careful consideration for exactitude. Even his movements seemed calibrated to the smallest of tolerances. The wood rasp he was working with now moved rapidly but always in strokes that were less than three inches long.

"Honorable Mr. Doo," said Too Much quietly.

Tryve Tron Doo's whole body stopped moving, froze, as Too Much made the first sound of his name. He remained bent for an instant, then carefully placed his wood rasp on the arm of the chair and stood up straight. He remained with his back to Too Much for another instant before turning to face her. His face, smooth as burnished stone, was without expression. He put his palms together under his chin and almost imperceptibly inclined his head.

Johnson Meechum always repeated the gesture with Tryve Tron Doo, and really enjoyed doing it. He thought it was funny. Too Much never put her palms together and bowed her head. She would have felt acutely dishonest had she done so. She was not the Chink. Tryve Tron Doo was the Chink, and the gesture was of his kind. Too Much could see that it obviously meant a great deal to him. She did not have the slightest notion of what the gesture meant. But she did not think it was funny. She waited until the old Chinaman had finished and carefully lowered his hands to his sides, both his thumbs exactly aligned with the outside seams of his flowing trousers.

"Rrrraaahhh," said Tryve Tron Doo, making the long, guttural growl he always made before strangling out a few English words. "Admirable Rady Too Much rike?" Without turning, he raised his right hand slowly until his forearm was parallel to the floor, and with his deeply lined palm, he indicated the chair behind him.

From the first time Tryve Tron Doo had spoken to her, he had always called her Admirable Rady Too Much. She did not take exception to it. She was convinced the expression was after the nature of his own kind and therefore natural to him.

"It's beautiful," she said. "But big. Very big."

"Rrrraaahhh," said Tryve Tron Doo. "Rarge chair for rarge soul of Admirable Rady Too Much."

Large soul, my sweet ass, she thought. But she knew the old man felt profoundly in her debt for work that meant something to him. He had even told her once, with eyes averted, that the work she had given him to do had made him feel alive, really alive, for the first time since age and a sick wife—a wife now dead—had forced him into Forever and Forever. It had taken some time for Tryve Tron Doo to work that many English words out of his mouth, and Too Much had stood silently listening and deeply embarrassed until he finished. Her first impulse was to try to set him straight and tell him that she had asked him to do the work because he was the only one she knew who was qualified to do it, and that she badly needed it done. And besides, she had no money. But she did not say this. It could easily have hurt him, to no point.

"It is a good chair, Honorable Mr. Doo," Too Much said, leaning to touch the place where he had been working with the wood rasp. "And I thank you for a beautiful job of work."

"Rrrraaahhh," Tryve Tron Doo said. Then his eyes rolled up in his head, as was his habit when he was trying to find the appropriate English words with which to respond. Sometimes it was difficult for Too Much to watch his struggle with an alien language, but she always waited it out. "Rrrraaahhh," he said again. And then: "Good chair, yes. Most velly good chair." He nodded his head rapidly in obvious satisfaction.

The Honorable Mr. Doo was not a modest man about his work. It was probably what Too Much liked most about him. He knew who he was and what he could do and he was happiest when he was doing it. Once he had taken a long and difficult time to tell Too Much that the worst job he ever had was no job at all.

Too Much heard the door close behind her, and she glanced over her shoulder and saw Johnson leaning against the wall, swabbing at his face and neck with his handkerchief. When she turned back to Tryve Tron Doo, he was already bent and working with his wood rasp in tiny, precise strokes.

Too Much walked over to Johnson and said, "I need your advice, Johnson."

"I think I've got enough left in me to talk," he said. "But that's all. I'll be damned if I know how the Old Ones stand it out there."

"That's easy enough to answer," Too Much said. "They don't think about it. It's thinking that grinds the heart out of you. And you spend entirely too much time thinking, Johnson. It's not good for you."

"Thinking?" Johnson said. "When's the last time you had to stand three or four hours in the kind of sun that's out there today?"

"Had to? Had to, Johnson? You haven't *had* to do anything."

"Oh, Jesus, don't start with me on that. You know what I mean."

"I don't know what you mean," Too Much said. "And I don't think I like that."

"I'm too tired and hot to argue with you about it," said Johnson. "Threaten me all you want to. But it's not going to work."

Too Much looked at him for a moment. Then: "Sit down."

His face and neck finally dried by the trailer's air-conditioning, Johnson was stuffing his handkerchief back into his pocket. He looked around the room, his mouth tight and grim, his eyes caught in a web of veins. "There's nothing to sit on," he said.

"Don't use that tone of voice with me," Too Much said quietly.

And then, in the same calm voice: "Sit on the floor; sit on the floor and lean back against the wall."

Johnson went to his haunches and then fell, rather than sat, onto his buttocks. He leaned against the wall and stuck his thin legs straight out in front of him. Too Much sat too, folding herself into the lotus position in front of him.

Johnson stared at her and shook his head slowly. "Look what you've done with your legs. I couldn't sit like that on the best day I ever had."

"You never tried, did you?"

"No, I never did."

"Therefore, you're reasoning contrary to fact. You don't know what you could have done, or could not have done, had you only tried, do you, Johnson? There are men older than you are who sit like this for hours. But never mind that. Put your head against the wall, pull your shoulders back, and breathe deeply."

Johnson breathed deeply and groaned.

"You're still breathing with only the top half of your lungs. Close your eyes and breathe deeply. That's right: pull your shoulders up and fill yourself with air and, for Christ's sake, relax."

He pulled his thin shoulders up and breathed, his eyes closed, and his head dropped back against the wall. "I already feel better."

"Shut up and breathe. Relax."

The only sounds in the trailer were the steady, precise rasping of the Honorable Mr. Doo's file and the thin whistling noise Johnson's breathing made. When his color looked better—his cheeks only slightly flushed, his lips no longer gray—Too Much said, "Now you can tell me how you feel."

"Fine. I feel fine." When he opened his eyes they were no longer shot with blood, and he did look better.

"You looked like shit when you first came in," she said.

"I felt like shit."

"I thought you'd have enough sense to figure it out, but since you obviously don't, I'll tell you. I don't want you standing in the sun until you're half dead."

"You gave me a job to do, and—"

"I gave you a job to get done. I would have thought a bank president would know something about delegating authority." A thin little smile played on her lips. "But then I don't guess you could delegate falsifying records so you could walk away with half the bank's money."

"That was uncalled for."

"But true."

"You know it's true, Too Much," he said. "But you're going to get my blood pressure out of control doing that to me, talking about the mistake I made."

"Let me give you something else to think about, then: money. I want to write checks on Stump's account. What's the easiest way for me to go about doing it?"

Johnson jerked, and his spine went straighter. "I won't have anything to do with that."

"With what, Johnson?"

"Stealing. I've done all the time I'm going to do. There's nothing you could do to me that would make me steal."

"Has the sun brought you to this, Johnson? Do you hear what you're saying? Both of us know you'll do anything I tell you to do, don't we?"

Johnson stretched his neck as if to breathe. And despite the chilled air in the room, he was sweating again. "I don't want to go back to jail."

"You're begging. I hate begging, Johnson."

"I couldn't stand to go back to jail."

"You don't know what you can stand." Then she leaned forward until she was only inches from his face and hissed, "Answer my fucking question, you son of a bitch. Will you now and will you forever do whatever I tell you to do?"

"Yes," he said, his eyes blinking rapidly. "Yes, I will."

"You will what?" she demanded.

"I'll do now, and I'll do anytime," he said, seeming to choke a little on the words, "whatever you tell me to do."

"Don't ever make me go through this with you again, Johnson." When he didn't answer, she said, "Do you hear?"

He could only nod his head, and he had his handkerchief out again, wiping at his face.

"You could have saved yourself all this. You could have saved *me* all this. I don't have time to jack around with you. Now, what do I need to do to be able to write checks on Stump's account? And before you get your blood pressure up again and blow a gasket, Stump knows all about it. You understand? We've reached an agreement, Stump and I. I'm managing Forever and Forever for him, and to do that I need access to his money unless I go to him every time I need a check signed and he doesn't want me to do that. He doesn't like checks. He doesn't like anything he has to sign his name to. So he wants to stay out of the whole operation and let me handle it."

"He agreed to something like that? My God, we could steal him blind."

"Old habits die hard, don't they, Johnson? But that's not what I have in mind."

"Exactly what do you have in mind?"

"I don't know."

Johnson's lips stretched into a smile around the stained, curving stem of Ted's old pipe, which he had put back into his mouth now that he was breathing easier. "If you don't know, then stealing him blind is still a possibility. At least a chance of ultimate possibility, right?" And then he winked broadly at her.

"Don't wink when you say that, asshole. You know as well as I do that anything's a possibility."

"Good," Johnson said. "Fine."

He paused, took the pipe out of his mouth, and looked over at Tryve Tron Doo, who still moved tirelessly and with machinelike precision over the same arm of the chair he'd been working on since Johnson had come into the trailer. "I don't think even Stump would give you power of attorney, not if his lawyer explained to him what he was doing, and any lawyer most certainly would. That would be ideal for your purposes, whatever those purposes turn out to be—frankly, they're not very clear. The easiest thing for you to do would be to get him to sign a simple signature card.

Of course, with a signature card on his checking account, you could walk in anytime you wanted to and take every penny out of it. But he probably doesn't keep enough in his checking account to make that worthwhile."

"I'd be willing to bet Stump has no idea how much he's got in his checking account. He could easily have a young fortune in it."

"How utterly delightful," Johnson said.

"I thought you didn't want to do any more time in prison."

"I don't. God knows I don't."

"You sure as hell don't sound like it. And you don't know what God knows, so leave Him out of it."

"I was only thinking out loud. You can't be put in jail for thinking."

"More people are behind bars for thinking than any other reason. I'd explain that to you if I had more time, but I want to get this over and done with. How many times does Stump have to sign his name?"

"Once."

"That'll work. Does he have to go to the bank?"

"He wouldn't have had to go to my bank, but I didn't bank in Florida. I don't know what the bank regulations are here. But all he'd probably have to do is make a telephone call, have the bank send him a card, which he would then sign and send back. Then you would have to go down to the bank, present some identification, sign the same card, and it's done."

She came out of the lotus position and stood up. Johnson struggled to his feet and leaned against the wall. He didn't look particularly good, but he looked like his old self again, Too Much thought. "You all right now?"

"I'm feeling pretty good, thanks."

"Try not to be so stupid from now on. When you go back out there, get in the shade to watch the work being done. Keep a thermos of cold water with you. You're no good to me dead. I'd only have to put you in the fire."

His eyes got bigger. "Did you say put me in the fire?"

"Have you cremated."

"Jesus, don't even talk about me being cremated. It scares the hell out of me. Being buried in a box is bad enough. But the last thing I want to think about is being burned."

"Then don't die in Forever and Forever. I'm in charge here now. And I've been thinking about figuring out a way to burn everybody in the place when they die and take what we save by not burying them to establish an activities fund for things like bingo and dances and big outdoor parties on holidays and such. Do you realize how cheap it is to send a person on his way in the fire?"

"Send him on his way in the fire? Jesus, what a horrible thought."

"Then try not to think about it."

"Too Much, what is it you want?"

"Want? How do you mean?"

"I mean bottom-line, end-of-the-road: *want*. What is it you're after?"

"If you're lucky, you'll never find out. And if you do find out, maybe you'll be lucky enough not to have to be part of it."

"That's no answer."

"It's the only one you're getting." She turned to look over her shoulder at Tryve Tron Doo, the sound of whose wood rasp had never faltered. "Right now I'd like you to see what you can do about getting the Honorable Mr. Doo to scale down that fucking chair he's building for me and the desk he's planning to build. I can't sit in something that looks like I think I'm God or I've gone out of my mind or both. Not and have Stump come in and see me in it. He might be on to everything then."

"And what is everything?" said Johnson.

Too Much gave him a full and open smile, showing her perfect teeth. "The chance of ultimate possibility."

"The chance of ultimate possibility about what?"

"I'll recognize it when it gets here," Too Much said, her smile still firmly in place.

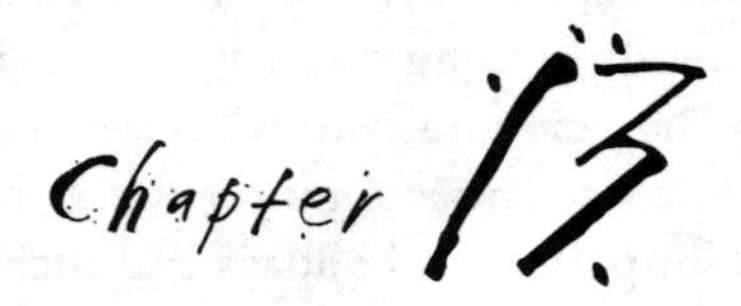

Take some, leave some, Too Much's grandfather always told her. Never scour the countryside and burn the bridges behind you and slay all the animals you can't eat or drive off. Because, he said, that's war. And nobody wins in war. And so it was that she found herself sitting in the thronelike chair the Honorable Mr. Doo had built for her, in front of her a desk that could sleep three people comfortably. There had been no way to get him to scale the chair and the desk down to a size that would seem a little more natural for an office without insulting Tryve Tron Doo, and she did not want to do that. He had been forced to scavenge, steal, and beg the wood the desk had been made out of, and that was more than insult enough without complaining that it was all out of scale, much too large.

The Honorable Mr. Doo was now at work building bookshelves to cover two entire walls of the trailer. Too Much had decided she missed having books around her, was hungry to see them, and to feel them in her hands, and most of all, hungry to know what it was like to be lost in a book again, a pleasure she had not known since she walked out of her grandfather's swamp with the little duffel bag on her shoulder.

She had no books, nor had she tried to acquire any, because since leaving the smoking ruins of her grandfather's cabin, she had not been in one place for very long. Now it looked as though she might be settling in for a while here at Forever and Forever. She did not know for how long, nor did she particularly care. It was not the sort of thing she had ever given much thought to. But she would stay in this place long enough to get the job done—whatever the job was, which was another point on which she was not entirely clear and that she did not think much about either.

But at least Tryve Tron Doo had not been forced to build the bookshelves out of materials he'd scavenged or begged or stolen. It was true the lumber was bought with stolen money, and Too Much was still not entirely sure how she felt about that. But she would never *have* to know how she felt about it, because she was very good at not thinking about that which she did not want to know. It was enough for her to know the money had been stolen from strangers, not from Stump.

She had never had any intention of stealing from Stump, but that didn't mean she wouldn't if she needed the money to run Forever and Forever the way she thought it ought to be run, to do for the Old Ones and the residents that which ought to be done. Her grandfather had told her time and time again, "When the ox is in the ditch, pull him out," by which he only meant that in this world you did what had to be done to stay alive and care for the ones you loved. Get the job done honorably or dishonorably. If it mutilated and caused great pain to the ox, what matter? What were pain and dishonor beside life? Did dishonor or pain matter if it meant avoiding death? Never. Let the imbeciles of the world hold to that proposition. She was blood of his blood, he had told her, and because of that very fact, she ought to know that blood was more important than any abstraction.

So far she had not had the chance to use any of Stump's money, stolen or otherwise. As it had turned out, she and Stump had to go to the bank together to get the signature card she needed validated, and she had been unable to get him out of his trailer to make the trip even though she had promised him that she would drive the pickup all the way there and back herself. All he would have to do was go along for the ride, sign his name, and ride back with her. Stump had remained unimpressed and unmoved.

She thought that before it was over she would probably have to threaten never to do her circus act for him in his bathtub again. But that smacked of blackmail, and even though she had done it before, she had never liked it. It made her feel like a cheap whore. And while she knew that an argument could be made that she was a whore, she certainly had never been cheap. That was what bothered her most, the notion of anybody thinking her cheap.

So remodeling Ted's old trailer had been a catch-as-catch-can affair: salvage this, borrow that, beg the other, or, finally, steal whatever was necessary if it came to that. Then one of the residents had shown up early one morning, walking right through the door without knocking and up to the enormous chair Tryve Tron Doo had made for her.

The resident looked like a retired midget from a circus or maybe a retired jockey, and without a word he walked up close enough that he could have touched her if he had wanted to. Too Much couldn't remember having seen him before, perhaps because he was so tiny, but she didn't see how she could have missed him, because he was splendidly and immaculately dressed in a snap-brim hat, a red bow tie—not one that had been clipped on but one that had been expertly knotted—a light-blue shirt, and a white suit that could only have been made from raw silk. His feet were shod in tiny wing-tip shoes with built-up soles and heels. He was very old, his face red, his cheeks filled with broken veins and smooth as a baby's.

He swept his hat from his head, which was also smooth and hairless as his face. His head was high-domed, absolutely symmetrical, and shaped like an egg. The curve of his chin reproduced exactly the curve of the top of his head. He made a tiny formal bow. When he looked up, his eyes were bright as a bird's and very blue.

"Jesus Christ," said Too Much. "Where did you come from?"

He waved his tiny hands. "Where we all came from—Forever and Forever."

"But I've never seen you before."

"Oh, you've seen me before. I was just wearing my Forever and Forever rags instead of my street-corner flash. You just saw a little old man and you'd thought I'd shrunk up to nothing, like the rest of these dying devils. But I've still got a lot of juice in me." He made a tiny gesture with his hat. "Nice chair. Very nice."

"This is the first time I've sat in it," said Too Much. "I thought I'd come over this morning and give it a try."

"It suits you," he said.

"Apparently Tryve Tron Doo thinks so."

"Ah," he said, glancing briefly behind him, where Tryve Tron Doo worked tirelessly at the bookshelves. "The Honorable Mr. Doo."

"The same," she said. "There didn't seem to be any way that I or one of the residents, Johnson Meechum, who helps me with certain things, could find a way to persuade Mr. Doo to reduce everything he was building to more, uh, human proportions without risking hurting his feelings."

The hairless egg-shaped face cracked into a smile. "Johnson the Swamp Killer! What a magnificent variety we have here at Forever and Forever. If not for the endless variety—rather like a zoo, don't you think?—I would have gone completely Berkshire long ago. But you must try not to fault the Honorable Mr. Doo for not building to human proportions, as you say, because I'm fairly sure he does not quite regard you as human. Can't be sure, of course. Chinese inscrutability and all that, you know. But he is not alone. There are many in the park who don't—that is, consider you to be quite human, Too Much."

"There will always be those who are incorrect in their assumptions," said Too Much. "But you seem to be one ahead of me, sir: you know my name, but I don't believe I've had the pleasure of yours."

"I beg your pardon. How gauche of me. My name is Fingers, and I'm here to lend my considerable talents to your enterprise. Forgive my unseemly pride, but I can be of help in finding the money you need. At no cost to you, of course."

"Well, Mr. Fingers, I don't really—"

"Not *Mr.* Fingers. Just Fingers. And before you make the protest that you sound as if you're about to make, let me say, I hear you need the money. Actually, I know you need the money. It would be my great pleasure to go out into the street and find a citizen walking around in nine hundred dollars' worth of suit and relieve him of some of whatever he's carrying."

"You'll have to run that by me again. I don't believe I understand."

"I'm a pickpocket without equal. Besides money, I can take a man's watch, or a woman's earrings. Once, on a bet, a very long time ago, when I was a young man and full of the pride of my art, as the young are wont to be, I took the panties off a woman in full stride, and she never felt a thing. I propose to, uh, acquire, shall we say—because it seems somehow less offensive—the money you need, and only relieve those of it who can obviously afford it."

"But that would still be theft, wouldn't it?"

"Of course, my dear, but theft with a difference. Back in the best days I ever had, I never touched anybody who didn't already have more toys than he could play with anyway. That may seem a fine distinction where theft is concerned, but then only fine distinctions matter, whether we're talking about theft—or redistributing the wealth, as I like to think of it—or anything else under the great vault of heaven."

"The great vault of heaven? You have a touch of poet in you, Fingers."

"No, you're wrong there. I only have a touch of larceny in me. Born with it, I have always been convinced, and therefore it is no fault of my own. And at the same time, fortunately for me, also born with the lightest fingers in the business."

"What is a man of your talents doing living in Forever and Forever?"

"My wife—a refined woman who somehow ended up with me—refused to let me work anymore."

"Work?"

"Do what I do best. Some people have five talents, some only one. Take my touch away and I'm nothing. But my fingers are pure magic; the rest of me's dead."

Too Much thought about that a moment, her lips pursed. "I wouldn't want to get you in trouble with your wife. So I think we'll have to find another way of coming by the money we need. I'll think of something sooner or later. It seems I always do. And that way you won't get on the bad side of your wife."

"She doesn't mind me working for you. As a matter of fact, she was the one who sent me. You see, she's convinced it's in a good cause. I do, too, for what it's worth. Hell, everybody's talking about what you're doing here at Forever and Forever. The place's not the same since you arrived, and it never will be again. Now, allow me to depart—I've talked entirely too long already—and get out on the boulevard and finger a little something for you," Fingers said. He turned on his elevated heels and walked out of the trailer, stopping at the door long enough to say over his shoulder, "Not a lot off any single person, mind you; just a little something to tide you over. And please don't think this is entirely altruistic. It's for me as well as for you. God, do I need to work again, feel the old magic working one more time! I'll be back with, as I say, a little something for you this afternoon."

And he was. He walked in later that afternoon, tipped his hat briefly, and put a roll of bills with a rubber band twisted around it on the desk, in front of Too Much. She could only stare at it without speaking.

"Two thousand and six hundred dollars," he said nonchalantly. "I encourage you to count it." He gave her his cracked little smile. "There are, after all, thieves in the world."

She only shook her head and said, "In one afternoon?"

He shrugged his tiny shoulders and again smiled his cracked little smile. "The economy is shot, or didn't you hear? There simply aren't that many nine-hundred-dollar suits walking around."

It was obvious to Too Much that the little man was enjoying all of this immensely. How curious the human beast, she could hear her grandfather say.

"Where are the wallets?"

"Oh, I always return them."

"You put the fucking wallets *back?*"

He gave his jagged little smile again. "I told you my fingers were magic. The master I was apprenticed to as a boy taught me to do it.

It takes the mark longer to find out he's been hit, so long as he still has his wallet on him, and also providing you didn't take every last bill he's carrying out of it. And I never do. Replacing the wallet is a great gag if you can work it. Not everybody can. But there are sloppy workers in every field, don't you know. I've met pickpockets who couldn't take a wallet off a dead man without waking him up."

"Did you take any of this from women?"

"The man who taught me the business—he was Japanese, by the way, and had the sweetest hands I've ever seen work—told me never to take money from women or mental defectives. They always draw too much heat when it's reported to the authorities. It's never worth whatever amount of money you lift from them. I would do it in less time than it takes to say it if it didn't draw so much heat. There are times when I think I might very well be entirely without scruples."

"But I thought you told me earlier you never took from anybody except those who had too many toys to play with anyway."

"Sweet Baby Christ, Too Much, that's sexist and elitist both. Where's your social conscious? My God, child, it's against the law to talk that way or even think that way anymore. You don't think there are women and mental defectives out there who are loaded with more gold than Fort Knox and have more toys than Santa Claus? You'd be surprised how many. But I leave them alone. Not worth it. Trick with them and you go to jail. I never served a day in my life, and I don't plan to start now."

Too Much watched him for a moment over the desk. "Leave the money. I'll be in touch."

"Anytime. Just working that little while this afternoon made me feel like God had just told me I was going to heaven after all."

"Don't count on it," said Too Much.

"I never have," said Fingers. "In my most twisted moments, that's not something I ever counted on."

As Fingers was walking to the door, Too Much said, "Thank your wife for me."

"Oh, she's the one who ought to be thanking you," he said. "Now I'll be fit to live with. At least for a few days, anyway. If I don't get into a pocket on a fairly regular basis, I turn into a real monster."

"Don't steal anymore until you hear from me," said Too Much.

"Oh, I lift stuff all the time, but I always give it back. It's how I manage to keep from turning into a monster with green teeth. It's also the way I keep my touch and stay light. I'm like a concert pianist: I have to practice every day."

"Believe me, I understand that."

He pulled his little hat lower over his forehead, winked, and said, "I never doubted it, Too Much. I always knew you were one of us."

Fingers had not been gone long before Too Much, staring idly out the window, saw a black Pinto pull up. The driver was wearing a black suit and a black flat-brimmed hat. He looked as though he ought to be in high school. And despite the black suit and the huge hat, he made Too Much think of a Domino Pizza delivery boy. She knew he was a delivery boy, but he was not delivering pizzas. He was delivering Ted Johanson.

The funeral parlor had kept calling saying that somebody had to come over and pick up the late Mr. Johanson, or they would have no alternative but to deliver him. They couldn't be expected, they said, to keep him forever. It was true, they had told Too Much, that the deceased loved one did not take up much room, but they did not have much room to spare. Too Much said that the one they had in the bottle was nobody's goddam loved one and that she would come down and get him as soon as she could find the time.

That had been yesterday when she told them that and it must have put somebody down there off their feed, because here came a high-school-looking kid bearing a container in front of him hardly bigger than a mason fruit jar, but for some strange reason it reminded Too Much of the chamber pot her granddaddy kept under his bed in the wintertime so he didn't have to go out into the cold to offer up his excremental sacrifices to the gods.

Fortunately, she had told Mr. Doo that Ted Johanson would be coming home pretty soon in a bottle, and the little Chinaman had built a low shelf on one wall to hold the bottle—which Too Much saw now was no bottle at all but a copper urn—and in front of the little shelf the Honorable Mr. Doo had fashioned a tiny shrine out of fieldstones he had gone out and dug from the ground and brought back to the trailer to honor the late Ted Johanson, whom Mr. Doo knew only by reputation. But that did not seem to matter. The shrine was a lovely, carefully crafted thing, and Tryve Tron Doo had kept a single stick of incense burning on it.

Too Much opened the door before the young man climbed the three steps to it, since he was carrying the urn with both hands and she couldn't see how he was going to manage to knock.

"Good day, ma'm," said the young man.

Despite his thin chest and beardless face, his voice was grave and deep and sounded as if he might be speaking from the bottom of a barrel. Too Much, her eyes fixed on the copper urn, wondered if people in the business of disposing of the dead had to have such a voice to be hired or if they were trained to have such voices after they were on the job.

Too Much did not answer him but only stood staring at the urn.

"Would this be the address of the lately deceased Mr. Theodore Sorrenson Johanson?"

"It would be his address, and would that be the lately deceased Mr. Theodore Sorrenson Johanson you're holding there in your hands?"

"Yes, ma'm," said the young man, and here he silently bowed his head. "This would be the late beloved Mr. Johanson."

"I don't know anybody that loved the motherfucker, but give him to me anyway."

The young man did not even blink. "Would you be the next of kin?" he asked. "Because somebody has to sign for him, and that would be the next of kin."

"He doesn't have any next of kin, but I'll sign for him. I run the place here."

"I'll need some identification," he said, still holding firmly to the urn.

"What you need is to hand over Johanson before I send him back with you."

"I quite understand," said the young man.

"What is it you quite understand?" she asked.

"Grief," he said. "It takes all forms, but it is all equally painful, and we do understand. We've been trained to understand grief."

"You've been trained to understand grief?"

"Oh, yes. We have a thorough understanding of grief."

"Jesus," said Too Much in pure amazement.

"Him too," said the young man. "We are required to have a firm foundation in Jesus." He handed the urn to Too Much and at the same time produced a small clipboard that had apparently been stuck behind him in his belt. "You'll just need to sign this," he said.

"This isn't even copper you've got Johanson in. It's colored plastic."

"I believe if you'll look at the form you'll see that the late Mr. Johanson had the economy plan," said the young man. "And the economy plan does not call for copper."

"I don't think Teddy would care one way or the other." Too Much looked over her shoulder and said, "Honorable Mr. Doo, could you perhaps put Johanson on his shelf while I sign for him?"

Mr. Doo was instantly at her side, his head inclined downward, his eyes apparently closed. He took the urn and backed away from her, now bowing slightly from the waist.

Too Much signed her name. The young man stared at his clipboard for a moment. "I'll need your whole name."

"That *is* my whole name."

"Too Much?"

"I hope to hell you don't find something funny about the Much family name or the fact that my dear old mama and daddy named me Too. Because my big brother, who is not but a biscuit away from weighing three hundred pounds, was given the name of Entirely Too by the same dear old mama and daddy, and if it's one thing Entirely Too Much does not think is funny is his goddam name. Besides that, he doesn't have a sweet disposition. I saw him bite a cat's head off once for pissing in the house."

"I quite understand," said the young man, taking his clipboard and marching back to his black Pinto.

"You don't understand a goddam thing," Too Much called after him, "or you wouldn't be delivering dead people in plastic urns."

When she turned back to look at the Honorable Mr. Doo, he had placed the fake-copper urn on the shelf, removed the stub of incense burning there, replaced it with a fresh stick, and lit it. He was kneeling on the floor and sitting back on his heels, his head bowed. She watched him for a moment.

"You don't need to do that, Honorable Mr. Doo."

Tryve Tron Doo did not move for another minute, and when he rose he turned slowly and said: "Rrraaahhh, onry say few words for Honorbal Mr. Johanson ancestor."

Too Much started to say something and then thought better of it. Whatever the old gentleman thought to say wouldn't help, but it couldn't hurt either. And she knew from her grandfather that Mr. Doo was speaking not only for Johanson's ancestors but for his own, and more than that, he was speaking for all ancestors of the dead everywhere, even hers. And the fact that nothing existed beyond the grave did not alter one whit the validity of his prayers. Her grandfather, profound atheist that he was, had insisted on that fact but had refused to explain it to her.

Too Much walked over and sat behind the beautiful desk that Mr. Doo had crafted out of discarded junk.

"Tomorrow we will scatter him in the swamp," she said, "and celebrate his going."

"We put Honorbal Mr. Johanson in swamp?"

"Tomorrow," she said, "all of Forever and Forever will put him there and sing him on his way."

"To his honorbal ancestor?"

"Maybe," she said. "And maybe not. But we'll sing him on his way to somewhere."

"Rrrraaahhh, I think I sprend time making some good thing to hold Honorbal Mr. Johanson. Prastic no good. I no rike."

Too Much could have gone across the room and kissed him for that, but she only smiled. "You do that, Honorable Mr. Doo. Make something good. Something good that we can hold in our hands and know is real, know is there."

"You most curious, Admirable Rady Too Much."

"Yes," she said, not smiling now. "I am most curious."

Chapter 14

Stump woke up to the sound of a piano, which caused gooseflesh to break out all along his spine. And it scared him. He was used to waking to the sound of mortar fire and screaming men. Sometimes to the sound of his own screams. The noise of war and the confusing chaos of battle had come back more and more frequently since Too Much had taken over Ted's trailer.

She still serviced him, or rather allowed him to service her. It was not the same, though. Nothing seemed the same lately, and he could not get comfortable with the difference because he couldn't put a name on it. War was war, and while he knew he would never understand it, he had experienced it. But everything seemed slightly off center now, and it only left him bewildered and with the feeling of being unequal to coping with the day every morning when he woke up.

And now, to add to the rest of everything else, a goddam piano. And it wasn't coming from a radio or off a record. He closed his eyes again and lay very still, because he heard now what he had not heard before: a babble of voices and laughter rising and falling around the piano, on which, he realized for the first time, somebody was playing scales.

He opened his eyes and could tell that Too Much had slept there on the other side of his bed last night. She had to have come to bed late, because he had not fallen onto the bed, fully clothed and very drunk, until midnight, and he had brought nearly a full bottle of

Turkey to bed with him. He rolled over and looked up at the headboard. The bottle was a little under half full, and he thought about taking a hit out of it but decided against it. He never had a hangover, a headache, or an outraged stomach. He sure as hell should have, but he never did. Maybe that was one of the reasons he drank so much.

Hangovers or not, though, he had to do something about his drinking. It had just about taken over his life. The thought occurred to him that he had to do something about a lot of things. Because he felt his whole life was being taken over. It was not just Too Much, but there was no question she was fixed solidly at the heart of whatever was wrong. He had somehow been pushed out of his place, off center. He ate, he drank, shit, pissed, and slept. And that was about it. There was a time—and it wasn't very long ago—when he thought that was what he wanted, thought that was *all* he wanted. But like a great many other things he had thought, he was wrong about that too.

And the plink-plink scale being played on the piano went on like a madness. The blind on the side of the room looking out onto the deck was drawn shut. But the light on the other side of the blind was bright enough for Stump to know it had to be at least midmorning. Stump got out of bed, went to the blind, and lifted one of the slats. What he saw was hallucinatory and reminded Stump of the first and only time he had ever dropped acid. Every resident of Forever and Forever was scattered about over the lawn that sloped down to the wooden dock that ran out over the saw grass of the swamp.

A black piano was on the end of the dock, with a very old resident sitting on a stool, playing the scale over and over. Tied up to one of the pilings just below the piano was a small airboat, the kind of boat that drew no water and could easily be driven over the saw grass of the swamp by the airplane propeller mounted on metal struts at the rear of the boat, so high that it was nearly even with the old woman at the piano. Johnson Meechum sat on the elevated seat at the front of the boat, where the controls were, and Mabel, her cloud of blue hair—which was normally carefully combed—blown and twisted about her freckled skull, sat in the rear of the boat just forward of the propeller, holding something that caught and reflected the sun.

She did not look particularly happy, but then Johnson's wife never seemed to look particularly happy to Stump unless she was somehow jerking her husband around and generally making his life miserable. But he had noticed that she had pretty much quit with that since she had moved back to the trailer from Ted's. Well, Stump had never thought so, and it certainly had not been so in his experience, but maybe it was possible for wives to change. Just as Stump was about to drop the slat of the blind he was holding open, Too Much ran down the dock barefoot and wearing her bikini. She bent to the ear of the woman sitting at the piano for an instant and then raced back toward the sloping lawn. The old lady at the piano began pounding out a rapid reggae beat. The Old Ones had herded up on the end of the dock, waiting, Stump knew, for Too Much to show them what to do.

Which is exactly what Too Much did. She lined the Old Ones up one behind the other and had each one place his hands on the ruined hips of the Old One in front of him. Then she went to the head of the line and started off, her hips popping from side to side and pumping back and forth like pistons. Minutes later, every last one of the Old Ones had the movement down pretty good, gimping and stumbling and hobbling and hopping and smiling for all they were worth, their old heads jerking to the music as they moved off in a single twisting line.

And in the time it took the Old Ones to get themselves strung out and going, the other residents had joined in the line with an enthusiasm that was embarrassing to Stump, twisting their bodies till they were—the obese as well as the bony—in such complicated configurations that Stump would never have believed it possible if he had not been looking at it himself. He didn't believe it anyway, he told himself. It was the whiskey coursing through his brain and blood that believed it. But he had to admit—and he was startled by the fact—the old lady at the piano wasn't bad. Stump thought that except for her ruined face and the terrible case of osteoporosis that she was carrying in the huge hump of her back, she could have played in most of the clubs in the country.

As the line swayed and jerked to the music, Stump saw the tables for the first time, wide and long and covered with what looked like white linen cloths. But what really stunned him was that the tables were loaded with food, some of it cold and arranged in clever little designs on beds of ice. And along with the iced dishes were steaming pots and platters kept hot with cans of Sterno burning beneath them.

The first thing that occurred to Stump was to wonder what in the hell was going on. And the second—because of the food, the airboat, and the piano—was to wonder where all the fucking money had come from to pull this thing off. Because the truth was that money had been much on Stump's mind lately. He really didn't like to think about it—hated himself for it in fact—but money seemed to be his last ace in the hole. That was why he had refused to go down to the bank with Too Much to validate the signature so Too Much could write checks on his account. Knowing Too Much and her attitude toward money, he had known all along that being broke by itself would not keep Too Much from leaving.

Meanwhile, for reasons of her own that he could not fathom, she really did want to make the lives of his dying residents full of laughter and joy and celebration, which was why he tried to keep his mind off it. His residents' ropes were played out, and all that was left to them now was to turn their ropes loose and die. They knew it and he knew they knew it.

How in the hell did she expect to get laughter and joy and celebration out of that sorry and inevitable fact? Besides, he had told himself more than once, it was not spending money he resented; it was lying through his teeth and telling people there was hope when there was none. Let'm die. It was their time. He couldn't see the problem. It came to everybody, the good and bad alike. Korea had taught him that if nothing else.

If it wasn't his money spread out there all over the lawn, whose the hell was it? And to what point, for Christ's sake? What were they doing? Having a party? They didn't have parties at Forever and

Forever, goddammit. They had funerals. Sickness and death were the order of the day. Not dancing lines and pianos and long tables covered with food and . . . Had he seen what he only now remembered seeing?

He went back and jacked up the whole blind. Yes, goddammit. Wine. A lot of it. There were wine bottles iced down in buckets, and other wine was sitting unstoppered along the sides of the tables. Jesus, white wine iced down and red wine breathing. And he'd be twiced damned if there, on the other side of the lawn, in the partial shade of a shrub, wasn't Justice toking on a bottle. And the old bastard didn't even have it in a sipping sack. It was right out there for the whole world to see. Stump could tell just by the way Justice was sprawled on the ground that he could not have got to his feet if somebody had a gun to his head. He was as fucked up as a ten-dicked dog. Well, Stump didn't know where the money came from or what they thought they were doing out there on the lawn of his Forever and Forever, but by God, as soon as he got out of the sour clothes he'd slept in last night and took a shower, he would go outside and kick some ass and take some names and get some answers.

He had just dried off from the shower and slipped into khaki shorts when he heard the front door of his trailer slam. Stump could recognize the footfall of Too Much even barefoot. He came out of the bedroom and they met in the hall.

"What the fuck's going on out there?" he said.

"Oh," she said brightly. "You've come out of your stupor. I thought you might have died of alcohol poisoning."

"It looked as though you were never coming in last night, so I had a few drinks before I went to bed."

"A few drinks, my ass. I slept in that bed with you last night, not that you'd remember, and I damn near died from the whiskey you were sweating out."

"Wait a minute. I'm the one that's got the beef here, and you're the one who's arguing. Am I hearing this right or what?"

"What's your beef? Let's start with that."

"I thought I might have a little talk with you about money."

"Now, isn't that curious? That's what I was coming to talk to you about."

She walked back into the kitchen, and he followed her. She opened a small paper sack, which he had not even noticed she had been carrying, and took out a roll of bills that had a rubber band around it.

"Two thousand dollars," she said, "unless I miscounted."

"Did you say two thousand dollars?"

"That's what I said."

"Where would you get money like that?"

"By taking care of business. Jesus, it's a wonder you're not in the poorhouse the way you've been fucking up."

"Don't stand here in my own house and tell me I've been fucking up. I am not an idiot."

"You brought up idiot; I didn't. But let's turn that loose, for Christ's sake. The only really important thing is the books are over in my office. At your convenience, you can look them over."

"Numbers give me a headache."

"Yeah, so you've told me before, but I just wanted you to know the books were there in the office anytime you wanted to see them. That way you won't have to jump down my throat every time I tell you you're a fuckup. You can go see for yourself."

"You can stop with the fuckup business. A little of that goes a long way." Stump rubbed the stubble on his chin with the purple end of his nub, looked out the window and then back at her. "I don't know why it never come to me to ask before, but where did somebody your age learn to keep books?"

"I didn't."

"If you didn't, what the hell are you doing keeping mine? Unless you've done something stupid like let Johnson Meechum do the work. Now, there's a bastard who can keep books. His prison time proves it. We'll both be dead in the water if you turned all this over to him."

That was precisely what she had done—or at least was going to do, when there were books to keep.

But Too Much said, "No, I didn't fall off the turnip truck yesterday. My shit's a little more together than that. But you do have a resident, one Mr. Guido, who has spent his entire life keeping books. And I made it my business to enlist him."

Stump rubbed his chin with his nub. "Guido? Guido, you say? I don't know a Guido."

"Doesn't surprise me," she said. "You don't know half the people in the park."

"I don't need to know'm. All I need to do is park'm and let'm die."

"Anybody ever tell you you've got a very unhealthy attitude?"

"More than a few. And in stronger language than that. But back to the point. So you found Fido. So what?"

"Guido. His name's Bruno Guido."

"Guido. Fido. Whatever."

"His name's Guido. Don't make fun of him, goddammit. You ought to show a little respect to a man who's keeping your books and probably keeping your ass out of jail at the same time. I let Johnson look over his shoulder, but I don't let him touch anything. He swears Guido is the real thing."

"How do you know he's not lying?"

"He wouldn't lie to me."

"Anybody'll lie to anybody."

"As a rule, I'd never argue with that. But Johnson owes me too much. I've got him like a fucking dog on a leash."

"The more I know you," said Stump, "the more I wonder why I let you hang around me."

"Check between my legs."

"See, that's what I mean. Dirty talk like that."

"A little crude maybe, but nothing truer in the world. And you know it."

"Yeah, I suppose I do. What's this Guido costing me?"

"Nothing."

"He's keeping my records for nothing?"

"Not exactly."

"Don't do this to me early in the morning," said Stump. "Say whatever you've got to say, and say it plain."

"He's working off what he owes you."

"Why's he owe me anything?"

"He hasn't paid any rent on the space where his trailer is parked since he moved in."

"What? Did he just move in?"

"Not hardly, Stump. He's been in the park for just over five years."

"Five fucking years!" said Stump, spilling his coffee. "Why didn't I know he wasn't paying what he owed me? I don't mind cutting these old guys a little slack from time to time, but I'm not running a charity here."

"No," said Too Much. "What you're running is a business that nobody has looked after and on which no records have ever been kept since you've owned it."

"You trusting him with keeping my accounts, when he hasn't paid anything on his rent in five years?"

"Mr. Guido tends to forget things—everything but numbers, that is. He's a walking calculating machine. He said if you'd asked him for the rent, he would have paid you. But since you never came around to ask for your money, it kept slipping his mind until it got to be a habit."

"Some habit. I ought to sue the old bastard."

"No reason to. That's his two thousand on the table. And besides, I charged him nine and a half percent interest on the money, and he was glad to pay it."

"Nine and a half? That's robbery. You shouldn't have charged him that."

"That's the going rate at the bank. Or at least he thinks so, because I told him. And besides, just a second ago, you were talking about suing him."

"You know I didn't mean that."

"It sure sounded like you meant it. But I'm glad you didn't. He's a great old guy. When I asked him if he could help me out, he would have jumped for joy, if he *could* jump for joy, which he can't, but he sure as hell jumped at the chance to have something to occupy his time. I happen to be very fond of Johnson, but I wouldn't let him get near books or money, yours or anybody else's. How stupid do you think I am?"

"Actually, I was wondering how stupid I might be." He looked at the money for the first time. "So the two thousand is back rent?"

"Now you've got everything right. That's what it is."

It was actually the money Fingers had stolen, all except six hundred dollars. But Stump would never know that, because he did not care enough to find out. Just as he would never know that somebody named Guido was not keeping his books. And he would never know that she put four hundred dollars in her own pocket for walking-around money and used the remaining deuce for the wake they were having for Ted Johanson.

"Is that how you paid for what's going on out there by the dock"—he pointed through the kitchen window to the place where the old people were gathered—"with part of Guido's money, which wasn't his money at all but mine?"

"As a matter of fact, I didn't."

"The kind of thing you've got going out there doesn't come free," he said.

"You'd be surprised," she said.

"Surprise me, then."

"Do you even know what everybody in Forever and Forever is doing out there today?"

"Too Much, I've only been out of bed for fifteen minutes. I don't have to tell you that it takes me about two hours before I know my name."

"Let me run it down for you, then."

"Would it be too much to ask you to make a little coffee while you're at it?"

She smiled. "Trust me with your coffee, but not with your money, right?"

"Don't start that feminist bullshit on me, Too Much. You know I can't take it late at night, much less in the morning before I've had some coffee."

"And you know me better than that," she said. "Most of the women I've ever known ought to be strapped into harness and hitched to a plow and beaten like a mule. At least they would have a certain dignity doing something useful like pulling a plow. And

God knows most of'm have the thighs and ass for it. At least it would be a hell of a lot better than spending their lives making up excuses why it's an inconvenient time for their husbands to get a little pussy or why it's impossible for them to give occasional head."

"Damn, that really rattled your cage, didn't it?"

"Women are only fit as beasts of burden, most of them anyway. It didn't have to be that way; they did it to themselves."

"As I understood it," said Stump, "you were about to run something down for me. Actually, what I thought was that you were going to explain what's happening out there on the lawn without spending any of my money."

"When did you get so tight about money?"

"I don't particularly give a rat's ass about money, but I happen to be goddam particular about getting fucked. It's the principle of the thing, and as strange as it may seem, I do try to hold on to a few principles."

"We're having a wake out there," said Too Much. "Today we're scattering Ted Johanson all over the swamp."

"Is that what Mabel's holding in the back of the boat?"

"That's right. She's holding Ted, or what's left of him. Might not even be Ted, for all I know. But that's what they delivered yesterday. It doesn't really matter. The ritual's the thing. Gets the grief out, lets it go."

"Is that why you've got a piano and dancing and drinking out there with his bottle full of ashes?"

She had put a cup on the table in front of him and stood now with a pot of coffee. He looked up and saw her eyes. "Don't pour that fucking coffee on me!"

"Is that what I looked like I was about to do?" she said, pouring his cup full.

"I'll just say that you didn't look like you were *not* going to do it."

"You mistook pity for anger," she said. "Sometimes you strike me as having room-temperature IQ, so to speak. Yeah, Stump, that's what we have out there. Music, food, dancing, and if the old parties get drunk enough before it's over, we might even have a little fucking."

Stump snorted. "It's been so long since any of the residents even thought about fucking, I doubt there's even a memory left."

"You convict yourself of ignorance out of your own mouth. But let it pass. The point I wanted to make is that laughter is the flip side of grief. Laughter and grief can, and often do, serve the same purpose. They're both cathartic. And don't look at me like that; cathartic only means, in this case anyway, relieving you of whatever emotional horror that may be gnawing you to the bone. Stick with me, Stump, and you'll get a liberal education."

"And you stick with me, Too Much, and you'll spend the rest of your life farting through silk. You believe that?"

"Based on my track record with men, I'd be a fool to believe it," said Too Much.

"You would also be a fool to think anybody is grieving over Ted Johanson's death. And horror? Nobody out there even mildly gives a shit."

"It really doesn't matter if there's grief or not. Everybody in Forever and Forever needed something to bring them together, some reason for a party. If there's no grief involved, all the better. But you wanted to know about money." She turned and looked out the window, where the old, cracked voices had become louder and a little drunken, and the piano more raucous, as if the notes were being beaten out with a hammer. "What's happening out there didn't cost you a penny."

She was lying. The two hundred dollars she had spent had gone to pay for cheap California wine. None of the residents had any taste buds left, and whether it was expensive wine or cheap did not matter. For most of them, it took about a cupful to get them drunk.

"Took'm most of the night, but they got the job done. The woman playing piano, you know who she is?"

Stump didn't even turn his head to look through the window. "Can't call her name right off."

"Never expected you to. The point is that lady played in Carnegie Hall. You know what Carnegie Hall is?"

"What do you take me to be?"

"You wouldn't want to hear me tell you. That piano, which is all she's got left in the world that is hers and hers alone, is a Steinway grand. And the food out there? One of the residents has a small catering business, and he offered to donate the food if the residents would prepare it. Took'm most of the night, but I'm here to tell you it's fittin to eat. The airboat there at the end of the dock had been in storage ever since the owner had to move here to Forever and Forever. He poached gators out of it in the Everglades until his wife died and old age forced him into this place. Said he couldn't and wouldn't ever sell it, said it would be like selling one of his own children. I could go on, but I think you see my point."

"All that," said Stump, "from people who gimp around all day, taking two or three hours out every now and then to lean on shuffleboard sticks. Who the hell would have thought it?"

"I would have," Too Much said.

"Yeah, I guess you would at that. Myself, I would've thought they would get tired, peter out, and give up, maybe even collapse."

"You sound disappointed they didn't."

Stump stared down into his coffee cup without speaking. Then, very softly, "I just want them to lie about, be quiet, and die."

"I can't help thinking you mean you wish you could lie about, be quiet, and die."

"If Korea didn't kill me, this place sure as hell won't."

"They're about to send Ted out to be scattered, so I guess I better get back out there. You coming?"

"I don't think so," Stump said. "I had all I wanted of Ted while he was alive."

"Whatever pleases you."

"I didn't say it pleased me."

"Nobody said it had to."

She had already walked across the kitchen and had her hand on the doorknob to let herself out when he said, "If you get through this today in time, we'll go down to the bank and fix it so you can sign for me."

"I was going to ask you again about that, but I didn't want to be a pain in the ass, and I figured this wasn't the right time anyway."

After she was gone, Stump got up from the table and went to

the window. As he watched, Johnson hit the starter button on the airboat, and it came to life with an incredible racket. Mabel put the urn between her knees and held to her hair with both hands as though it were a hat that might blow away. All of the residents had gathered down by the water's edge at the foot of the dock. When Johnson pushed the throttle forward and the airboat leapt away across the saw grass, a ragged cheer went up from the residents.

About two hundred yards from the dock, Johnson pulled the throttle back to trolling speed and Mabel stood up, the urn held under the crook of one elbow. Her other hand went into the urn and came out with a handful of ashes. As she flung the ashes abroad over the saw grass, the sweetest, purest soprano voice Stump had ever heard fell into a tone-perfect version of "Amazing Grace." Every other voice there by the dock was utterly quiet as the high, beautiful voice went to meet Mabel's hand scattering Ted's ashes over the mud, the shallow black water, and the saw grass. The singing voice reminded Stump of the young Joan Baez, only purer. He searched to find who was singing. It did not take long. She was very old and frail, with thin hair, and she held herself between a four-legged walker, her head dropped back, her eyes closed on the sky, singing.

Stump rushed to his bedroom, snatched the bottle of Wild Turkey off the headboard, and never put the bottle down until it was empty.

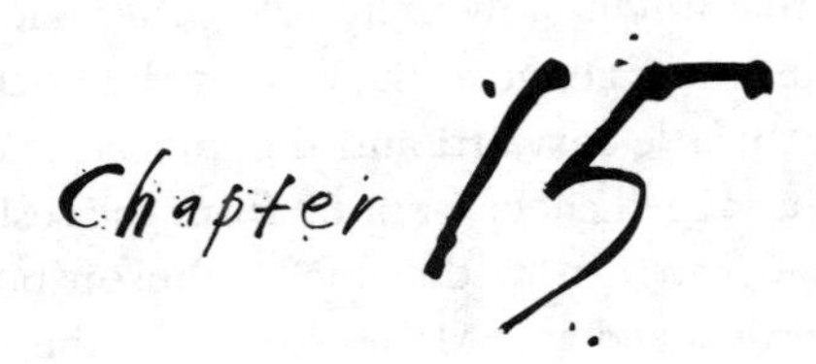

It didn't take long to scatter Ted, but it took all day to scatter the party. For a while right after Too Much left, Stump went to the blinds from time to time, lifted a slat, and looked out. But finally it got longer and longer between times when he glanced through the slats. It didn't look as if anything out there was slowing down at all. Maybe the key to the swirling movement was the dancing line that would come together, snake around through the grounds, and break apart, only to take up and join again.

At some point, Stump saw that Justice was sitting with another bottle. He had no idea how Justice had got it, but from the way he kept knocking it back, he wouldn't have it long. Just watching him made Stump want a bottle of his own, so he went to the closet in the hall and got out a new fifth of Wild Turkey, uncapped it, and took a drink. He thought about getting a glass and some ice, but it was the briefest of thoughts, and it went away as quickly as it had come, and the notion of a glass or ice never occurred to him again.

He drew the blind halfway up, and for some long time—he had no idea how long—he felt a wonderful peace and contentment watching the residents frolic and swirl about the tables, eating and drinking as though there might never be anything to eat or drink again, and watching, too, the Old Ones herded up around Too Much as she drifted slowly about the grounds, hugging first one resident and then another, patting a shoulder affectionately or touching a hand, the Old Ones bunched about her and following closely.

Without Stump even noticing them doing it, a group of residents had drifted down the dock to the piano, where they started singing gospel songs, one song segueing into another, all of the old people from time to time pointing out toward the fastness of the swamp where Ted had been scattered, sometimes pointing for a very long time, sometimes weeping. From this distance, it was a while before Stump realized that some among them were crying, although by no means all of them. It was one of the strangest things Stump had ever seen: they leaned cheek by jowl on the back of the piano, one resident crying, his face contorted and wet with tears, while people on both sides of him would be smiling, singing, or broken up in laughter.

About halfway through the bottle of Wild Turkey, Stump found himself laughing, crying, singing, and finally howling like a dog. And it was all for Ted, whom he had never liked, but the worst part of it was that he had never stopped to consider why he had never liked him. But now he did stop to consider Ted, the man, and considering him now that he was gone was devastating: someone who had spent his manhood in the woods and ended his life no longer able to climb a tree, a man who had lived breathing the cold, clean air of the North Woods and then finally was exiled to a land that was stifling and hot and filled with the combustion of engines and filled, too, with trees, very nearly all of which had sticks propping them up and lights hanging in them. His strength gone, his wife gone, everything gone, irrevocably gone, everything gone but the rage of the words that he could still spit out of his toothless mouth. But even the words were to no effect, because everyone who heard them thought them a joke. He, Ted Johanson, was a joke.

It was unbearable, so Stump went to get another bottle. Then he came back to sit on the bed and look out the wide window, which had come to seem like a movie screen to him. That is what he wanted the window to be, a movie screen full of people he did not know, acting crippled, and deaf, and senile, and incontinent—maimed in every way that counted. Maimed and alone. Abandoned. But shortly the movie would be over, the director would dismiss them, and every last one of them would be whole and happy again.

He was fumbling with the cap of the bottle—which he was unaccountably having difficulty getting off—when he saw Too Much walk up to Justice, sitting now in the shade of shrub with his bottle. She stopped and looked down at him. The Old Ones had herded up close to her back. Too Much turned and gestured briefly toward them. Justice only shook his head and took another sip from his bottle.

His legs were splayed out straight in front of him where he sat, and she kicked him hard on the bottom of one of his long, narrow shoes and inclined her head slightly downward. The tendons stood out in her neck and her perfect teeth gleamed in the sun, but they were not pretty in her twisted mouth. They looked savage and dangerous.

Stump took a drink and his vision blurred. When it focused again, Too Much was gone, but Justice was on his feet, though not as steady as he might have been, a long, limber stick in his hand, chasing the herd of Old Ones about the lawn. From time to time, he rapped them lightly across their thin shanks.

With the Wild Turkey bottle still held by the neck, Stump felt himself slowly fall backward on the bed, and at the same time wondering what was going on with Justice and the Old Ones.

When Stump woke up, the sun was in his eyes and he seemed to be floating. The floating didn't bother him. Drinking often made him float, and he had floated more during his lifetime than he liked to think about. But the sun, although low in the sky, was still fiery bright and made his eyeballs feel cracked. Stump was stinging over the whole surface of his body, and he recognized the stinging as fire ants. He could only have been lying in a bed of them. Then he saw why he was floating, and it had nothing to do with whiskey. Three Old Ones had him by each leg and three by each arm, and Justice was chasing them with a stick, screaming as he went.

"Rat off de end ob dat dock! Chunk him in! Dat'll do de trick. Soba his ass up, I'm tellin yo. White man's whiskey be more harder to run off dan nigger wine. Chunk his ass in!"

With Justice laying the whip to them now and again, the Old Ones staggered toward the dock as fast as they could.

"Justice," screamed Stump. "You black motherfucker."

"Whoa! Whoa up dere. Dis white man done come to life."

"I'm gone come upside your fucking head with a two-by-four is what I'm gone do. Tell these bastards to put me down." Stump struggled briefly, but he was still too weak from the alcohol he'd drunk to have much effect on the Old Ones holding him, who didn't look at him but rather stared at Justice. Stump had had time enough now to think about where he was, and it occurred to him that it could very likely be a nightmare. None of this could possibly be happening. "Are you gone tell these bastards to put me down, Justice?"

"Yo damn right," said Justice. "Put yo right in de fuckin wata. Soba yo ass up. Dat where yo gone now."

"I own you, you black piece of shit!" Stump screamed.

"De cat done own me. Yo time be ober, Mistuh Stump. De cat own me and yo and dese crippled-up mofos I be drivin here wit my stick." He lashed out and caught the three nearest Old Ones with his stick, and they lunged forward in a staggering lurch. But not a one of them made a sound.

"If you throw me in that water, you're dead meat," screamed Stump. He couldn't seem to say anything without screaming. He thought it might have helped if he could talk in a normal voice.

"De cat got me, you don," said Justice, lashing out again at the old ones.

"What goddam cat you talking about, Justice?"

"Dat be fo Justice to know and yo to fine out."

"Why the hell are you doing this?" They were getting nearer to the end of the dock, and Stump sure as hell didn't want to go off the end of it into the mud and muck waiting right there under about two feet of water.

"Cause yo come out here sleepin drunk in my shade jus lak

trash. Miss Too Much don tol ol Justice, say git erry piece ob trash out dis place and clean hit up. Now yo unnerstan? Miss Too Much done gib Justice dese Old Ones an say, she say, make'm clean it up. Be good fo dem. Git dere ol tickers ticking. Mr. Stump, yo lyin out here all fucked up, so I got to git yo too. Justice caint run no risk wit Miss Too Much. Now yo unnerstan?"

"No, goddammit, no! I don't understand. And—"

"No matta. Dat cat in de groun wit me in his ahms, unnerstan. An you still goin in dat wata, white man. Now dat signify an gone stretch yo ass out. Miss Too Much seen you, she say, Stretch his ass out so he signify. He caint signify lak he be under dat bush. Now yo got it, white man?"

"What's this 'white man' shit? Since when you calling me white man, Justice?" They were very nearly to the end of the dock, and Stump knew he was about to go into the shallow water covering God knew how much mud. "We like brothers, you and me, Justice."

Justice stared at him as the Old Ones stood poised on the end of the dock to throw him in. "Brothers? Me an you? Sheeeiit! Now ain't dat jus lak a white man. Worse'n a damn cat. You think ole Justice lak bein de nigger all dese years in Forever and Forever fo nothin but a little taste from time to time when yo think yo can spare it or jus git to thinkin doin a little sumpin fo de nigger make you less a asshole dan you be. The shit done turned on yo, Mr. Charley. Chunk dis white fool in!" Justice cut the Old Ones across the legs with his whip, and for the first time they made a sound—a kind of long, groaning sigh—and sent Stump flying.

He felt himself go over the side and through the air. The mud was so soft, it didn't even slow him up when he hit it. He went down and under into total blackness. If he hadn't been as drunk as he was, he might have got out sooner. As it was, he thought he was going to die. He was so disoriented, he couldn't discover which way was up. He could get no purchase with his feet in the mud it was so deep, and as he flailed about, his air giving out, he thought—even in his rage—what a low-rent piece of business it was, after all he had gone through in Korea, to be thrown by a bunch of mindless cripples, at the direction of a nigger drunk on cheap wine, to die in a mud hole on his own property, property he had only been able to buy because he had been forced to cut off his own fucking hand caught in a corn picker.

But he did get out by accidentally finding one of the pilings under the dock with one of his flailing arms. By the time he had managed to drag himself onto land, gasping and heaving like a beached fish, he caught just a glimpse, after digging the mud out of his eyes, of Justice whipping and herding the Old Ones around the far corner of a trailer, leading them back into Forever and Forever. When he did finally struggle to his feet, he could barely walk, because he thought he must be carrying about thirty-five pounds of mud from the crown of his head to the soles of his shoes. And stink? Goddam, that mud stank! He had only managed to stagger two or three paces before he—who prided himself on never puking—sent a stream of sour whiskey and bile down the front of himself.

Fucked-up and so full of a stink that he would have driven a dog off a gut wagon, he was still entirely focused. All he could think of was Too Much. Every bit of this was her doing. Her circus act might be good, but by God, it wasn't this good. He headed straight for Ted's trailer. The chill and the stink of the mud had sobered him up, that and his anger. He didn't know what he was going to do. But he'd find out—and she'd find out—when he got there. His rage would not turn him loose, nor did he want it to.

There was nobody left on the sloping lawn where the wake had been held. And even when he reached the narrow macadam streets dividing the trailers, there were only a few of the residents still out in the late evening heat. None of them spoke, nor did they pay him the slightest attention. He thought they probably didn't even recognize him and consequently decided to ignore this muddy and stinking apparition that had found its way into the place where they lived. So the few that sat on the steps of their trailers or stood about on the edges of their small yards just kept on with their newly acquired habit of scratching themselves vigorously in private places, while they talked and avoided even looking at him.

Stump was coming across the courtyard where Ted had topped the Australian pine and then pitched out of the tree onto his head and broken his neck. He was exhausted from fighting his way out of the mud and hungover and in desperate need of a drink, staring at the ground, not looking where he was going, his shoes making a sucking sound with each step he took and his mouth still full of grit that he could not spit out. If he had not nearly tripped over the tiny stump with the black cross painted across the top of it, he would not have looked up and seen what had once been the ratty place where Ted used to live.

He stood stock-still, trying to figure out what had happened to Ted's trailer, what *could* have happened to it in so short a time. It now had light-yellow siding and a yellow roof. A short widow's walk had been built onto the front of it with a door opening onto it. The gardens that surrounded the entire trailer glowed like a light with hundreds of plants in bloom in blinding splashes of color. Stump stood in his muddy clothes, his feet making squishing sounds every time he shifted his weight, and thought of his own trailer. Christ, where he lived looked like a sharecropper's shack compared to this. What he was looking at was like magic, but a magic that scared him, a magic he did not like. It definitely did not look like anything anybody lived in, or at least anything anybody he had ever known had lived in.

This was her fucking office? This was what she needed to have a little space of her own? To come and think? Or, as she had said, *not* to think? What kind of goddam books did she think she was going to have to keep to need a place like this? He slammed his purple nub into the open palm of his other hand. Everything about this had a very bad smell. And thinking that only reminded him how terrible he himself smelled, and somehow he seemed to smell even worse knowing that the Old Ones, deaf, toothless, and nearly blind, had picked him up bodily and thrown him into his own swamp.

Keenly aware of the sucking noise his feet were still making as he walked, he went up the three steps of Ted's trailer and pushed open the door. But he didn't go in, only stood there looking, mainly at Too Much sitting in a chair that would have dwarfed his old mama, whose whiskey-bloated body at the time of her death from cirrhosis weighed two hundred seventy-five pounds. Too Much had her head down, poring over some papers, and Johnson Meechum was standing beside her, bent forward and looking over the same papers.

A tiny Chinaman was sitting on his heels, chipping away at a huge stone at the far end of the trailer. There were framed pictures, what looked to be original line drawings, hanging on the lime-colored walls. The whole place was as clean as an operating room. Against the wall directly in front of Stump, a small, dark man with a mouthful of tacks and a ball-peen hammer was working on a very long, very deep sofa. He seemed to be covering it in red velvet. At either end of the couch stood two very large dark men in tight double-breasted wool suits, black hats with the tiniest of brims on their heads, and their massive arms crossed over their chests. They were not sweating. Heavy wool suits in this weather, and not even their upper lips were damp. Amazing! They were the only ones who had seen Stump in the doorway. They stared at him for a very long time without speaking.

Then one of them said, "Who da fuck you?" Neither man's lips had seemed to move.

Everybody else in the room turned at once to look at Stump: the little man on his knees in front of the couch, Johnson and Too Much from the desk, and the diminutive Chinaman who was chipping as regularly as a clock ticking at his huge stone at the end of the trailer.

"Who are these two bozos?" asked Stump, indicating the large men at either end of the couch.

"Mr. Guido's sons," said Too Much.

"And where's he?"

"That's him on his knees, doing the couch."

Stump shook his head as though to clear it. "I thought he was the one doing the books."

"He is."

Stump was incredulous. "You got the guy doing the books doing your upholstering?"

The little man on his knees turned briefly to Stump, the points of tacks sticking out of his teeth. "Meetcha," he said.

"Jesus," said Stump. "I'm in a madhouse here. The fucking bookkeeper's doing the upholstering?"

"You got a problem wit dat?"

"Yeah," said Stump. "I got a fucking problem with that."

One of the big men, presumably the one who had spoken, unbuttoned his double-breasted coat and let it fall open. A holstered .45, which the suit had been designed to conceal, was strapped to his chest. "Don't have no problem wit dat."

"But if he's my bookkeeper, what the hell's he doing tacking cloth to my couch?" Stump was speaking to Too Much, but one of the large men answered. Stump still could not tell which.

"Some men he got one talent, my papa got more dan some talent."

"Your face," said one of the large men.

"What?" said Stump.

"Your face."

Stump opened his mouth, but Too Much said, "I wouldn't answer him again. They have a thing about being answered twice. They come over from Miami once a month to see how their father is doing, have been since he's been living here. They'd rather he not live here, but he likes it."

"Hell," said Stump, "I'd like it too if it was free. Why haven't I seen him before?"

"We've already been through that," Too Much said. "You only see what you want to see."

Stump gave a great snort of exasperation and said, "Could we get these people out of here?"

"My God, Stump," said Too Much, "what on earth happened to you anyway?"

"Looks like he fell in da fuckin mud," one of the men said.

"Yeah, he got da fuckin mud all in'm. I'm bettin his fuckin ears full a da mud, cause he don't hear good."

Stump still did not know which one was doing the talking.

"Shut up, Dominic," Too Much said.

"Yeah, shut the fuck up, Dominic," Stump said. "You're getting in over your head."

"Lissen to him," said one of the huge men in the tight suits.

"I don't know you," said Stump, "but you bout to piss me off. And I guess you got just enough sense to know I been pissed off once already today."

"What in the world happened to you, Stump?" Too Much asked again.

"They thrown me in the swamp."

"They who?"

"The Old Ones."

"Why would they have done that?" Johnson asked.

"Justice told'm to."

Too Much said, "What made him do that?"

"Said you told'm to," Stump said.

"You know I would never do that."

"I don't know any such thing. But I do know you subject to tell a lie."

"She never lied to me," said Johnson.

"Just wait awhile," Stump said. "She'll git around to it."

"How long you had da mout you got?" It was one of the big men at either end of the couch.

Stump's clothes were drying to him, and he was beginning to itch. "Too Much," he said, "you think you could get these people out of here?"

The old man kneeling at the couch stood up, spat the tacks out of his mouth into his hand, looked from one huge man at the end of the couch to the other, and said softly, "You boys." They followed him out of the trailer without a word.

"Honorable Mr. Doo," said Too Much.

Tryve Tron Doo got slowly to his feet, placed his chisel and mallet on the floor beside the stone he had been chipping away at, turned, and walked directly to Stump. Putting his hands together under his chin, he inclined his head slightly and passed through the door.

"Johnson?" said Too Much.

"Me too?" Johnson said.

"You too," she said.

He glanced at Stump and then sidled, crabwise, out the door.

Too Much sat looking at Stump, who leaned as though to step into the room.

"I'd rather you didn't come on that parquet floor with all that mud on you."

Stump saw for the first time that it was, in fact, a parquet floor, the squares of wood fitted so perfectly together they appeared seamless and so highly polished they glowed like light.

"A parquet floor in a goddam trailer? Ted must be spinning in his grave."

"I think one thing or another in that swamp's already swallowed his ashes, so I don't imagine he'd be doing much spinning by now. Besides, the floor wasn't my idea."

"If it wasn't your idea, whose was it?"

"You wouldn't know her."

"Her?"

"Never put down anything but parquet floors her whole life. Worked at it forty-five years before she ended up here. I watched her work and couldn't believe the skill it took to put it down."

"Give me her name. You'd be surprised at how many I know here in Forever and Forever."

"I'm surprised at how many you don't know. But her name is George."

"Oh, I know that one. The little fagette with the monster husband named Sarah."

"It's too bad there's not a hell, a man like you needs burning so bad."

"How you know there ain't a hell?"

"I got it from a good source."

"Don't guess it was God."

"If he wasn't God, he'll do till God comes along."

Stump was staring at the floor. "Guess it must of took as much money as it did skill to put that floor down."

"When you get around to looking at the checks I've written on your account, you'll see I didn't pay for the floor."

"I don't plan to be looking at no checks, but if you didn't pay for it, who did?"

"George."

"How many times did you have to let her fuck you?"

"Try to remember who you're talking to. This isn't Justice. If I put you in that fucking swamp, nobody'll ever see you again, because nobody will ever find you. Besides, she doesn't have a nub. You know that nub's all I want. What the hell ails you anyway?"

"Being buried in mud tends to ruin a man's disposition."

"That was a mistake."

"Justice lost his fucking mind when you put him in charge of the Old Ones."

She looked briefly at Stump. "All he was told to do was clean up where we had the wake."

"Did you tell'm to use a whip on the Old Ones?"

"You know better than that. He must have misunderstood."

"He didn't misunderstand a damn thing."

"Did he do a good job?"

"He damn sure didn't clean me up, but he put me in the swamp. He damn nearly got rid of me forever. Nothing but luck is why I'm standing here now."

"You're also dripping a puddle of mud on my new floor."

Stump looked down at his feet. "You mean *my* new floor."

"Not really," she said. "You didn't pay for a damn thing in here."

"None of it?"

"None of it. It'll come as a surprise to you—it did to me—but half of these old folks still have ninety-five cents of the first dollar they ever made. I didn't spend a nickel for anything in here, and you didn't either. It's all the residents' money and labor."

"Now, tell me why they'd do something like that."

"They thought I deserved it. I never asked them. They just showed up and did it."

"Sure!"

"You see those bookshelves up there?"

"Is that what they are? Never had much to do with bookshelves myself."

"Come back this evening and they'll be full of books."

"Coming from . . . ?"

"Retired college professor down the lane with a trailer full of books. Insisted I have them."

"Why doesn't he want'm anymore?"

"Blind."

"That'll work. But if he's blind, how'd he know you were down here in Ted's trailer with a bunch of empty bookshelves?"

"Word of mouth, Stump, word of mouth. Might surprise you to know I'm all over the park. At least stories of me are. Some of'm are even true. And when more stories are a lie about you than are true, then you're right on the edge of being a legend."

"You already a legend," Stump said.

"I didn't think you knew."

"No way I could have missed. You're a fucking legend or a legend fucking."

"You'll pay for that, you bastard."

"We all pay for everything in the end."

"Not necessarily. Go run a tub, and I'll come clean you up."

"A kindness I wouldn't have expected."

"It's not a kindness. I'm getting sick over here smelling you."

"I'm getting sick smelling me too. You think you can get me clean enough to do me?"

"I can get you clean enough to be done. Too Much needs to be done too. All work and no nub makes for a dull threat."

"Threat, Too Much?"

"Threat, Stump. You figure it out."

"I don't have to. It's a threat to use my nub to stop my heart." The mud on his face, dried into a mask now, cracked when he smiled. "You're nothing, Too Much," said Stump, "if not a fucking double threat."

"You said it, Stump," Too Much said, "so try not to forget it when the payback comes. Like you say, we all end up paying."

"If I forget that, I deserve what comes to me."

"You won't deserve it, but you won't like it when it comes."

"Damn, couldn't you even smile when you said that?"

"I'd be lying if I did."

Chapter 16

Mabel and Too Much were sitting in the living room of Mabel's trailer. Mabel was feeling good because she was eating bonbon candies, which she only allowed herself when she had a serious problem. The problem she had was that she wasn't sure she had a problem, and that was always the worst problem for her to deal with, the kind she didn't know if she had or not. Too Much was herself feeling better than she had felt in a good long while. She had managed to get Stump cleaned up enough to do him. He always seemed to feel so good when she was doing him that he failed to realize she was doing herself at the same time.

This never caused Too Much much trouble, because she had long since resigned herself to the fact that where sex was concerned, most men were mindless fools, thinking as they did that any self-respecting woman would lie there humping and pumping and sweating and grunting for no other reason than to do *them.*

"Baby, that street runs both ways!" she'd always tell herself when she was getting off.

She damn sure was not going to give any man alive his jollies if she didn't get her jollies in return. Turnabout was fair play. Dig it and believe it.

And Lord, Lord, did she ever properly do herself this last go-round. So she was stretched out and feeling better than good, watching Mabel go after those bonbon candies. As she watched, Too Much languidly scratched those intimate places she remembered best after her violent encounter with Stump in his special bathtub.

It was probably the bonbons that made Too Much so unprepared for what Mabel said around the sucking sounds she was making with the candy.

"You know, honey," said Mabel, the sucking sounds getting louder and louder as she tried to dislodge the candy stuck between her teeth, "when I went in that urn and got that first handful of Ted, I smelled that man all over again."

Too Much had been sitting there thinking that she had, in fact, probably taken Stump all the way to his elbow. Of course she couldn't be sure, but if she had, it was a record, and that was what she had her mind on when Mabel brought up going into the urn after a handful of Ted.

"I'm sorry," Too Much said. "I missed what you said. Guess my mind was wondering."

Yes, Too Much was sure now. She'd taken him all the way to the elbow. A fucking record—a pun, for Christ's sake, she thought, and the last thing she had on her mind was a pun, but she was incredibly proud of herself and she smiled her secret smile anyway. God, she must be deep. The notion thrilled her. Before she was finished, she'd find out just how deep she was, discover the length of what she could take. What if she managed to take his whole arm? In a flash of fantasy, she saw Stump just disappear from the sudsy bathwater as she, in one mighty effort, sucked him all the way up inside her.

"You remember when you took me over to Ted's trailer before you made the place your office that night when Johnson went over the edge and fell off his mind and commenced mopping me down in the bathtub with the Baby Rose Bud? That was a big event in my life, and I hope you haven't forgotten it already."

"Mabel, I won't ever forget that, the night of the bathtub. I mean," Too Much said. But she thought, Not for the reasons you think, though, and she smiled her secret smile again.

"Well, like I said. I smelled Ted as strong as if he'd been sitting there beside me. I couldn't have smelled him any stronger if he had been a fresh-dropped cow patty, no disrespect intended, if you get my meaning."

"I do get your meaning, honey," said Too Much. "I've seen that movie myself, wrote it, produced it, directed it, and starred in it. There are men in this world that the more they stink, the better they smell. But believe me, I am sorry."

"Don't be sorry," Mabel said. "You came right to my main point without missing a beat, Too Much. Before I threw in that first handful, I was wet. By the second handful, I had a wet-on you could've drowned a puppy in. And poor old Johnson sitting up there running that boat had no idea about what was going on."

"I wouldn't let it worry me," said Too Much. "Nobody talks about it much, but that kind of thing happens all the time. It's as common as field peas."

"And I can only say thank God for that. The last thing in the world I'm doing is worrying about it. On the other hand, there is a problem." But Too Much had already seen the problem. She just didn't know how she would go about solving it. So she let Mabel talk on. "The man I'm honing after . . . Do you know that saying, 'honing after'? Learned it from one of the socials the ladies and I have on Wednesday afternoon."

Sure that's where you learned it. A social, my ass, thought Too Much. Dishonest bitch. And then she wondered if she really disliked Mabel or just thought Mabel ought to be mutilated and then killed.

"But I'm getting right off my point."

"Don't think twice about it. I've got your point. I had your point before you ever made it," said Too Much. "As I told you, Mabel, I've been around most of the blocks a woman can go around."

"Girl, I sometimes think you're touched with magic!" exclaimed Mabel. "It's hard to believe, a young girl like you knowing what you know, being where you've been."

"Honey, just between you and me, I've always thought I was touched with magic too. And you're not the first one to think nearly everything about me's hard to believe."

Mabel leaned forward in her chair and hissed, "You're not even married to that chewed-up Stump either, are you?"

Too Much, who was working at her gum, didn't miss a beat. "I believe we were having a little talk about the man you're honing after. The one that's already been eaten by whatever lives at the bottom of the swamp."

"Precisely! And it's a hard thing, me honing for a man that's been burned up and eaten besides by all them blind things."

"Blind things?"

"Johnson told me all about it. Everything that lives at the bottom of the swamp is blind."

"If Johnson said it, it's most likely true. He knows more about that swamp than anybody else in Forever and Forever, including Stump. Stump likes to pretend it's not even out there."

"Johnson knows more about it than's good for him, I always thought."

"Probably," said Too Much. "But I don't think he can help it."

"God knows," said Mabel. "It's a lot in this old world we can't help. Now, you take Ted. I guess I've got to kiss his beautiful ass goodbye—I guess I can talk like that with just the two of us here—him being dead and already in the fire besides. But God knows I sure would have liked to feed in his lilies. 'Feed in his lilies'—that's another one I learned at our Wednesday afternoon socials. God, that's a good one. I can just say it out loud and get damp." She put her hand to her mouth. "And me a lady of a certain age too." And then she actually blushed.

Too Much only watched her blush and said nothing, but she thought, No, I don't hardly think so. You pulled that one right out of the hat where all the rest of us keep ours. If you could only manage to live without being ashamed of everything you think or want, you wouldn't be blushing now; if you could only come to peace with the hard truth that all the men and women of the world spend their lives looking at each other's asses. Nothing very strange in that. It seems to be a natural law, like gravity.

"No use waiting for it to stop," Too Much said. "Be grateful for what you've got. You could, you know, be suffering from a terminal case of dry socket. Women your age sometimes do, you know; not uncommon at all."

"Dry socket?"

"A minor nuisance that can be solved with a tube of K-Y lubricating jelly."

"What in the world's that?"

"Damn, Mabel, where'd you live your life?"

Mabel shifted on her haunches and took another bonbon, then said, "I'm not sure I ever had a life until Johnson mopped me in the tub." She put her chin in her hand and with the other hand rummaged through the box of empty bonbon wrappers. If Mabel was ever *really* in a pinch, Too Much wondered how many of those bonbons she could eat. "Being mopped in the tub woke something up in me," she said in a musing voice, almost as if she were talking to herself. "It was like being . . . I don't have the words for it. I can't say it."

"I can't either," said Too Much. "But I know. I surely know the place you're talking about."

Mabel looked up from the bonbon box, which was apparently empty, and said, "Damn, child, is there anywhere you haven't been?"

"My head tells me yes," said Too Much, "but my heart tells me no."

"Does your heart tell you what I'm going to do with this problem of mine?" Her voice was suddenly rough-edged, almost barking.

"I hope that's not sarcasm I hear."

"No such thing," said Mabel, dropping the bonbon box to the floor, the little empty wrappers spilling out on the rug. "Just occurred to me we didn't seem to be getting anywhere with my problem—some sort of solution, I mean."

"You got as far from your problem, and as close to it, as you're ever going to get when they torched Ted and sent him home in a bottle."

"What a horrible thing to say!"

"Why is it every time I tell the truth, that's what somebody says to me?"

"It was still horrible."

"And still true."

"I guess."

"Not guess, goddammit, you *know.*"

Mabel looked at the floor. "I know."

"That's better. Much better," Too Much said. "Now, what does that tell you?"

"What does what tell me?"

"What you said."

"Nothing."

"Which is why you have me. What it tells us, Mabel, is that our best shot—our only shot—is Johnson."

"It hurts me to say it, but there's been a falling-off between Johnson and me."

"I gathered as much when you started honing after a jarful of ashes."

"If you were my daughter, you wouldn't put things in such a dreadful way."

"If you were my mother, you'd be dead. Makes us even."

"The devil lives in your mouth. He could be the end of you yet, child."

"A lot of people have commenced calling me child. And I can't say as I like it. My goddam name is Too Much. And there's a good reason for me having that name. I know and see and feel and hate and love too fucking much. For instance, you didn't throw away all of Ted Johanson's ashes, did you? You didn't scatter all of Ted out there on the swamp. And you can go on and tell the truth, because I know it anyway."

"How did you know that!"

"It wasn't really hard to figure out."

"The devil does more than just live in your mouth, Too Much. He lives in your heart. You scare me sometimes."

"How much do you have left?"

"Of what?"

"Ted?"

"Lord God, I don't want to talk about that."

"You want me to help, do what I can? Then talk to me."

"I've got about one good handful of Ted left. He's in a Ziploc baggy over at the trailer. But I've got him put up real good, so Johnson won't stumble up on him."

"Johnson's not the sort of man who would care one way or the other about a man who's burned up and in a bottle anyhow. But you, Mabel, are the sort who might think about it a lot. Do you ever wonder what part of old Ted's in that Ziploc?"

"I don't know what you mean," Mabel said.

"Sure you do. You know exactly what I mean, thinking about it as much as you have. Could be a hand or maybe part of a foot, but late in the middle of the night, with old Johnson snoring away there beside you, we both know what's in that Ziploc, don't we, Mabel? At three o'clock in the morning and you burning up in a cold sweat, tossing in those sheets, it's Ted's cock in that Ziploc, am I right, Mabel?"

"You're the devil, doing the devil's work."

"Tell me something. Have you ever, in the middle of the night with the sweat running cold over your body, gone to that Ziploc bag, opened it, and touched it?"

"For mercy's sake, Too Much, touched what?"

"Mercy's got nothing to do with it. And you know exactly what you touched. You did touch it, right?"

Mabel averted her eyes. "Yes, I touched it."

"And that, Mabel, is precisely why you need my help."

"I don't see where it's any help you or anybody else can give."

"Ah," said Too Much, "but I'm not just anybody. I'm Too Much."

"Always something to be grateful for," Mabel said in a voice that was nearly a whisper.

"You've picked up Stump's way of talking."

"No offense intended."

"None taken. We've got more important things to do than sit

around being pissed off. We've got to get off our asses and go to war."

Mabel's wrinkled brow stretched as her eyes flared wider. "Did you say go to war?"

"I said it and I meant it, if that's what it takes. But it won't take war. A few threats maybe, but not war."

"I was never very good at threatening my brothers and sisters."

"One of my greatest virtues has always been threatening the human beast."

"Human *beast?*"

"Manner of speaking. And you really ought to have your ears checked one of these days. But right now, shut up and listen. Where's that fucking husband of yours?"

"You ought not to speak of Johnson like that."

"Probably not, since his whole problem seems to be fucking—or in your case, not fucking."

Mabel was blushing again. "None of this should have ever been brought out in the light of day. Some things were never meant to be public. We all have our crosses to bear."

Too Much leaned across on the couch and took Mabel's thin, birdlike shoulder in her hard little hand. "Mabel, you interested in the light of day and what ought to be public and bearing crosses, or you interested in nights loud with groaning and wet with the slap of sweating flesh? Now, which is it?"

Her eyes averted and blood running to the roots of her blue hair, Mabel said, "That other."

"Which other? I can do a lot of things, but I can't read minds. Say it! Which is it?"

"That last," she said, her voice soft, her eyes holding a thousand-yard stare at the far wall.

"Sorry, old girl, but that doesn't tell me enough. We'll talk again when you can speak English. When you know what you want and you're able to say it, say it all."

Mabel's head suddenly whipped around, and Mabel turned a face on Too Much she had never seen before. The lips were pulled back in a thin little snarl. Her hair seemed to have gone wild on her head, as her eyes, caught in a fine web of veins, leapt madly in their sockets. Tendons stretched and stood like wire in her thin neck. Her false teeth moved, and a little trail of drool slipped down her chin. Mabel took no notice of it.

When Mabel spoke, it was a sharp hissing a snake might have made. "You can't leave anybody anything, can you? You've got to take everything and leave us naked and hurt. All right! I want the slap of wet meat in the middle of the night. I want to be out of my head, lost and not even caring, in the middle of groaning and moaning, and then . . . then, by Jesus, I want to come like the end of the world. Fucking come like the end of the fucking world!"

Too Much reached out and put both her arms around Mabel's thin shoulders and drew her into a tight embrace. Mabel was crying now, making no sound but crying still, tears running on the horribly twisted, snarling face. Mabel allowed herself to be drawn in and comforted much as a child might do, but her own arms were rigid at her sides.

Too Much's voice was soothing and gentle again, much like a mother might have used with a child. "There, you've said it. You've got it all out. Do you know what you just told me? Do you understand what you just admitted to me and to yourself?" Mabel did not speak, but her rigid arms went limp at her sides and her face fell back into its old lines of despair and desperation. Too Much said, "You've just said what the whole race of beasts want to say, scream for, beg for, even: They want to be young again and stay young forever, with the blood pumping all over again the way it once pumped, pumping again that way and never stopping."

Mabel drew a little way back. "I never said nothing about wanting to be young."

"Hush," said Too Much. "It's all right. It only makes you part of the beast in all of us."

"Even if what you said was true—and I'm not saying it is—it wouldn't do me any good. There's nothing to do for what I am: old and worn out." She made no sound, but tears burst from her eyes again and wet her cheeks. "And it's the worst, bitterest thing that ever happened to me."

"You don't have to be anything you don't want to be."

"Why not?"

"Because you've got me." Too Much held up her small, thickly muscled hands. "Because we've got these. These and *belief.* There's life and death in these hands, Mabel, if you believe there is. Can you believe, Mabel?"

Mabel looked into Too Much's eyes for a long moment. "Yes, I can believe. With you to help me, Too Much, I can believe anything."

"Let's go find Johnson and the Old Ones and Justice, and straighten out some things around here."

Chapter 17

They found Johnson sitting on a warped wooden bench in the partial shade of a dying magnolia tree on the high ground that sloped down toward the dock on the edge of the swamp. His thin legs were crossed at the knees and his hands were behind his head, his fingers interlocked.

"There he is, the old fart," said Mabel, as soon as she saw him, "wasting his time just as hard as he can, just as he always does."

"You let me handle this, Mabel," said Too Much.

Johnson was watching the Old Ones being herded about a hundred yards or so down the slope by Justice, swatting first one of them, and then another with a thin stick he carried, swatting them not hard but not easy either, directing them to pick the tiniest bits of debris—pieces of cups, napkins, plastic spoons and forks, bits of white paper sacking—out of the grass and place them in a five-gallon metal bucket.

He carried his stick—a thin, limber branch he'd found somewhere—like an officer's swagger stick, and as he strutted about, he slapped it against the loose folds of his denim trousers from time to time and called, "Come on now dere, git it up and git it out! Man don't pay you to move lak yo sleepwalkin out here. Bend to it! Justice want to see him some sweat, want to see sumpin happnin. Git it and go, by God! I ain't got dis whup to make me look purty. Come down on you an put a hump in yo back is whut I do. Wanta see nothin but assholes an elbows."

Too Much and Mabel moved up behind the bench on which Johnson was sitting without him hearing them. He had his face tilted back, taking the sun.

"Johnson, what do you think you're doing?" Too much asked in a quiet, almost conversational voice.

Johnson did not even turn to look at her, and when he spoke, it was obvious he had been dozing. "Taking my ease, Too Much. Just taking my ease." He paused and yawned, the old flesh that hung along his jaw stretching thin. "Taking my ease and taking care of business, just like you see out there, doing exactly what you told me to do." He unlocked his liver-spotted hands from behind his head and waved one of them toward the Old Ones.

In a voice sudden and strident, Mabel said, "Who told you to let Justice beat those poor souls, Johnson Meechum? You're in a world of hurt and don't even know it."

Johnson jumped at the sound of his wife's voice, and his head swiveled on his thin neck as he looked up at her, his eyes wide and suddenly very much awake. "Didn't know you were back there, honey. Thought it was just Too Much. Too Much told me to delegate authority to save me strain on myself. Ask her if she didn't."

"I don't have to ask. And don't be honeying me, sitting out here bossing the helpless and the hopeless."

"I asked you to let me handle this," said Too Much in the same quiet voice.

"I've spent sixty years trying to handle him. He can't be handled. The space between his ears is all air. He was never in his whole life anything but a walking dick, and now he isn't even that."

"Now, Mabel, don't act like this out here in front of Too Much," Johnson said.

"Besides a walking dick, he was a thief as well, but the jailhouse squeezed the larceny right out of his blood, just like you'd squeeze the water out of a mop." She looked about wildly for an instant, as though she had just suddenly remembered some horror she had forgotten, and then said, "*Mop!* I ought to wring your skinny neck like a chicken and throw you in a pot for the dogs to eat."

"Mabel," said Too Much, whose voice was entirely too calm to be anything but scary.

"What?"

"Shut up. Now! Right *now!* I don't want to hear another word."

Mabel's red face went a shade darker, but she kept her thin lips clamped together as she looked from Johnson to Too Much and back again.

Johnson said, "You ladies can go on back in the trailer, where it's cool. I've got everything covered out here." He turned to focus on Too Much. "Don't I have everything looking just like you said you wanted it? You said you wanted it clean, and it's just about as clean as it can get, wouldn't you say?"

"What I'd say you wouldn't want to hear," Too Much said.

Johnson opened his mouth as though he would speak but seemed to think better of it and clamped his lips tightly together.

Too Much looked down toward the water's edge and called, "Justice."

Justice, who had had his back to them since they'd come out to stand behind Johnson sitting on the bench, jerked his head around and dropped his switch at the same time. "Sho now, Missy," and he ducked his head as though avoiding a blow.

"Pick that stick up and get on up here."

"Whut stick dat, Missy Too Much, ma'm?"

"Don't make me say it again," said Too Much.

Slowly, as though it hurt him to bend, he picked up the stick he had dropped and came slowly up the slope, his baggy pants flapping about his legs. He stopped a good ten yards in front of the bench, his head still dropped forward as though he were searching for something on the ground.

"You like to hit people with sticks, Justice?" Too Much asked.

"Say whut?" And then he looked at the stick in his hand as though he were surprised to find it there. When Too Much kept silent, he finally looked up at her and said, "You mean this here stick right here?" he said, holding the stick as far away from himself as he could.

"Don't play with me, Justice," Too Much said, for the first time with considerable heat in her voice. "You know I don't play."

"Ennythin Justice know, he know Missy Too Much don play."

"Then talk straight to me. I don't have time to jack around out here with you all day."

"I know dat ain nothin but de truf."

"Then tell me what was going on when I came out here and saw you on the old people with that stick? Have you lost your mind, for God's sake?"

"Mistuh Johnson done gib me dem Old Ones an told me to git errythin clean as a houn's tooth round about down in here, to git it cleaner dan I had it."

"I delegated authority to you, Justice," said Johnson, a little desperate. "Now, didn't I tell you that? Didn't I say I was delegating authority to you to get the job done, get everything cleaned up right and proper?"

Justice only stared back at him, nothing showing in his old black face. Then he looked up at the cloudless sky for a moment before he turned to look at the Old Ones, all of whom had stopped stock-still and herded closer together.

Too Much said to Johnson, "Did you actually use that word with Justice? Did you really tell him you were *delegating* authority to him?"

Johnson looked confused for a moment and then said, "I think I did. Yes, that's what I said. God, that was wrong, wasn't it?"

"No wonder you were a bank president. You're just about that bright. You might as well have spoken to him in Russian."

"You sorry sack of—"

"Hush, Mabel." Too Much turned back to Johnson. "And I don't guess you saw what he had in his hand and was using on the Old Ones?"

Johnson didn't say anything. He looked off toward the far edges of the swamp.

"He seed me," said Justice. "How he *not* gone see me? An he ain say sheet. Sides, you got to prod dem Old Ones hard to git dere tention, leastwise what Mr. Johnson say, git'm movin lak dey means it."

"And you thought that was a good idea, did you?" said Mabel.

Johnson thought about that a minute, or seemed to, and then said, "I didn't think about it that way, but I guess you're right."

Too Much said, "You didn't think about it *that way*? You didn't think about it. Period. And the stick, Johnson? Did you give it to him?"

"Of course not. It would never enter my mind to do such a thing."

"My God! I've known dips and I've known dips, but you are entirely in a class by yourself."

"Try to shut up, Mabel," said Too Much, without looking at Mabel. "Put your mind to it and just try."

"I'd appreciate it," said Johnson.

"Right now I don't care what you'd appreciate," said Too Much. "I've just heard her too many times already."

"I guess I bettuh git on back to dem Old Ones," said Justice, pointing off behind him, where those he had been driving with the stick were herded even closer around their five-gallon metal bucket, looking apparently at nothing, not even each other, with their rheumy, glazed eyes.

"I guess you better stay right where you are. If I look, I don't even want to see you breathing," Too Much said. "We got something to get to the bottom of. On the whole scale of what's going on in Forever and Forever right now, this doesn't even register, but we've still got to do something about it."

That seemed to startle Johnson. "How's that again?" he said. "What?"

"You dimwit," said Mabel.

Too Much glanced at her but said nothing. She looked back at Johnson and then turned from Johnson and studied Justice. "You picked the stick up, then?"

"Sho now. How else it come in my han?"

"Why?"

His eyes opened a little wider, and he turned to glance at the

Old Ones before looking back at Too Much, his face closing on itself in a brief fist of wrinkles before he finally lifted his thin winglike shoulders in a shrug.

"You posed to."

"Why?"

"If you be waking folks, you posed to have you a stick. You lay it on'm, dey wake lak de debil den. You got to poke'm and whup'm. Whup'm good an dey wake good. Errybody know dat."

"Tell me, Justice," Too Much said, as though talking to a child of her own whom she loved but whom she recognized as being a little retarded nonetheless. He had to be taught, but taught slowly. And she was doing it with the tenderest kind of concern. "In your whole life, did you ever have a stick in your hand to poke and whip the work out of people?"

"What the hell is this?" demanded Johnson.

"Shut up, Johnson. I'll tell you when to talk."

Justice looked at the ground. "You know I ain nevuh had no whup. I be de nigger in Forever and Forever." He paused and looked directly into her eyes. "I be de nigger since my ole ma bloodied me into de world, and I be de nigger when dey put me in de hole and shovel de dirt on my nigger face."

His voice had grown stronger as he talked, and even his bony spine straightened; his thin shoulders pulled back, raising his chin. It was as though some unthinkable revelation was trying to take form somewhere in the recesses of his mind.

"But the stick came natural to your hand today when Johnson turned over the Old Ones to you?"

Justice said nothing, but his dim eyes held hers.

"Did it feel good?" asked Too Much.

The answer was immediate and strong. "It be de mos wonderful thin in de world to me. Howsomever, it be de mos terrible thin in de world to me."

"Don't let it rattle you, Justice. You just played white man for a while. A natural thing. You understand?"

"Not one wade you say, if yo wants de truf."

"Ditto for me," said Johnson.

Too Much glanced briefly at Johnson. "If I'd thought you would have understood, I'd have been talking to you." Then she turned back to Justice. "Don't worry about understanding. You will. Believe me, you will. Now, go take the Old Ones home." As Justice turned to go, she said, "And Justice." He stopped and looked back at her. "The cat comes out of the ground today. I'll dig'm up and burn him myself. And I'll burn the picture with him. It's over. The cat's out of your life forever. I give you my word."

Justice said, "How come dat?"

"Because now you're the man you always were but didn't know it. Nobody has a claim on Justice but Justice."

Justice shook his head. "I don know nothin I didn't know when de sun come up dis moanin."

"Oh, but you do," said Too Much. She went around the bench and hugged him briefly. "Now, go get the Old Ones."

"Thank you, Missy Too Much, ma'm."

"Just Too Much, Justice. To you, forever and forever, Justice, my name will always be Too Much. And *only* Too Much. You remember that."

Justice turned and looked down toward the old people and then back at Too Much. "I member." Then he inclined his head toward her in a simple formal gesture and said in a quiet statement, "Too Much."

"Justice," she said.

Justice turned and, his trousers flapping about his thin shanks, moved off toward the Old Ones.

"Well," said Mabel, "that's that. At least we cleaned up the mess you managed to make, dipshit."

"How much longer you plan to call me that?" said Johnson.

"As long as it feels good," said Mabel, slapping Johnson on the shoulder.

"I think you've made your point," said Johnson. "I think we can go now."

"Not quite," said Too Much. "We're not finished here."

"What else is left to be done?" He stretched his neck to look around, the tendons standing out in the wrinkled skin of his throat.

"You," said Too Much.

"I don't understand," said Johnson.

"I know you don't," Too Much said. "That's why you still have to be done."

"Done, you say?"

"And Mabel."

Mabel, who had been grinning at Johnson's confusion, frowned and barked, "What?"

"Keep a civil tongue and watch that tone of voice with me. You're warped, Mabel, and I mean to straighten you out. I mean to straighten both of you out. I've got too much invested in you to watch you keep acting like beasts."

"Beasts?" demanded Mabel.

"Shut up," said Too Much, almost kindly. "It's object-lesson time."

"What's an object lesson?" asked Mabel. "That is, if I'm still allowed to talk."

"You spent all these years with me," said Johnson, "and you don't know what an object lesson is?"

"You could have taught me, you know," said Mabel. "It's not against the law to talk to your wife."

"Precisely," said Too Much. "Follow me."

"Where are we going?" asked Johnson.

Too Much did not look at him when she said, "The time for talking is over. It's time to act."

Johnson licked his dry lips and said nothing. He and Mabel followed Too Much down the slope to the edge of the swamp. Too Much stopped and looked into the shallow edge of the water for a long minute. Then she shook her head. "I don't think this is the place." She walked slowly on around the weedy shoreline, with Mabel and Johnson following. Finally she stopped.

"This is it," she said.

Mabel and Johnson stared hard at the water. And then Johnson said: "What?"

"The place."

"And what place would that be?" said Mabel. She was beginning to sweat, and tiny insects bumped about her face, which was red and frowning. Too Much looked at her and suppressed a smile. Mabel was not a happy camper at the moment, thought Too Much, if, indeed, she ever had been.

"What is this place you've stopped here at anyway?" Mabel said, pointing down toward the swamp.

"The place your entire married life with Johnson has been leading you."

"You're not making sense," said Johnson.

"And neither has your life," said Too Much. "But don't beat on yourself too much about it. Most lives don't. That's why they get warped now and then and have to be straightened out. And I've found that sometimes you have to go straight to an object lesson as a last resort."

"I wish you'd quit saying that unless you're going to tell me what it means," said Mabel.

"You never *tell* an object lesson, Mabel. That's the beauty of it. A lot of learning but little talk. Talk's so cheap it buys nearly nothing. At least with some people. And with people like that, the last thing it buys is understanding. Now get in there."

"What?" said Mabel. "In where?"

"If I had to guess," said Too Much, "I'd say it was a hundred-odd thousand acres—give or take—of swamp behind you. I think you can figure it out."

"You're not making sense, Too Much. You haven't made a whole lot of sense all morning."

"Let's make it easy," said Too Much. "Turn and face me."

Mabel turned around and, with her back to the swamp, faced Too Much.

Too Much said, "Now take about four good steps backward."

Mabel glanced briefly over her shoulder. "Do, I'll be in the water."

"Now you're getting the idea. But not even up to your knees, I wouldn't think."

"It's things in there that are slimy and squiggly," said Mabel, her voice dropping into a little girl's whine.

"Blind too," said Johnson. "Blind as a bat and slimy and squiggly, that's what's in there all right." His fake teeth fairly danced in his mouth as he smiled and talked at the same time. He didn't know what was happening and he didn't give a damn. Watching Mabel being made to back into the swamp was more than he could have hoped for on the best day he ever had.

"I wouldn't think that bottom was none too safe," said Mabel, turning her head to stare at the black water.

"I can tell you for sure it's not," said Johnson. He was about to lose his teeth; the look that had come on Mabel's face might just cause him to break a rib. But hell, it was hard to have any sympathy for anybody whose shit always carried the faintest scent of almonds. "That bottom's liable to swallow you like quicksand," he said. "Then again it might not. I hear Stump went under and nearly didn't get back out again. But you won't know till you try it. That's what an object lesson's all about." He didn't have the foggiest notion of what he was saying, but he sure did like the way it was scaring the hell out of Mabel.

"Since you know all about it, you can go first," said Too Much.

"How's that?"

"Get your ass in that water, Johnson."

"A damn cottonmouth moccasin couldn't make me get in that water."

"But I could, couldn't I?"

Johnson thought a minute. "If you can't have it any other way."

"I can't. Take Mabel's hand."

Now there was no hesitation. Johnson reached out and took his wife's hand. Mabel's hand caught his and gripped it hard enough to turn her misshapen knuckles white.

"Now, I don't want to hear a goddam word. Just back into that water."

They had only taken two steps back into the black and brackish water when they both began to sink.

"We're sinking," said Johnson.

"Yes, you are, aren't you?" said Too Much.

"We may never get out," said Mabel.

"This could be your last chance of ultimate possibility. And the last one is always death. And the blind slimy things will eat your eyes."

"You're scaring me."

"You wouldn't be human if you weren't scared."

"I thought you were my friend," said Mabel.

"And so I am," said Too Much. "But friendship sometimes has to be a very hard thing. For instance, you have to take another step back now."

"I'll be damned if I will," said Johnson, his voice cracking.

"You'll be damned if you won't. And you know it."

Johnson immediately took another step back, and so tightly did he hold Mabel's hand that she had no choice but to step back with him. Their feet made sucking sounds as they pulled them out of the mud to step back. It was only with great effort that either of them was able to do it.

Mabel looked down at the black water swirling at her feet. "How far do we have to go back in this? It can't be very sanitary."

"The last thing it is is sanitary," said Too Much. "But you have to keep going until you get to where you need to be."

"Well, how far is that, dammit?" asked Johnson.

"I think I'll know when you get there."

"You think? Is that what you said?" asked Johnson, a vein of rank fear and anger forking over his nose and across his forehead into his freckled scalp.

Too Much did not answer. She only squatted on her haunches and chewed on a blade of grass, watching as they sank at a fairly even rate now, about an inch a minute. They were both over hip deep, and Mabel's skirt ballooned around her as she went down.

"You don't know what you're doing," said Mabel, as she tried to push her skirt down but gave it up as impossible now that it was was spread out all around her chest, just below her armpits. Tears had started in her eyes. "We could die in here."

"That's not my intention. I brought you here to teach you something, not to kill you."

"Then you don't have to do all this," said Johnson, trying to make his voice calm and reasonable but not succeeding. It was full of terror. The water was at his collarbone. Beside him, Mabel had forgotten all about her dress ballooning around her, because even with her neck stretched as much as she could stretch it, the water was lapping at her chin. "No. Hell, no," said Johnson, right on the edge of screaming and no longer trying to hide his fear. "This is not necessary . . . necessary . . . necessary . . ." He'd got momentarily stuck on the word and could not get off it.

"Try not to babble, Johnson," said Too Much calmly.

"I'm not babbling. I'm about to die, goddammit," Johnson screamed.

"You're not going to die. I'll get you out in time," said Too Much. She took the blade of grass from her mouth and looked at it for a moment. "If I can, that is."

"What the hell happens if you can't?" said Johnson, his voice breaking in a glassy way that Too Much had never heard before.

Mabel, her wide-eyed face as immobile as a death mask and her complexion slightly greenish, said nothing. If she had tried to speak, her mouth would have filled with swamp water. But then, as if on some silent command from Too Much, they stopped sinking as suddenly as though they had hit solid stone under the mud.

Mabel leaned her head back and spoke directly toward the sky to avoid getting a mouthful of water and said, in the happiest voice Too Much had ever heard from her, "We stopped. Praise God, we stopped."

"You did," said Too Much. "You stopped."

"Why, do you suppose?" said Johnson. "I thought we were goners for sure. I know there's a sandstone bottom under this whole swamp, all at different depths though. Maybe we just got lucky and hit it."

"Could be," said Too Much. "But I don't much think so. Luck for me has always come in one flavor: bad. No, I think this is something else."

"Where are we, then?" asked Johnson.

"Right where you need to be, I'd say." Too Much took the blade of grass out of her mouth and stared at the frayed end she'd been chewing.

"And where's that?" asked Mabel, her head back, but still risking a throatful of water.

"Chin deep in the rankest shit within a hundred miles in any direction."

"This is no time to be joking," Johnson said.

"If I sounded like I was joking," said Too Much, "that's all right with me. But do you feel like where you are right now is a joke?"

"It feels like suicide," gasped Johnson.

"Murder," said Mabel, ignoring the water trickling into the sides of her mouth. "And if we die, it's on your hands. You killed us." Then she spouted water out of her mouth in an arching column over her head like a breaching whale.

"That wouldn't be a whole lot of consolation to you, I wouldn't think," Too Much said. "You'd still be dead as anybody's likely to get."

"Oh, God!" gurgled Mabel. "I feel'm." And then she sent a thin stream of water into the air again. "They slick and slimy." This time she swallowed the water before she could spit it out.

"Most likely blind too," said Johnson with some satisfaction.

"They'll get you too, you bastard," she said, swallowing the swamp water that had filled her mouth with hardly a pause.

Too Much could see that Mabel seemed to be getting the technique of disposing of the swamp water down pretty good. And the look in her eyes as she cut them toward Johnson was filled with rage and outrage. The human beast, thought Too Much. The miserable, implacable human beast was as predictable as the tides of the sea it had crawled out of in the long ago. Too Much knew in her blood and bone that Mabel would have killed her husband in that instant had it been possible. And the knowledge surprised her not in the least.

"Can't," said Johnson, his eyes on Mabel now. "Nothing slick and slimy and probably blind too can get me." It was as if both of them had completely forgotten that Too Much was squatting on the shore directly in front of them and that they themselves were in imminent danger of death. "I got britches on and my shirt tucked in. Your dress is floating over your head, and that ass of yours is hanging out for every slick and slimy thing that wants to take him a bite. Just your good luck they all blind. If they could see, that ugly shitter of yours would scare every living thing in the swamp to death."

"You are a goddam sorry man, Johnson Meechum." She got the entire sentence out before she had to swallow a mouthful of water.

Too Much couldn't help noticing that Mabel's rage was so maniacal that she no longer seemed to mind having to drink swamp water if that was the price of keeping the argument going between her and her husband.

"And you are the sorriest woman that ever shit behind two shoes," Johnson said.

Too Much thought "the sorriest woman that ever shit behind two shoes" was a pretty damn good line, but her point had been made, and besides, whatever patience and compassion she had ever had with either Mabel or Johnson and their predicament was gone.

In the quietest of voices, Too Much said, "Johnson."

His head snapped around and he looked at her, his face filled with surprise and astonishment. Too Much had been right. He had forgotten all about her squatting there not twenty feet away. And Mabel's reaction was so violent that she actually went underwater, and it was a long moment before she could get her face back up to breathing again, spouting water as she surfaced.

"Did you hear what that son of a bitch said about my . . . well, my dress being up and what was showing and what the slick and slimy things might do?"

"Slick, slimy, and blind," said Johnson. "Don't forget blind."

"I haven't forgotten a goddam thing," said Mabel. Then, after a pause to spit a long stream of water into the air, "And you won't forget either, once I get out of this stinking mess."

"Good choice of words, Mabel. Maybe you can go on with your lives now that you both understand that sixty years of living together has brought your marriage to a stinking mess. And if it's one thing I can't stand, it's a stinking mess."

"I'll do what I goddam well please. And Mabel will too," said Johnson.

"No you won't, because I live in the same world with you. And the world right now happens to be Forever and Forever. I tried everything I could with both of you, and you beat me. I don't like to get beat, but sometimes I do. There's no shame in getting beat, though, only shame in staying beat."

"Jesus Christ!" said Johnson suddenly. "I believe I'm beginning to slip!" And he was. Almost imperceptibly, the last of his skinny neck sank, and the black swamp water lapped at his chin. He stared wildly at Too Much. "Do you mean to help us or just sit up there and watch us drown?"

"To tell you the truth," said Too Much, "watching you drown doesn't seem like such a bad idea right now."

"You can't mean that," said Johnson.

"The hell I can't. Sixty years married, and the two of you can't find anything better to do than to stay in a constant fight."

"We'll change," said Johnson, "won't we, Mabel?"

Mabel rolled her eyes from Too Much to Johnson, but she couldn't speak without risking drowning.

"This is murder," Johnson said.

"More like suicide, I'd say," said Too Much. "I didn't put you in that water. You backed into it of your own free will." She paused a moment. "Just about the way you fucked up your marriage."

"Thank God, there's Stump," said Johnson. "Stuuummmppp!" he called, making a sound like a bull moose in high rut.

Too Much turned and looked back up the slope, where Stump stood with his camera pressed to his face.

"Yo, campers!" called Stump. "Say 'cheese.'"

Johnson smiled, and his teeth floated out of his mouth and sank in the black water. Stump walked down to where they were and dropped onto his haunches beside Too Much. His breath was strong with the odor of whiskey.

"That's gone make one helluva picture," Stump said. "Johnson, how'd you and your old lady come to be in the swamp like this?"

Johnson looked toward Too Much. "She's trying to kill us."

Stump sat on his haunches very still for a very long moment and then said, "Somehow, I could believe that." He turned to look at Too Much, who had her arm stretched back through her legs and was giving her stretched cheeks a brutal workout, making soft moaning noises deep in her throat as she did. "You thinking to kill'm, Too Much? Is that what you doing?"

"Nope," she said without looking at him. "I was trying out a little marriage counseling on Mabel and Johnson."

"Well, I'll be damned. Marriage counseling, you say? Is it anything you can't do?"

"If it is, I haven't found it. But I don't think I've had much luck here. These two have been disturbing my tranquillity. Now that Forever and Forever is mine, my tranquillity is not allowed to be disturbed. Everybody's got to toe the line, so we can have celebration, joy, maybe even happiness."

"Get us out, or Mabel'll drown here in a minute," Johnson said.

Stump ignored him. For the first time since she had started working with her arm reached back between her legs, plowing the mellow yellow furrow between her stretched cheeks with her long fingernails, Stump raised his eyes to her face, his forehead knotted and wrinkled now in what could have been only confusion or the beginning of anger. "Either my hearing's gone bad or you misspoke yourself."

"I never misspeak myself."

"The last time I checked, Forever and Forever belonged to me."

"When's the last time you checked?"

With his mouth already open to speak, Stump saw Justice, not thirty feet away, coming toward them, carrying a coiled rope in his hand. Stump's face flushed with blood, and his eyes were suddenly caught in a web of veins.

"Come on, you black fucker," cried Stump. "I'm gone show you what happens to niggers that throw this ole boy into a goddam swamp."

Justice stopped and dropped the rope he had been carrying. "Ain't de nigger no mo," Justice said softly. "Used to be de nigger. Now I's Justice. Too Much took de nigger off me an made me nuttin but Justice."

Stump started up the slope, saying, "I'll show you what you are, by God!"

Justice bent to his shoe. When he straightened up, the sun glittered off the blade of a straight razor.

"Come on, mofo. Justice be takin dat other hand off. Hell, yo don need it. Yo don do shit roun about down in here wit it nohow."

"Now Justice ain't even the nigger no more!" said Stump, grabbing his head with his good hand. "What's going on here anyway?"

Behind him, Too Much said, "Among other things, I think Mabel's drowning."

Justice hopped from foot to foot and waved his thin arms and started screaming, "Wherebouts Miz Mabel?"

Stump looked up the slope toward the rows of trailers and shouted for somebody to call 911. Some residents were playing shuffleboard by the pool, but they didn't even turn to look at him. Only Too Much remained utterly calm. It was as if she were accustomed to having people drown in front of her every day.

"You two get Mabel," she said calmly, slipping out of her sandals. "I'll take care of Johnson. And you can stop yelling about 911. If somebody happens to look down here and figures out what's going on, maybe they'll call. But otherwise have you forgot where you are? This is the land of the blind and mute, the dead and dying. Along with everything else, nobody's ears work."

As she talked, she had eased into the water, never touching the bottom but rather floating on her flat little belly on top of the black water, but when she got to Johnson and took his head in her hands to turn him face up so he could breathe freely, his arms, muddy and covered with green algae, grabbed at her to pull her down with him. She easily avoided his arms and at the same time gave him a short, chopping right on the point of his chin with her hard little fist. When his arms dropped, she put her hand on his forehead and held him underwater.

"Christ," said Stump from where he knelt on the edge of the shore. "If you want him to die, just leave him alone and the swamp will take care of it."

"At least I'm in the water with him," Too Much said.

"Looks to me like you trying to drown him."

Too Much gave him a cruel, thin, little smile. "With some people you have to do something radical before you can hope to help them with whatever trouble they may be in." She jerked Johnson's head out of the water and spoke loudly into the ear nearest her. "Do you want me to drown you?"

Johnson's wild eyes rolled, and his tongue, black with mud, hung out of his mouth. He shook his head no, apparently unable to speak.

"Then relax," she said. "Too Much has never lost one of her own in a crisis."

On the shore, Justice was not cooperating at all. Stump ran up and got the rope Justice had dropped in the grass. He handed it to Justice.

"Git in there and see if you can get it around her and under her arms. Maybe we can pull her out."

"Maybe yo can shit too," said Justice. "Yo *know* whut all be in dat water."

Stump said, "I'd do it myself, but that rope'd be hard to wrap around her with only one hand and this nub. Too Much is in there, and she ain't nothing but a yearling girl. If she can do it, you can do it. Now git on in there."

"Yo don know whut Too Much be. She be born knowin errythin bout slick and slimy thins dat be blind besides and stay in de swamp. Ain't nothin in de swamp or out de swamp gone mess in Too Much's shit."

"Git in or git dead," said Stump. "You owe me. I took you off the streets when you had nowhere to go."

"I *know* dat be right. You take ole Justice in to be yo nigger. An I been de best nigger I could. But dat shit gone now. I taken and given up bein de nigger. Yeah, dat shit be gone now fo shore. Over de hill an far away. Sides, Johnson shoot dis swamp erry day, but he ain kilt it yet. Errybody in Forever and Forever know dat."

Too Much, who was using a kick that made her feet beat in a blur of black froth, had Johnson's shoulders out of the water. Suddenly, her feet slowed, and she turned to look at the shore over her shoulder. "Justice, get in the water and get the job done," Too Much said, her voice so soft, the words hardly carried to the shore. "And get in *now.*"

He responded so quickly that he didn't even stop to take his shoes off his sockless feet. With one end of the rope in his mouth, he dog-paddled out to where Mabel had gone down. Quicker than Stump would have thought possible, Justice had the rope securely tied about her.

"Awright," said Justice, "pull er on outta here."

Stump held the other end of the rope in his hand but did not move. "Why did you do that?" he asked Justice. "You weren't gone do it when I told you to."

"Pull er out, you white mofo," said Justice, coming out of the water covered with stinking mud and algae. "She probly daid by now anyway, but I got er tied on, so goddammit, pull."

Stump looked at Too Much and said, "Why'd he do that for you and not for me?"

Too Much was gasping for breath as she finally pulled Johnson out of the water. She stood up quickly and took the rope attached to Mabel and wrapped it around her waist and backed up, snapping it taut. "I told you. I own the place and everybody in it. You plan on helping me here or just keep standing there hustling your balls with that one good hand and spitting?"

"We've got to talk," Stump said.

"All we've got to do right now," Too Much said, "is pull an old lady—who's more than likely dead—out of your swamp."

Chapter 18.

On his way down the narrow hallway from the bedroom to the kitchen, Stump paused at the open door of his bathroom. The huge tub seemed even bigger empty than it did filled with water. It had been four days now—or at least this was the morning of the fourth day—since there had been water in it. Stump could smell the stink in the tangled hair of his armpits and the sour odor of his crotch, urine-tainted and stained by dirty-handed pissing and by three days and four nights without a bath. But by God, he'd promised himself he would leave off with the whiskey, which he had been not so much drinking as pouring down his throat steadily and savagely the last three days—leave off with the whiskey and scour himself down with hot water and soap. Not by sitting in that goddam monster tub alone, though. He could not bear that. For the first time ever, he would use the showerhead he'd had installed above it when he knocked down a wall and put in the huge tub to accommodate Too Much's circus act.

He glanced briefly at the showerhead now before his eyes dropped again to the tub, which yawned monstrously before him like the scariest question God ever imagined. But he thought he could at least stand in the fucking thing without Too Much naked beside him.

Too Much naked beside him!

Just the thought was enough to make every cell in his body scream for a long—really long—drink of Wild Turkey. But he could not stay in this mothering trailer another day, or he would surely go crazy. He had to sober up and get up! Dry out and get out! It was balls-to-the-walls time!

He tried to tell himself he was overreacting. But that didn't work. That *hadn't* worked. That *wouldn't* work. The seams of his world had come unraveled. There was madness everywhere, down all the narrow macadam streets of Forever and Forever. He did not know the face of it. He did not know the reason for it. But still it was snarling—growling and prowling—out there, just beyond the walls of his trailer. He knew it was, even though when he cocked his head and listened, the explosive silence made him feel stranded, abandoned on the planet.

Stump suddenly turned and walked down the hallway to the kitchen and on into the sitting room. Every blind was drawn. He put his whiskey-betrembled hand on the bottom slat of one of the blinds as though to lift it, but he knew he would not. Even drunk he had done it only once, and he knew there was not enough whiskey in the world to make him do it again. He would have to be sober and do it on sheer guts and will . . . maybe. The only way to know if he could or could not, was to try it.

First he had to take a sane shower, sanely shave his sane face, put on some sane—completely sane—clothes, open the sane door to his sane trailer, and step out into a world of what he could only think of as complete *madness.* He turned from the drawn shade and went resolutely back down the hall to the bathroom and stood in the door and watched the empty tub and felt his resolve leave him as he saw her all over again: Too Much rising out of the steaming water, her muscled belly beading and flexing.

"What? What the . . . ?" he had said, seeing her.

She reached for a towel and started drying herself. For the briefest moment, she stopped and looked at him, the towel held now between her legs with her right hand while with her other hand she caught and rigorously scratched each of her nipples, first the right one, then the left. But she did not answer as she passed the towel on between her legs and up the flexed jaws of her ass, at the same time shaking her head in a way that made her hair whip about her face. Stump stood in the door naked and confused and intimidated in a way he did not understand. She seemed angry. And if anybody should be angry, it was he, Stump. That she was angry—or just pretending to be angry—made no sense. None at all. She had told him to run a hot tub so she could clean up from the swamp, and he'd done just that. But she didn't come until the water was cold, so he had drained it and run another. He'd been running fucking hot baths for three days and four nights, avoiding cleaning up himself so that he could go into the tub with her and pray that she would feel inclined to work her circus act. And when she got around to coming back, she slipped into his trailer and into his tub while he lay naked and drunk in his bed. She'd already stripped herself of mud and algae before her splashing woke him and brought him staggering down the hall to stand in the door and watch her rise out of the tub into the steaming air.

"You're not making sense," he said, and as he spoke, he was surprised to feel his face go numb with what he recognized as the numbness of fear. He could remember screaming in the middle of an exploding firefight, screaming and screaming, with flares hanging in the night sky over some meaningless hill in Korea, but never being able to feel his deadened lips move in the screaming. And that was the same numbness that had him now as he watched her not making sense. None at all.

"None at all," he said. And then, "Sense, I mean."

She stopped with one beautiful foot up on the side of the tub, where she bent and did not so much dry her long, thin, suckable toes as she scratched them with the towel. She looked up at him through the thick wet strands of her hair.

"Did somebody tell you that something—or anything, for that matter—would make sense?"

"You know what I mean," he said.

"No, I don't," she said. "But what I did was the only sensible—if you insist on talking about sense—the only sensible thing I could have done."

"Johnson and Mabel could've drowned," Stump said.

"But they didn't," Too Much said.

"What if I hadn't looked out the window and seen what you was doing and come running? What if Justice—a goddam nigger that don't make sense no more neither, now that I think of it—what if Justice hadn't seen the same thing and come running with that rope?"

She was out of the tub now. The water was dark with swamp mud. The huge new tube of K-Y that Stump had put out in an unjustified moment of optimism just that morning lay untouched on the flat rim at the head of the tub.

"But you did," she said. "And he did."

"Mabel and Johnson all right?" said Stump. "Where you got'm at anyhow?"

She had a fresh pair of cut-offs in her hands. Stump had not seen her get them. He had not seen *anything* since she had come in and it infuriated him.

"If they weren't all right, would I be here?" she said. "And the two of them are in their trailer. Where else would they be? Go over there and have yourself a look. You won't believe it. In there together and happy as pigs in shit. On second thought, go a little later; they hard at work right now. Least they better be. But in a while, check'm out."

"That'll be the last place I go," he said, staring at the K-Y. "And happy? Them? In the same trailer? You must think I fell off the turnip truck yesterday. I don't believe a fucking word of it either."

"That's just how come I've decided on my course of action," she said. "I don't think you believe in anything, least of all happiness and joy and laughter. I thought I could make you see the way but now I know different. So I had to get me a course of action."

"Course of action?" He wasn't sure what she meant, and he didn't even like the sound of the words.

"Some of us have to get up and *act,* Stump," Too Much said. "It's been too much thinking around here for me." She stared at him a long moment. Her eyes had gone cold and flat and angry. "When in doubt, act."

"I know," he said. "I've seen you act." He looked at the bathtub of dirty water. She had not pulled the plug to let it drain. He looked down at her lying on her back at his feet, squirming and wiggling into her cut-offs. "But I don't understand you taking a bath without me. And it ain't even a proper bath you took, for a fact." He shrugged and tried not to look hangdog or whipped. He knew women didn't like that. But that *was* the way he felt. "I just don't understand."

She was standing now, her naked young-girl's breasts cantilevered ninety degrees from her rib cage. Without leaning more than a foot, he could have taken a nipple in his mouth. At that moment, he would have given his other hand to know that she would have welcomed him to do it.

"You don't understand?" she said, reaching to get her ribbed tank top.

"No," he said. "I don't."

"Give it time, you will," she said. She had stepped into her sandals and brushed past him and headed toward the front door.

"When will I see you again?" he said.

"You'll see me when you see me coming," she said. "Somebody around here's got to goddam *act,* and it looks like it's *me* or nobody. I can't stand this kind of sloppy shit."

Stump stood naked in a kind of trance after she was gone, hearing all over again the sound of the front door closing and at the same time hearing all over again the last thing she had said, which was precisely the last thing she had said down on the edge of the swamp when they—he, Justice, and Too Much herself—had finally got Johnson and Mabel on shore.

Mabel hadn't drowned, but she looked damn near dead to Stump when they got her out of the water. Her eyelids were blue and her thin lips were wrinkled and purplish. Johnson, who had a lost and bewildered look about his eyes, did not so much stand as hang between Justice and Stump, a hand on each of their shoulders.

"I've got to get up to my place and call a goddam ambulance," said Stump.

Too Much did not answer or even look up from where she knelt beside Mabel. She put her fingers on Mabel's neck, and Stump knew she was searching for a pulse in the carotid artery.

Too Much smiled and whispered, "Oh, yeah, you sweet bitch, you're not going to die on Too Much."

Johnson was making sounds that were not words but were obviously meant to be. Too Much grabbed Mabel by the hair and pulled her head straight back and jammed her fingers in Mabel's mouth and pulled her black tongue out over her lower lip, at the same time flipping her onto her stomach and straddling her lower back, a knee on each side. Stump did not believe Mabel was breathing, and he could not help remembering medics in Korea working over dying men—or men that were already dead—working with a calm ferocity and savagery, working tenaciously and with a kind of mad perseverance, refusing to give up, refusing to accept death and the sorry fact that they had lost one of their own.

With a spread palm on each side of Mabel's spine, Too Much slammed her entire weight forward and downward, causing a great belching gush of dark water to explode from Mabel's mouth and nose. Turning Mabel's head to the side, Too Much began sucking her nose and mouth and spitting great mouthfuls of water onto the ground. The water Too Much sucked out of Mabel's nose and mouth and spat onto the ground stank of vomit and bile. Too Much gave no notice at all if she smelled it, but it sickened Stump.

Too Much rolled Mabel onto her back, pinched her nose closed with thumb and forefinger, covered Mabel's mouth with her mouth and began to pump air into Mabel's lungs and draw it out again. At irregular intervals she would stop and strike Mabel a vicious lick on the chest with her bony little fist.

Stump did not believe he had ever seen CPR administered in quite that way, but by God it was working. Mabel began to move, only faint stirrings at first, then wild flounderings, her old legs pumping as though she were riding a bicycle, and at the same time she gagged and coughed and sneezed so that mucus, dirty and gritty, hung from her nose and chin.

The first time Mabel pushed Too Much away, Too Much stood, reached down, and with a hand under each arm, dragged her to her feet. But Mabel's knees wouldn't hold her, and she went back to the ground, caught in a great spasm of coughing.

Too Much made a half turn and struck Mabel in the hip with the point of her heel, much the way she might have spurred a horse. "Come on, goddammit, Mabel, take your feet. Either die or git up. You bout to piss me off."

Johnson made grieving sounds as he watched Mabel, her knees drawn to her chest, puke down the front of herself. During the entire time Too Much worked on Mabel, Justice stared off toward the far horizon, where the swamp met the sky. He looked bored by what was happening around him. Under her breath, not even loud as a whisper, Too Much was viciously cursing Mabel for either not getting up or else dying. But it was now clear Mabel was not going to die, not from what she'd suffered in the swamp anyway. Stump had seen this kind of thing done by medics in Korea too. Medics invariably got meaner than God when they had *not* lost one of their own to death. Stump had never understood why, but then he had never understood anything about that terrible little country that was filled with maimed and dying slopes and dinks and filled, too, with maimed and dying teenage American boys, a surprising number of them black, who had to be told over and over again that they were not in a war but in a police action.

In a sudden bending action, Too Much went down over Mabel, and when she straightened up, Mabel was slung across Too Much's shoulders. Seizures of coughing still tore at her, and dirty swamp water still trickled from her mouth.

Too Much said, "Justice, you think you can get Johnson up to his trailer?"

"I can git'm up dere, Too Much," said Justice, his eyes never leaving whatever he was focused on where the cloudless blue sky dipped into the black swamp.

"Drag the son of a bitch if you have to," she said.

"Drag'm or roll'm. He be dere when yo git dere."

"Good," she said. When she started to move off up the slope toward the trailers, Too Much walked smoothly, even lightly, giving no indication at all that she had Mabel draped across her shoulders.

"What about me?" said Stump. "What do you want me to do?"

Too Much turned to regard him for a long moment, and Stump

couldn't help thinking that she was looking at him the way she might look at her foot if she had just stepped into a pile of fresh dogshit. But what made him sick to his stomach was that her look did not anger him. It only broke his heart.

"Go up and run a goddam tub. A *hot* tub. I'll take care of the rest of it. Somebody around here has got to goddam *act*, and it looks like it's *me* or nobody. I can't *stand* this kind of sloppy shit."

That's what she said she wanted, and that's what she got. With Mabel slung across her shoulders and Justice cursing and half carrying Johnson, who staggered blindly and silently beside him, they disappeared into the narrow macadam lane leading to their trailer, and Stump went up to his place and ran a scalding tub, and his cock got hard as soon as he saw the first steam rising. But by the time the water had cooled in the tub, his cock had shrunk and was hidden in its nest of gray hair, hidden in an embarrassing and disappointing way.

So Stump took a long, fine hit of Wild Turkey, turning the bottle up and not bringing it down until it had bubbled several times. That didn't cure anything, but it helped. When the tub cooled, he drained it, took another drink, and wondered what the fuck was going on. He did not want to go over to the Meechums' trailer. If he could have his way, he would never lay eyes on the Meechums again. But he did want to see Too Much, in the worst kind of way, and even though he kept telling himself lies to the contrary, he knew the main reason he wanted to see her was that he needed, and needed badly, to watch and feel her do her circus act.

So when the tub cooled, he filled it again with hot water out of the biggest hot-water heater he had been able to find and have installed at the same time he had knocked down a wall and brought the tub into his trailer to accommodate Too Much and her circus act with himself immersed in the water with her, a willing partner and participant. When it had filled, he lifted the Turkey and worked it hard.

All that first night and the next day, he filled the tub and emptied bottle after bottle. And after three days and four nights had passed, Too Much showed up at his trailer when the water was hot and he was in a light whiskey coma in his bedroom. He missed the bath and circus act, and he missed helping her out of her tight cut-offs, she squirming on her back on the rug and he pulling them down over her twisting, moving hips. He missed it all. He was sorely grieved, and pain ran all along the nerves of his body.

Too Much had not been gone but a little while when he walked to the front of his trailer and looked out the window. What he saw was like taking hold of an electric wire. His blood went hot, and it felt like his brain was expanding inside his skull. Standing about thirty yards down the lane in front of the window, three of the residents were in animated conversation. Their arms flew about, waving in the hot air. From time to time they poked each other in the chest with a pointed finger, apparently emphasizing what they were saying, and their feet moved in little bouncing half-steps. And they were smiling and laughing.

But what caused the shock that jolted Stump was the way they were dressed. One old lady, her hair pinned in a bun on top of her head, was wearing a spangled leotard that fit her badly. Stump had loved circuses all his life, and he recognized the leotard as something a woman flier on a high trapeze might wear. Beside her was a clown in a red-spotted suit. He had a huge rubber nose, and his face was covered with startling white greasepaint. Another man was dressed as a lion tamer. He cracked his long leather whip from time to time.

Stump had never had DTs in his life, but he had been drinking harder for a longer period of time than he could remember ever having done before, especially without eating. And what he saw scared him. He had to find out what the hell was going on and exactly what he was looking at. So he burst through his front door and down the steps and nearly ran over a cowboy. Stump stopped dead still in front of a little man wearing a cowboy shirt that was a faded blue and embroidered with tiny roses, and leather chaps, boots, and a black ten-gallon hat. The chaps were worn almost through in places, and the hat was old and dented and it obscured the face of the cowboy.

"Don't reckon you'll ever see another one of these," said the cowboy in a cracked, wheezing voice that Stump recognized as that of one of the residents. But he could not put a name with the voice. The cowboy turned his wide belt buckle until it caught the sun like solid silver, and Stump could read what was on it: a huge bull done in exacting detail and over the bull the legend WORLD BULL RIDING CHAMPION, 1914. CHEYENNE, WYOMING.

The little cowboy said, "Guess you never thought I never had a life before my goddam family dumped me in Forever and Forever, didn't you, you scum-sucking dog?"

Stump turned and fled back into his trailer and drew every blind before he had another long pull of whiskey.

When he did bring the bottle down and quit breathing so hard, his face darkened, and he said into the silence of his trailer, "That little ruined piece of shit called me a scum-sucking dog." That was when he decided to sober up and go out, by God, and put the fear of God into Forever and Forever.

Chapter 19

Stump tried to put his mind on hold, just think about absolutely nothing, while he scrubbed himself down, then put on a fresh white shirt, with the end of the right sleeve folded and pinned together over his nub, and dress slacks instead of shorts, and his best pair of shoes. If he was a businessman going out to take back what was his, reclaim his business and make everything orderly and sensible again, then the least he could do was look the part.

Stump checked himself one last time in the ceiling-to-floor-length mirror nailed to the wall in his bedroom and then walked to the front of the trailer, where he took a deep breath, stood taller and straighter than he normally did, opened the door, and stepped outside. It was just getting dusk dark and yet there were groups of residents standing about in front of their trailers, chatting in voices old and cracked but unmistakably happy, unmistakably joyous. Now and again, laughter, a little breathless and often ending in a spasm of coughing, but nonetheless lilting, floated over the night air.

Stump was stunned and stood stock-still there at the top of the three steps leading down to the macadam lane. Since he had bought Forever and Forever, during that whole time, he had never seen more than maybe five of the residents out after dark. And he could not remember laughter at all, day or night. He knew there must have been some, but he could not for the life of him remember it. A peal of high laughter broke from the group nearest him, and it sent a jolt of fear to seize his spine. It was the same kind of fear he had felt the few times he had heard the Chinese bugle blowing in the middle of the night in Korea, blowing for an attack.

Suddenly, four men, wearing straw boaters, striped shirts, and white trousers, came out of one of the lanes, their arms over each other's shoulders, doing a fluid and synchronized soft-shoe dance while they sang "That Old Gang of Mine." Stump's eyes had adjusted to the darkness now, and it seemed as though the entire goddam camp was dressed in one costume or another. And more than that, every resident he could see was engaged in a little leisurely scratching, and all the males were making significant adjustments to their crotches by hustling their balls. Even the singing quartet was into it. And on every fourth beat, they all simultaneously snatched at the seat of their ice cream pants.

Stump felt somehow outrageously dressed in his neat, entirely normal—not to mention sane—clothing. Goddammit, he was getting it from every angle, a total gang fuck. As his anger grew larger than his fear, he went down the steps into the lane and nearly had the life scared out of him by Justice leaping from behind a hedge and landing right in front of him. Stump would have screamed, but his throat was too constricted to make a scream possible.

But when he was able, he yelled, "Get back!"

Justice had on black high-topped tennis shoes with no socks, black Everlast boxing trunks with *Kid Lightning* stitched on the right leg, a headgear that was too large, and boxing gloves. His legs—and especially his knobby knees—were gray instead of black. As Stump stood in an incredulous trance, Justice, bobbing and weaving, danced entirely around him, feinting with first his left and then his right before he caught Stump in the solar plexus with a left hook. Stump gave no sound at all but only a great rush of air as he sat straight back on the seat of his trousers. Justice, after some effort, managed to get the mouthpiece untangled from his mismatched teeth and with great formality began to count over him.

"One," said Justice. "Two," he said.

"Justice," screamed Stump, "you've lost your fucking mind!"

Justice stopped counting and said, "It ain jus boxin yo cain do neither. Caint read, can yo? What dat say right dere?" He kept tapping the leg of his shorts with his gloved fist. "Say Kid Lightenin whut it say. Nobody wan none a Kid Lightening. Cause he be bad to de bone." Justice had stopped talking to Stump. He was talking to himself now. "Be Kid Lightenin den, be Kid Lightenin now." He paused and then looked down at Stump. "Don blame yo fo takin de count. Hell, I mout a kilt yo, yo got up." He held up his left hand. "It be de horspital in dis han." Then he held up his right hand. "Be de graveyard in *dis* han." He turned and cat-danced away into the darkness on his old skinny legs, snorting through his nose and throwing slow, labored punches as though he had a weight in either glove.

Stump got up and dusted off the seat of his pants. Justice might be old and skinny, but the fucker could hit. Stump gingerly probed his stomach and solar plexus with the ends of his fingers. Nothing seemed to be broken, but he knew he'd be bruised badly and he knew exactly where to put the blame: Too Much. He didn't know how she was directly responsible or even how she had managed it, he just knew in his bones that she was somehow responsible for Justice's hitting him.

But it wasn't time for Too Much yet. The first thing he wanted to do was go to Johnson and Mabel's trailer. He didn't know if both of them, one of them, or either of them was living there. He had not seen them since Too Much went up the slope from the swamp carrying Mabel—who still puked dirty water from time to time—slung like a sack of shit across her shoulders. Justice had Johnson tied to the end of the muddy rope they had used to save Mabel and led him staggering and stumbling like a blind mule.

Hell, they could be dead for all Stump knew, but if they had gone and died on him, he would surely have been told about it. And since he had not been told about it, he assumed they were alive and could tell him why everybody in Forever and Forever was tricked out in a costume of one kind or another. Maybe, too, they could tell him why everybody was so goddam hostile: the little cowboy calling him a scum-sucking dog and Justice punching the holy shit out of him over nothing.

And then there was the scratching—everybody scratching as though they had fleas. Stump did not think he wanted the answer to that one tonight. Not right now anyway. One thing at a time. Besides, if push came to shove, he could live with everybody in the park scratching as if they had fleas just as long as it was not contagious and he, Stump, was not in danger of coming down with a dose of whatever was making them do it.

Stump turned a corner, and there at the end of the lane was the Meechums' trailer. It was ablaze with light. Every lamp in the place must be turned on. For some reason, that made Stump feel good. He went up the steps to the door and knocked.

Immediately and simultaneously Johnson and Mabel called, "Coming."

Their voices blended as if they had been doing nothing all day long but practicing saying the word together so they could sing it out when Stump knocked. But what was more startling, they sounded happy. That was good. The last thing in the world he needed was to get in the middle of the two of them fighting. Getting in the middle of a fight and settling it so that everybody was happy was the kind of thing Too Much liked. Stump did not give a fuck who fought who, or for how long. Just so he was left out of it.

The door opened and both of them, Mabel and Johnson, stood shoulder-to-shoulder in the doorway. It made Stump move back and down to a lower step. He had never seen two people stand in a doorway like that. Johnson was wearing a three-piece pin-striped suit. Mabel had on a floor-length gown that was blue and trimmed in white lace. The lace had the yellow tinge of age about the edges of it. It was also strapless and emphasized Mabel's thick, humped shoulders. Stump had never noticed her shoulders being so heavy and meaty. Her breasts hung like long, thin flaps, and Stump wondered what was holding the dress up. Then he saw that it had what looked like a wire rim under the top of it that cut into her flesh. Under her left collarbone and parallel with it were six brown warts the size of a match head, an inch apart, and in a line so straight that at first Stump thought they were something she had stuck on herself.

They both stood smiling for all they were worth, which caused their teeth to move ever so slightly behind their stretched lips. Stump could not speak. He knew he was staring in an unseemly way and that his mouth was open, but he could not move his eyes or close his mouth. They were the damnedest two things he had ever seen, and he was waiting for an explanation. The skin over his heart seemed to go cold. He felt that anybody who looked as they did owed him an explanation.

"Well," said Mabel in a loud, braying voice, "aren't you a sight for sore eyes."

Stump had never heard such a voice come out of her mouth. And they were both still smiling as though it were something they had been sentenced to do as a penance. In a long life of feeling himself in a mad world, this topped everything that had come before it.

"Don't just stand there," said Johnson. "Come in and be welcome."

"Don't just stand there," said Mabel in the same braying voice Stump had never heard until tonight. "Come in and be welcome."

Stump felt a little dizzy. Hadn't they both said the same goddam thing? And why were they wearing those clothes? Jesus, he wanted to know what was happening in Forever and Forever, but he didn't think he wanted to know badly enough to get involved in whatever the fuck they were doing.

"Get in here, Stump, and I'll give you a cup of coffee," said Mabel. It was a command, not a request.

Stump took the top step again and was about to go into the trailer when he saw the heavy red line painted on the floor. Mabel stood on one side of it. Johnson stood on the other. Stump actually had his foot raised to step into the trailer, when he stopped. His foot stayed frozen in the air. There was something savagely wrong here. He looked at Johnson, who still held his smile, but he was now using his tongue to adjust his teeth in his mouth. Stump had never seen that done before. And for reasons he could not have named, it made him remember who he was. He owned this goddamned place. He was the one who said what happened and what did not. He answered to nobody. In Forever and Forever, everybody answered to him. He had bought this place and come here to live to start with to have a place he could control and to get the fuck out of the world, over which he never had any control at all.

Johnson looked down at the red line. "It takes a little getting used to. But by God, it works. Mabel and I are pulling in double harness for the first time since Carl was born."

"Double harness," said Stump. He knew what pulling in double harness meant, but he would not have thought for a minute that Johnson did.

"That's one of Too Much's sayings," shouted Mabel. "It means—"

"You ain't got to holler," said Stump. "I didn't lose my hearing yet, but I may lose my mind if—"

"Anyhow, pulling in double harness means—"

"I know what it means," said Stump, surprising himself with the anger in his voice. It was only then that he realized he still had his foot in the air. He put it down and stamped it beside the other foot, because it felt like it had gone to sleep. "But there's a hell of a lot of other things I don't know. And it's starting to piss me off."

"Anything we can do to help," said Johnson, "we'll . . ."

Stump pointed to the thick red line painted on the floor between Mabel and Johnson. "That," he said.

"It takes a little getting used to," said Johnson, "but it works."

"I think you already told me that," Stump said, "and it didn't help a damn bit. You playing a dangerous game here, Johnson. I ain't in the frame of mind for this."

"It's not hard to understand," said Mabel. "Too Much split us up to keep us together."

Stump reached up with his right hand and squeezed his head, his eyes pinched tightly together. "Is it me?" he said in a soft voice. "Have I finally gone round the bend and lost my mind?"

"You haven't lost a thing," said Mabel, "but your common decency. Which you may never have had to start with. But of course you may have lost it because you're afflicted!"

Stump was silent a moment, pinching the bridge of his nose

with his thumb and forefinger. He finally took his fingers away from his nose and looked at Johnson. "Can you tell me what the hell she just said?"

"She just told you what Too Much said," Johnson said pleasantly.

"She said that about me?"

"Oh, she said a lot more than that," Mabel said. "For instance—"

"I don't need to hear it."

"I thought from what you said, you did."

"I don't." Stump forced himself to be calm. "I just want you to answer a few simple questions. You think you could do that for me, Johnson?"

"I can try," said Johnson. "But if it's about Too Much, I don't think there is such a thing as a simple question as far as she's concerned."

Again Stump took several big breaths and made a conscious effort to stay calm. "Let's just give it a try, all right?"

"I don't see any harm in that. Fire away."

"Coming over here to your place, I passed Justice, and—"

"Actually, his name's Kid Lightning."

"Well, Kid Lightning was tricked out as a boxer, and he knocked me on my ass." Stump fingered his stomach. "Something may be broke in there for all I know. Now, why would he do that?"

"Kid Lightning was ranked fifth in the world when he was twenty-three years old."

Mabel came right behind what Johnson said, with "Bet you didn't know that."

Stump felt his face flush with anger. "No, I didn't, but I didn't ask that either. Let's get a little closer to home. How come the two of you are dressed like . . . like the way you are?"

Mabel and Johnson looked at each other before looking back at Stump.

"We could tell'm that," said Mabel, "couldn't we? I don't think Too Much would mind. Wouldn't be talking about anybody but ourselves."

"I used to be a banker and never wore anything but pin-striped suits," Johnson said, and then inexplicably winked at Stump.

"And this was my favorite gown when I was known as the Queen of the Ballroom."

Stump only shook his head. "You're both nuts. Maybe all three of us are."

"Nobody's nuts," Johnson said. "We wore these clothes during the happiest times of our lives. So when we dug'm out and put'm on, it was like being back there where we were happiest again, just like Too Much said it would be."

"You should never have done that," said Mabel. "You went too far."

"Jesus," said Johnson.

Stump stood thinking about the old lady in the leotards, the clown, the cowboy, and Justice knocking him on his ass. He could and would take care of Justice later, and as for what the residents wore, he couldn't think of one reason to give a shit. But what the fuck was the point of it all? That's what he wanted to know.

"Do you think it would be breaking Too Much's law," said Stump, "since she seems to be running things around here, to ask if you know just exactly what it is she wants?"

Mabel glanced at Johnson and then said, "Happiness."

"Happiness?"

"And joy," Johnson said.

"Joy." Stump was getting dizzy with the idiocy of this.

"Celebration," Mabel said.

"And celebration, you say?" Stump reached up and squeezed his head again. "And just who the hell is keeping anybody from any of that?"

"She says it's you," Mabel said.

"Well, the cat's out of the bag now," Johnson said, fear unmistakably in his voice.

"I don't know who would believe that," Stump said.

"Everybody in Forever and Forever believes it," said Johnson. "If you'd been to any of the meetings in the square where Ted fell dead out of the tree, you'd probably believe it too."

"Not probably," Mabel said. "You'd be a hundred percent believer."

"In what?" Stump said. "You mean like God?"

"Never heard her mention God," Johnson said.

"Then what? A believer in what?" asked Stump, trying to keep his voice calm.

"You'd best keep your mouth shut," said Mabel. "She said he'd come asking."

"She said I'd come asking? She mentioned me by name and said I'd come asking you?"

"I didn't say that."

"To hell you didn't."

"I might have said it," Mabel said, "and then again, I might not. Believe anything you want. It's just your nature to be that way."

"And you heard all that from Too Much, right?"

"Take it any way you want to," Mabel said.

"That young bitch," he said.

They both visibly flinched, but it was Mabel who first recovered enough to speak. "I surely wouldn't want to be caught saying anything like that about her."

"Caught? Caught by who?"

"Her."

"Damn," said Stump.

"Before you get in any deeper," said Johnson, "come on in here and let me show you how that little girl's mind works."

"Believe me," said Stump, "I know something about how that little girl's mind works." He was thinking about her hooking his hips tightly with her bony little heels and crying, *Look out, Old Son, I'm about to go round the bend!*

"But you haven't even seen this," Mabel said.

"What?"

"That," said Johnson, pointing to the neatly painted strip of red paint on the floor between Johnson and his wife.

"First thing I saw when you opened the door," Stump said. "Even asked about it. Just never got a answer."

"Guess we all had other fish to fry," Mabel said, and then went into her startled braying laugh and kept on with it until she was nearly bent over, while Stump and Johnson watched the brown spots on her skull that her wispy blue hair never quite covered up.

Stump looked over at Johnson. "If that was a joke, I missed the funny part."

"Wasn't a funny part," Johnson said.

"Oh, I see," Stump said. He did not see anything but maybe a crazy woman.

"No," said Johnson, "I don't think you do. What it is is Too Much told Mabel that she was holding her laughter in, had her foot on it, so to speak, and she ought to take her foot off and let that laughter of hers out."

Stump could only stare at Johnson in amazement. Her foot on her laughter? She ought to take it off and let the laughter out? Jesus, something had gone seriously wrong in Forever and Forever when he wasn't paying attention! But he had only himself to blame. A man couldn't expect things to be in order when he'd been laid up drunk for three days, drunk and longing for a young girl, who wasn't normal in any way that mattered, to sit in his bathtub with him and do what he had come to call her circus act.

"Actually," said Johnson, "Too Much told everybody at one of the meetings in the square that we all had our foot on our laughter and that we ought to take our foot off and let that laughter out. I think Mabel's better at it than just about anybody else, if I do say so myself."

As suddenly as a door closing, Mabel's laughter stopped, and she straightened up to look at Stump. Her face was its same old sorrowful self. There was not a sign anywhere in it that she had been laughing. Or even smiling, for that matter.

Mabel looked at her husband with what could only have been affection. Stump had never seen her do that. Ever.

"I think Johnson gives me more credit than I deserve."

"You do it better than any of the other residents."

Mabel said, "I don't know if that means much or not."

"That's the wrong way to think, and you know it."

"Oh, I believe. You know I believe."

"Not when you talk like that, I don't."

Taking a step back, Stump said, "Well, I know what *I* believe. I believe I better get on over to Ted's old trailer, where Too Much's been hanging her hat for too long now, and get a few things straightened out."

"I don't believe I'd do that if I was you, Stump," Mabel said.

"I *know* I wouldn't do it," said Johnson. "Besides, you haven't seen what I've been trying to show you since you got here." He reached out and caught Stump by the arm and pulled him into the trailer.

As soon as he was inside, he saw that he and Johnson were walking between red parallel lines painted on the floor about a yard apart. There was something very goddam wrong about this. He did not like it at all. He turned to look over his shoulder to see if Mabel was following. She was not. She was going the other way, walking between blue parallel lines painted on the floor toward a door at the other end of the hall, leading to the living room. When Stump and Johnson went through an arched passageway, they found Mabel standing at the other end, with her arms folded across her flat, hanging breasts. Stump looked at her just long enough to see that she seemed very satisfied with herself.

He was dumbstruck by the blue and red lines that had been painted on the linoleum floor. One pair of lines led to one of the sliding glass doors; another pair led to the other of the sliding glass doors. Some blue parallel lines led to the plants in the room. One pair of blue lines led to a plastic-covered easy chair in front of the fake-fieldstone fireplace. And there were other lines, going every which way, crisscrossing each other.

While Mabel and Johnson beamed upon the grid on the floor, Stump's stomach and head felt as though he were turning over and over on a runaway Ferris wheel. He knew who the mother of this madness was, and it had the stamp of her name all over it: Too Much.

"See," said Johnson, "Too Much figured this whole thing out—keeping us together by keeping us apart. It's the damnedest thing I've ever seen, but it *is* keeping us together. And it goes without saying that hurled objects that violate somebody else's space is forbidden. What do you think, Stump?" Stump opened his mouth and licked his lips. That was as close as he could come to talking. "But of course you haven't seen how it works, have you? Watch this."

Johnson stepped up to the edge of one of the blue corridors of paint, looked over at Mabel, and said, "Permission to pass."

Mabel, who had been watching him with shining eyes, said, "Pass."

When Johnson stepped between the blue lines, Johnson and Mabel took off toward each other as fast as they could in the get-along gait of the arthritic and the enfeebled old. But their faces were transformed by the flush of pleasure and delight. They didn't stop until they slammed into each other in a tightly locked embrace.

Mabel looked at Stump and said, "When we come together like this, every time is like the first time. Am I right, honey?" she said, looking into Johnson's face.

"You sure are," said Johnson. "And I haven't had to shoot the swamp since Too Much nearly drowned us and then had the trailer painted like this."

Stump turned and headed for the door.

"Wait," called Johnson. "You couldn't believe what Too Much has done with the bedroom and the bathroom."

"Yes, I can," shouted Stump over his shoulder.

Chapter 20.

When Stump got to Too Much's office in Ted's old trailer, it was ablaze in light. Apparently every light in the place was turned on, and the screen door slammed nearly constantly as strangely dressed men and women came and went. Stump stopped in the darkness of the square only a step or two from what was left of the Australian pine tree Ted Johanson had fallen from and killed himself. What had stopped Stump was the men and women who went in and came out of the trailer wearing such curious costumes. *Costumes* was the word that suggested itself to Stump just before he realized that those going up and coming down the steps of the double-wide were not men and women at all. *They were residents!*

It took him a long time to recognize them as residents, because nearly all of them wore hats of one kind or another. At least one of them had on a full headdress of feathers that spilled down his back to within inches of the ground. The women had their faces so heavily made up that they appeared at first to be wearing masks. Flamenco music and rhythmic clapping started up in a sudden burst inside the trailer. And now an incomprehensible babble of voices rose and fell with the music and poured out onto the night air every time the door opened. Stump thought it sounded like a nightmare.

"Yeah," he whispered, unconsciously putting his right foot up on the little nub of Australian pine with the black cross painted on it. "It sounds like a nightmare, all right. And I know whose nightmare they think it is. Well, we'll just see about that."

He stepped up on the pine tree stump with both feet and stretched his neck to see inside the trailer through one of the front windows from which the curtain had been lifted. And then he wished he had not, because he looked directly into the face of Too Much where she sat in the huge, thronelike chair. A green, leafy wreath of some sort sat on her head. Her eyes—looking directly into Stump's—were so bright they seemed to glitter in her deeply tanned face. Stump flinched and quickly stepped to the ground before he realized she could not possibly see him where he stood in the dark. In spite of the fact that he knew she could not have seen him, her gaze felt like a weight where it had touched him. And he was afraid.

Jesus, he thought, how could this have happened? And what *had* happened anyway?

He shook his head and tried to smile at himself, at how he was acting. He felt his lips stretch, but he knew it was not a smile. He was too old and beat up and, yes, afraid to lie to himself. Something was going on here, and he did not know what it was. Standing there in the middle of an incomprehensible mess, he was reminded more than a little of Korea and what had been done in that dreadful, shit-smelling country. Some of the soldiers had seemed to know what was going on and some had not. Some had believed and some had not. But the ones who had seemed to know and believe had died just as alone and bewildered and terrified as those who had not.

"Well, you didn't die," he said aloud to himself. "You were there and you got back. That was then. This is now. Now you're a businessman taking care of business." That made him feel better. He took a deep breath. "You're only taking care of business, so don't get it mixed up with a lot of other stuff you don't understand and don't need to understand. Now, go in there and do what you came to do."

He was in full stride toward the door of the trailer—concentrating on taking long, decisive steps—before he realized that he didn't know *exactly* what he had come to do. Not *exactly.* He knew he wanted to set things right, whatever that meant. Things could not stay as they were. That much he knew. Forever and Forever felt foreign, and he felt an alien in it. "No reason in the world to get twisted over this," he whispered to himself as a well-dressed midget he did not recognize stopped on the steps coming down from the trailer and stared at him.

"Damn, it's good, really good, you've finally come," said the midget, taking his fine panama hat off and holding it at his chest. The midget looked friendly, even deferential. He tilted his symmetrical, egg-shaped head, and the light from the door gleamed on his polished and utterly bald scalp.

Stump stopped. "Do I know you?"

The midget smiled and seemed to consider the question. "No," he said finally. "No, I don't think you do."

"I didn't think so," Stump said.

The little man stepped aside for Stump to pass and said, "But go on in. Everybody's waiting for you."

Stump glared up at the wedge of light falling from the door. The flamenco guitar and the castanets that had joined it seemed to have grown louder, more frantic, as did the clapping hands and the cries of laughter and shouts of joy.

Stump said, "Nobody's waiting for me."

"Whatever you say," the little man said.

Stump could feel his heart pounding and he thought, You're going up the steps of Ted Johanson's trailer, not up a hill. But he remembered the feeling of going up a hill in the face of enemy fire, and this was the feeling he remembered. The little man reached over and pulled open the screen door. There didn't seem to be anything else Stump could do but go on up the steps and find whatever was waiting for him and see what he would or could do after he found it. He stepped into the room, blinking against the light. The guitar and castanets and the sounds of clapping and shouting quit as suddenly as if everybody had practiced stopping on the same beat. The silence met Stump like a wall, and he stood looking at what seemed to be just about every resident in Forever and

Forever. They were all back against the walls, some standing, some sitting on folding chairs or else on the floor. They all looked happy and they all looked ridiculous. Stump felt better immediately, better and stronger, because of how ridiculous they all looked.

"You *all* look ridiculous," Stump said with more satisfaction than he felt.

Nobody said a word or made a sound. They only grinned at him and grinned at each other. Stump walked out into the open space in the middle of the room, stopped, and slowly turned, having himself a good hard look at each of them as he did. There were nurses, three of them, in spotless white uniforms and little peaked caps, a cop, two baseball players with the names of teams Stump had never heard of stitched across their chests, a gambler in a green eyeshade with a deck of cards in his long, nimble fingers, and beside the gambler sat a surgeon with a white mask over his nose and mouth. But many of them were dressed for something Stump could not identify.

"Hello, Stump. Good to see you."

Stump had avoided looking directly at Too Much. But he turned to face her now and was stunned by the shock of recognition. Blood rushed up out of her tank top to flood her face, her breathing was rapid and shallow, and her quick and darting eyes glittered. It was the look she had when she did her circus act.

Stump said, "What is it you're tricked out as, little girl, with that bush on your head?"

She reached up and touched the wreath on her head. "Oh, this," she said. "Guess it does look strange." Her voice was good-natured, even sweet. With one of her fine, muscular little hands, she gestured toward the residents. "It's just something they wanted me to wear because we're finally celebrating May Day and—"

"So *that's* what you're doing: celebrating," said Stump. "I wish somebody'd told me—because I was beginning to wonder."

He felt himself on ground that was a little safer now that he had a name to put on what they were up to.

"We're not celebrating yet, but we're due to start anytime now."

That put Stump on slippery ground again. But it wasn't as bad as before, because now he was angry. She *couldn't* and *wouldn't* act like this in Forever and Forever!

"If you're not celebrating, what the hell are you doing in here?"

"What I've been doing all along," she said. "Looking for the chance of ultimate possibility." She stiffened on the chair, and her lovely mouth went thin, and when she spoke, her voice was thin, too, and brittle. "What are *you* doing in here, Stump?"

"I've come to take back what's mine!" He had not meant for his voice to be so loud, loud and angry. After all the misery she had caused him, he did not want to lose her and her circus act. He forced himself to smile and speak softer. "That's all: take back what's mine, and nothing else."

"I don't believe anybody here would deny you that," Too Much said, looking around the room. "Take what's yours and welcome to it."

Stump looked at the residents and then at Too Much, finally ending with his eyes locked in a thousand-yard stare on a wall twenty feet away. This wasn't working the way he thought it might. His own fault, he guessed, but he wasn't really sure even about that. He felt as though he might never be sure of anything again. Still, as far as he was concerned, music and laughter and unseemly dress and faces a quarter inch deep in paint, powder, and eyeliner had no place in Forever and Forever. Why couldn't they all accept that the next thing left for them was death? Five minutes after he'd seen what was now Forever and Forever, the equation that presented itself to him was this: Forever and Forever equals quiet and solitude and stillness and death. To Stump, the equation did not offend; rather, it was one in which he could and did take refuge.

"Stump," Too Much said, "you still with us?"

Stump, who had moved farther away from the residents in the room and deeper into himself, did not answer. Any answer he could think of would have been a lie.

"You seem to be having trouble," said Too Much.

"No," Stump said. But he was having trouble, all of it with himself. He had lost his way. At least that was how he felt: lost. "No, none at all."

"Don't guess you came to join the party," she said.

"I told you what I came for."

"And I told you I wanted you to have it. We all want you to have whatever you came for, whatever is yours."

"It's not that easy," Stump said. He wanted things to be the way they were, but he couldn't think of how to say it without sounding silly or else have her misunderstand the way things were. Did he mean, she might ask, the way they were before she came to Forever and Forever? The answer was yes, but not if it meant having her leave his tub, his bed, and his trailer park.

"Maybe this is yours!"

Stump turned in the direction of the voice and saw the man with the guitar holding the instrument out toward him.

"I thought it was mine, but maybe I was mistaken," said the man. He struck a savage flamenco chord on the strings, and it shook the air. The residents burst into laughter and shouts of encouragement for Stump to take what was his. The man struck the strings again and said, "Do you play?"

"I never play," said Stump. "And I'm not playing now."

"Sure you play sometimes," cried the Gypsy woman. "Maybe you play these! Maybe they are yours!"

The castanets burst into sound on her blurring fingers as she raised her hands above her head. The residents were on their feet now, clapping and screaming at Stump.

"Take the guitar!"

"Strip her of what belongs to you, Stump!"

"Strip all of us!"

"Don't be afraid. Take us and make us dance your jig!"

Then all of them together, laughing, made their voices a single derisive taunt: *"Take us and make us. Take us and make us. Take us and make us."*

"Enough."

Too Much spoke softly, and Stump wondered how a word spoken so quietly, with no suggestion of anger or even of demand, could have so effectively and so suddenly cut off the noise of the hysterical voices as neatly as if it had been a string that she had snipped with scissors. All that was left in its place was the sound of labored breathing and wheezing and a few random coughs.

"Stump," said Too Much, her voice sounding much louder now in the quiet room, "as it happens, I do have something of yours." She stood up from her enormous chair and held out a pair of boots. "They came from your closet," she said. "I found them and I took them." They were a pair of combat boots that had never seen combat. They had been issued to him after he got back to the States. Stump was stunned into silence. There was not a single response he could think of to make. She held the boots away from her as if they might be dangerous. "Honorable Mr. Doo, if you would, please."

Mr. Doo stepped forward, took the boots from Too Much, and made a slight bow before heading straight toward Stump. But Mr. Doo turned before he got to him and went out the door, his footfall as light as that of a fox.

Stump, who had watched him leave, turned back to Too Much. "He took my boots," he said, and he hated himself for the weak lament in his voice and the inadequacy of what he'd said, but he could think of nothing else to add. He watched Too Much, the joyous climax of her circus act back upon her face again. A rapid, but not loud, rapping started somewhere outside, and every head turned to look at the door. A soft, guttural sound rose from the throats of the residents.

"What's that?" said Stump.

Too Much said, "That would be the Honorable Mr. Doo, Stump, nailing your boots to the stump."

"What stump?" he asked, but he already knew.

"The maypole stump," she said. "We've got the stump. But we don't have the pole. And everybody in Forever and Forever decided they would do you the honor of making you the maypole."

The guttural sound in the throats of the residents turned into a single violent noise, and he felt what seemed like hundreds of hands grab him and lift him high and carry him, struggling and twisting, through the door and out into the night, which suddenly burst into light from dozens of torches carried by residents, skipping and dancing—Jesus Christ, skipping and dancing!—around the stump, onto the top of which his combat boots had been nailed. And even as they carried him, he thought, I've lost it.

The residents started chanting in a singsong voice: "Tra la la, the first of May! Tra la la, we'll have our say!"

And on it went like a madness, as they stuffed his feet into his boots and laced them hard to his ankles and calves and stood him up straight. When they took their hands off him, his knees buckled and he fell over backward. He was stunned after he hit the hard-packed earth, but they—still chanting—lifted him and set him standing again. Terrified as he was, he held his balance this time as best he could. Another fall like that might break his back. Loops of satin ribbon—dozens of them in all colors of the rainbow—were dropped over his head and neck and shoulders and pulled tight. A single resident held the other end of each ribbon, stretching twenty feet or more from the stump he was nailed to. He struggled briefly, but the ribbons held him as fast as if they had been ropes. His eye caught Too Much where she stood almost beyond the light of the torches. The troop of Old Ones leaned in out of the darkness behind her.

The ribbons, radiating from Stump in every direction, had been pulled tight now, and he could not fall. If he leaned too far to the left, those on the right straightened him up. If he started backward, those in front held him fast. They had begun circling him, wrapping him tightly in a cocoon of satin ribbons.

"Too Much," cried Stump, "for God's sake."

"Talk to them, not to me," she said, her voice surprisingly low and surprisingly clear. "I was in Forever and Forever but never of it. I'm never of anywhere."

"Don't go," he begged, terrified.

"I told you to talk to them."

"Where will you go?" His voice did not work right. His chest felt like it was being bound by metal bands. "Tell me where you'll go."

"Where the road leads."

"They'll hurt me."

"Probably."

"But I never did anything."

"What?"

"I never did anything."

"Tell them."

He looked at the faces, red in the light from the torches, circling him. Dust—red, too, in the refracted torchlight—rose like smoke among them. Stump's eyes swept the circle as it moved.

"You can all leave Forever and Forever if that's what you want to do." Stump spoke as loudly as he could, but the bands of satin were at his throat, on his face. He caught the burning eyes of the man dressed as a surgeon. "You! You there, doctor! I'll help you move! I'll do anything you want."

The doctor snatched off his white cap and pulled his mask down. "What is my name?"

Stump didn't know his name, although he knew he'd seen him many times over the years.

Stump's eyes shifted to a man who seemed to be enjoying himself immensely. He recognized him as the midget he'd met on the steps. The little man stared directly back at him, and his smile seemed to grow bolder as he demanded, "What's my name?"

A woman behind the midget screamed, "What's *my* name?"

"You're a resident," answered Stump, because he had no notion at all of what her name might be. "You're all residents. Isn't that good enough?"

"Wrap him tighter," someone yelled. "Wrap him much tighter."

One of Stump's eyes was still clear, and he was able to move his chin. He cut his eye toward Too Much, who already had her back to him and was moving off into the darkness.

"Too Much, what will they do to me?"

Too Much stopped and looked back over her shoulder. "They have fire in their hands and water in the swamp. It depends on how good or how bad their imaginations are. But between fire and water, there has to be the chance of ultimate possibility. Try to trust in that, Stump. It's all that's left you now. I have to go. I'm finished here. The rest of this is up to you." A pause. A slow smile. "And, of course, to those whose names you do not know."

Stump saw her turn and stride away into the darkness, until the single eye that could still see was wrapped and wrapped again. A chant started up, but he couldn't make out what it was. It grew dimmer and dimmer as layer after layer of satin wrapped his head. Finally he was standing in the dark in complete silence, and it was getting harder and harder to breathe.